MW01616483

Praise

Kee Sloan spins a compelling story that draws readers into a web of beloved and quirky characters. His signature wit and daring reflections on faith—spiced with the warmth of Southern mannerisms and culture—will make you laugh, cry, and wonder about the big questions of life. People familiar with Sloan's writing and preaching, as well as those new to his unique voice, will be drawn into Buddy's world and the revelation of important universal truths. In short, it's a delightful and worthwhile read!

—*The Rev. Mary Bea Sullivan*
Interim Rector of All Saints' Episcopal Church
Homewood, Alabama
Author of Living the Way of Love

Author Kee Sloan does that rare and wonderful thing in his new novel, *Prodigal,* presenting delightful tales about utterly realistic characters whom readers will truly care about. This story is one you will not want to put down.

—*The Rev. Dr. C. K. Robertson*
Author of A Dangerous Dozen *and* Barnabas vs. Paul

Kee Sloan's wonderful fictional priest, Buddy, reminds a particularly skeptical friend, "My job is to offer, to invite people into a deeper awareness of the love of God." That is exactly what author (and bishop) Sloan does with his fantastic new book, *Prodigal.* Readers will find themselves drawn into the stories of Buddy and the fascinating people he encounters in Alabama and perhaps find a little hope in these pages as well.

—*The Most Rev. Michael B. Curry*
Presiding Bishop of the Episcopal Church
Author of Love is the Way, Crazy Christians, Following the Way of
Jesus, *and* Songs My Grandma Sang

In the quintessential spirit of Southern storytelling, Sloan's *Prodigal* brings fully to life an eclectic cast of small-town residents who provide us a window on faith and morality. You certainly need not be Christian, nor of any religion for that matter, to find this page-turner inspiring.

—*James B. McClintock, PhD*
Author of Lost Antarctica *and* A Naturalist Goes Fishing

Prodigal, Kee Sloan's latest effort, is a compelling narrative with profound theological insight. Hope, faith, and above all, love, make the book's title most fitting. Set in Sloan's native South, in a small cabin under a perigee moon on the longest, coldest, night of the year, the story reaches its crescendo. Anger, fear, resentment, pride, doubt—the manifestation of every form of human imperfection—gather in a moment of confrontation and ultimately of grace, reminding the reader of William Faulkner's keen observation: "You don't love because: you love despite; not for the virtues, but despite the faults." This book will touch believer, doubter, and nonbeliever alike and may introduce a new term, "gumbo theology," to all who seek to understand both the human condition and the meaning of unmerited grace.

—*John M. McCardell, Jr.*
Former Vice-Chancellor and President
The University of the South

PRODIGAL

Peake Road Press
6316 Peake Road
Macon, Georgia 31210-3960
1-800-747-3016
©2021 by John McKee Sloan
All rights reserved.

Library of Congress Cataloging-in-Publication Data

Names: Sloan, John McKee, 1955- author.
Title: Prodigal : a sequel to Jabbok and Beulah / by John McKee Sloan.
Description: First. | Macon, GA : Peake Road Press, [2021]
Identifiers: LCCN 2021026090 | ISBN 9781737323600 (paperback)
Subjects: GSAFD: Christian fiction.
Classification: LCC PS3619.L6274 P76 2021 | DDC 813/.6--dc23
LC record available at https://lccn.loc.gov/2021026090

Kee Sloan

PRODIGAL

A Sequel to *Jabbok* and *Beulah*

Also by John McKee Sloan

Jabbok

Beulah

for family and friends
who remind us that we're loved
no matter what, no matter what

Acknowledgments

I continue to be grateful for the many people who have shaped and guided me, who have touched my mind or heart, people who have taught me, people who have encouraged me, and people who have just put up with me. I know I've been too progressive for some, and too conservative for others, too outspoken and too quiet and too fast and too slow, all at the same time; thanks to all of you who've pointed out my various shortcomings and flaws, and to all of you who haven't.

And always—first and last—I am grateful to Tina Brown Sloan, the love of my life.

CONTENTS

PRELUDE

In 1964, I was nine years old, and my brother—four years older and infinitely more sophisticated—had a collection of 45 rpm records, including "Don't Let Me Be Misunderstood" by The Animals. There was a lot that I didn't understand in that song, but the refrain has stuck with me ever since:

> "I'm just a soul whose intentions are good.
> Oh Lord, please don't let me be misunderstood."

After thirty-nine years of preaching, I think I've figured out that being a faithful person is not about getting all the facts right or devising a comprehensive systematic theology. It's not about what you know; it's about whether you let yourself love and be loved; it's about who you trust.

I hope you'll find some truth in this book. Not facts, not an accurate accounting of my life, but some glimpse of the truth of God. I hope you'll laugh a little bit and maybe cry a little, too. If you're looking for something to make you angry, maybe you'll find something here you can get really steamed about—not that it will do you any good. Most of all, I hope you'll think about some of what you read in these pages, and if that causes you to consider what you believe, I will have done my job.

I don't claim to have all the answers, but I've asked a lot of questions. I am, all these years later, "just a soul whose intentions are good," still praying that I won't be misunderstood.

1

My Privilege

It was a little after two on Tuesday morning, and the phone was ringing. I don't know how long it had been ringing; I picked up the receiver before I was completely awake, ridiculously hoping I could catch it before the intrusive noise woke Beulah and our sweet little boy Jude asleep between us. A moment or two later, my waking mind caught up with my reflexes and my hands, and I realized I was talking to Guy Ray Gregory, a member of the parish whose wife, June, had been teetering on death's doorstep for months. He was saying, "Well, that little Pakistan doctor says she ain't got long. I know it's late, Father Buddy, but . . . well, could you—if you could . . . it would mean a lot to me and . . . you know, a lot to June."

"Guy Ray," I croaked. My voice was hoarse, still waking up. "I'll be right there."

"I'm sorry, Father Buddy—I know it's late, but—"

"Don't worry about it. It's my privilege. I'm on my way."

Beulah sat up a little, careful to not wake our two-year-old son, who had recently decided that sleep was his personal adversary. She whispered, "June?"

"Yeah. Go back to sleep, honey."

"Give Guy Ray my love."

"I will."

"And come back soon."

"I'll try."

She straightened the coverlet over Jude and lay back down, sinking back into sleep. She murmured, "Love you, Buddy-boy."

"I love you right back. Go back to sleep." I wished I could go back to sleep, too—sink down with her, under the covers, with our precious son between us. But I had to go; it was my privilege.

I pulled on the same pair of khakis and black clergy shirt I'd worn the day before and checked myself: wallet, keys, pocketknife and bandanna in my pants pockets, collar buttons still in the shirt—I was ready to go. There was a little silver cannister holding the oil for anointing in the car's glove compartment, and I always had a Book of Common Prayer on the back seat, just for moments like this.

The hospital was across town, which in West Branch, Mississippi, was not really all that far, but it gave me some time to prepare myself for what I was doing and to think about June and Guy Ray Gregory. I'd been the vicar of the Church of the Holy Incarnation for about ten years and had known the Gregory family the whole time. I'd done the wedding services for both of their sons, L.G. and Vinnie, and baptized Vinnie and Carol's two daughters. L.G. had married Tammi Boykin, a Church of Christ girl whose mother was enthusiastically scandalized at the prospect of baptizing babies, so their three children were destined to be heathens until they were old enough to be baptized as adults—usually eleven or twelve in that tradition. The two Gregory boys worked at their father's garage now; Gregory and Sons Automotive was the finest auto repair place in Northeast Mississippi.

It had been a terrifying three months since June was diagnosed with bacterial meningitis, an inflammation of the tissues protecting her brain and spinal column. She was treated at the West Branch Hospital, and for a while it seemed like she would recover completely, but earlier that week she'd taken a turn when a seizure in the middle of the night had forced them to bring her back to the hospital, and now I was needed.

It was their son Vinnie who'd taught me about privilege. Eight years before, when retired Army Colonel William Albert Porter Junior died, his family found the directions he'd left in his will specifying how he wanted his funeral to be. Even though they hadn't been involved at the parish for years—he was unwilling to join the Methodist Church and his wife couldn't make herself become a Catholic—they hated "the liberal direction of the Episcopal Church" in ordaining women and in revising the Book of Common Prayer. Whether they liked it or not, though, they were still on our books and came occasionally, usually on Christmas and Easter.

I went to their home to visit the widow the day after the Colonel died in a hospital in Memphis. She sat very stiffly and told me he had directed that the funeral was to be at the Church of the Holy Incarnation. We talked about the readings and the hymns that he had selected; he had instructed that the service should be from the 1928 Book of Common Prayer, and he wanted the minimum number of the shortest readings allowable. He directed that we would sing "My Country 'tis of Thee," and we were not, in his words, to "drag it out." Then she told me that he had specifically stated that he wanted a young person from the parish to be an acolyte at his funeral, reminding whoever might be reading his posthumous note that he had been an acolyte there when he was a young man. He had told her several times that it had meant a lot to him to lead the stately procession into the church as the first words of the funeral service were spoken by the priest: "I am the resurrection and the life, saith the Lord: he that believeth in me, though he were dead, yet shall he live . . . ."

So later that afternoon, I called our Number One Top Acolyte, who said she'd love to help but couldn't miss school the day of the funeral because she had a big test. The second-best acolyte, not nearly as reliable as my preferred choice, was in the same class dreading the same test. And that left me with Vinnie, who at the time had long, out-of-control, bushy reddish hair that usually shrouded his eyes. He slouched. He would not have been the Colonel's first choice, either.

Vinnie was a sweet kid but easily distracted, so I always had to remind him when he was supposed to give the collection plates to the ushers or close the gate at the altar rail. But the Colonel had left instructions, and this was my last chance to help his family obey his final orders: I had to find an acolyte, and Vinnie was my only remaining option.

The morning of the funeral, I received the body into the church and met the Colonel's son, who'd arrived from Germany the night before. Captain William Albert Porter the Third stood as straight upright as a living human can. When we shook hands, he squeezed my hand with effort and purpose, as if to let me know he was in control, establishing his manly superiority. I squeezed back, not trying to win a contest of gripping masculinity, but just to let him know that I wasn't the wimp he undoubtedly assumed I ought to be, as a member of the clergy.

The Captain nodded approvingly, and then he saw Vinnie the acolyte. Well, I think he mostly saw his hair, and that was all he needed to see. Vinnie represented everything the Colonel and his son the Captain found wrong with America today, and I think he was about to protest when his wife interceded: "Not now, William. This is not your watch." He allowed a tactical retreat but gave me a glare, letting me know he would hold me personally responsible if Vinnie the shaggy acolyte ruined his father's service.

The funeral was at the parish, just the burial service—no Eucharist so we can get this over with—and Vinnie led the procession up the aisle, just as the Colonel had all those years ago. Any sign that Vinnie was touched or moved in any way was well concealed, possibly by all that hair. The homily was brief, as per instructions, and we marched out singing "My Country, 'tis of Thee," distinctly up-tempo.

After the service, I told Vinnie he didn't have to go to the graveside, that he could go on back to school. When he said he'd be glad to go the cemetery, I assumed he just wasn't in a hurry to get back to algebra or history or something. I chuckled a little to myself, remembering that I'd done the same thing when I was an acolyte. I told him to bring the processional cross and said he could ride with me in the funeral procession, just behind the hearse.

The service of committal at the graveside is usually brief, but at a burial of a former member of the military, it can get somewhat more complicated. I'd seen it before, but I'm always moved by the soldiers removing the American flag from the casket and folding it—slowly, precisely—and giving it to the family. Then there was the twenty-one-gun salute, always a bit jarring for me, and then the bugler blowing Taps, which inevitably brings tears to my eyes.

At the Colonel's burial, the family waited for the cemetery crew to lower the casket into the concrete vault, and then each of them threw a shovelful of dirt onto it. It took a few minutes to accomplish this, and while they were still trying to coax some of the younger grandchildren to take the shovel, the Colonel's widow made her way over to me carefully, leaning on a walking cane and a grandson. She said, "Thank you, Father Hinton. The service was nicely done—the Colonel would have approved." I said, "Thank you, ma'am."

Then she turned to Vinnie, who was standing next to me and whose mind seemed to be wandering. She said, "And thank you, young man." I thought "Okay, this is it—the moment for Vinnie to do or say something nonconformist or goofy, something to ruin the Colonel's funeral." I glanced across the gravesite to see the Captain sending me a preemptory glare.

But Vinnie nodded his bushy head politely and said, "Yes ma'am—it was my privilege."

Mrs. Porter smiled and patted Vinnie on the cheek, and said, "You're a good boy. You need to get a haircut."

To which Vinnie smiled very slightly and said, "Yes ma'am."

Now it was eight years later, and that good boy had grown up and gotten married and had two beautiful daughters who would soon be invited to be acolytes at the Church of the Holy Incarnation. I sighed as I pulled into a parking place at the hospital, knowing I wasn't going to be there to see those little girls grow up.

Beulah and I had accepted a call to go to Alabama, where I would be the rector of St. Thomas Episcopal Church in Greene. I'd told the wardens at lunch on Monday, just fourteen hours earlier, and broken the news to the Vestry that evening. None of the rest of the parish knew it yet, but a letter had been put in the mail, and the whole town would know by that afternoon.

I took the elevator to the third floor and found June's room. L.G. and Vinnie were standing out in the hall; when they saw me coming, Vinnie came to hug me but L.G. went into the room. L.G.—whose birth name was "Little Guy Gregory"—had also been an acolyte at Holy Incarnation when I arrived, but he didn't have anything to do with the parish or with me since he'd married Tammi. It seemed like it made him nervous for me to be there, but there wasn't anything I could do about that.

There is a beautiful service in the Episcopal Book of Common Prayer to be used when someone is dying or has just died—Ministration at the Time of Death. Much of it is written to be a litany, so that the person leading the service says something and everyone else responds. In my experience, I'm usually the only one in the room with a Prayer Book, so I have to tell them what they're supposed to say, but it works out pretty well.

Two or three weeks earlier, I'd come in response to a call from Guy Ray to administer last rites, and we'd used this service from the Prayer Book with the expectation that June would die that night. But she rallied and was released from the hospital, only to be readmitted a week or so later. I'd come by earlier that night, after the Vestry meeting; the doctors had run tests, but they couldn't say with any certainty what was going on, and I'd told Guy Ray to call me if there was any change or if he needed me.

I was heavy with the idea that June was going to die and burdened by my announcement that I was leaving Holy Incarnation. They would all find out later that day; I felt like I was deserting June and her family.

One of my favorite prayers in the Book of Common Prayer is in this service to be used at the time of death. I think I like it because it's direct and simple. It is A Commendation at the Time of Death: "Depart, O Christian soul, out of this world; In the Name of God the Father Almighty who created you; In the Name of Jesus Christ who redeemed you; In the Name of the Holy Spirit who sanctifies you. May your rest be this day in peace, and your dwelling place in the Paradise of God."

That prayer hit me especially hard that day. Maybe it was because it was three in the morning, or maybe it was because it seemed absolutely sure that June was going to die soon. Or maybe it was because I was the one departing, and I was feeling guilty about it.

It had been my great privilege to serve as the rector of the Church of the Holy Incarnation for a decade, and now it was time to leave.

2

If She Likes You, You're Okay

One of the most difficult things for a priest is knowing when it's time to move on to another parish. You love the people at the congregation, all of them—although of course there are always some people you enjoy and others you'd rather avoid; we're all just people, after all. And you love the work, most of it. Now, after a good long time at the Church of the Holy Incarnation, it had been more and more feeling like it was time for me to go. I'd loved most of it, but now I was starting to feel too comfortable. Complacency can quickly become debilitating to priests and to congregations.

A few months before, my friend Rusty, a classmate from seminary, had called and asked if he could put my name into consideration to be the rector of a substantially larger parish in Alabama. I never thought I'd leave the Diocese of Mississippi, but it was a real opportunity that I had to consider, especially with a wife and child. And the unhappy truth was that after almost thirteen years of ordination, I was still making the minimum salary prescribed by the diocese.

So I told Rusty, who was serving a large church in Birmingham, that he could put my name in, and they sent me a packet of information, including five questions to answer with two hundred and fifty words or less. I showed it to Beulah, and she suggested I should fill it out, just to see how far it might go. She asked, "What could it hurt? What's the worst that could happen? They write a letter and tell you thanks for participating? They come over here and listen to you preach and then take us out to lunch?"

I took some time to answer the questions and mailed them back. The following week, I received a call from the chair of the search committee, who told me they wanted to send a couple of the members of the committee to hear me preach. Beulah and I talked, and I wondered if we should call and tell them they didn't need to come. She asked, "What are you afraid of?"

"Do we really want to leave Mississippi?"

"Buddy, it's Alabama! It's not like we're talking about moving to Norway, or Boston, or someplace foreign." And then she suggested, "Let's just be who we are and not pretend to be anything else. If they like us, and if we like them, we'll go ahead with the process. If they want to drop us out of the process, or if we want to get out of it, that's fine. We don't have to go anywhere."

Several weeks later, two people from St. Thomas Episcopal Church in Greene, Alabama, came to hear me preach. Somewhere in my nervous preparation for the sermon, I read in a Bible commentary a quote from the English poet Robert Browning that seemed to illustrate the point I wanted to make: "Leave now for dogs and apes! Man has Forever." In some circuitous process I could never fully explain later, this led to me telling a story about going fishing with my mother's Uncle Benny, who wanted to make sure that my brother and I understood sex, that we were not dogs to chase after females in heat but young men who would have relationships with women whom we loved and trusted. I told that story in the sermon; I don't remember the point now, but I thought it made sense at the time. It certainly held the people's attention.

Beulah thought it was a good sermon, but she had to admit she was a little surprised that I talked about dogs having sex while a search committee was listening in the pews. "Maybe there ought to be some limit," she gently suggested, "on being who we are."

After the service we took them to The Cedars, a nice but pricey restaurant in town. We didn't go there often, and usually just when somebody else was picking up the tab. I didn't realize until it was too late that half of the congregation ate there most Sundays; before we were through with our coffee and lemon icebox pie, the news was all over town that a search committee had come to visit.

Our friend JoJo McCain, whom we'd met when he was a camper at the Special Session for people with mental and physical disabilities, seemed especially anxious about us moving. He wasn't intellectually disabled; he'd just grown up being treated like he was because his brother Bobbo had been, and they were always together. When his brother was killed in a traffic accident, along with his mother and aunt, he'd moved to West Branch, mostly to be with us. Now he was upset that we might be moving to Alabama. "I ain't never even been to Alabama!" he fretted.

We tried to tell him that it wasn't decided, that he would be fine, that he had friends and a place to stay and his work, but he was worried. He told Beulah, "It just make me so sad."

Miss Elizabeth, a prominent and influential member of the parish, cornered me after the Bible study the next Wednesday morning. "So, are y'all moving to Alabama?"

I tried to keep it light. "Oh, I don't know. We'll have to see."

She declared, "You know, there's only two kinds of priests for a little parish like this one: the ones who don't stay long enough, and the ones who stay too long."

"Which one am I?"

She threw my words back at me: "Oh, I don't know," she said airily. "We'll have to see."

Our last Sunday at the Church of the Holy Incarnation in West Branch, Mississippi, was in late August of 1993. The time between the visit of the search committee and the arrival of the moving trucks was insanely busy and was made even more wonderfully bewildering by the news that we were expecting our second child the following February.

I did reasonably well at my last service at the Church of the Holy Incarnation, but it was very emotional for all of us. I got a little choked up during the sermon, but they were sweet and good-natured people, and I felt their support as I tried to get the lump in my throat to go back to wherever throat lumps come from so I could continue speaking. I was excited to go to a different parish, but I felt like I was being disloyal to these people who'd been patient with me for such a long time.

June and Guy Ray Gregory were there with Vinnie and his family; June had rallied again and was strong enough to come to church. She couldn't climb the steps to the altar to receive Communion, so I carried it down to her. She took my hand and kissed it as I was trying to give her the bread and said, "Thank you, Buddy." I wanted to tell her that it had been my privilege, but the thought of saying it threatened to choke me up, so I just nodded and said, "Yes ma'am."

Miss Elizabeth drew me aside during the reception and said, "Well, I guess you've turned out to be one of those priests that didn't stay long enough. It's better that way; we have had some who stayed too long, you know."

In the fall of 1993 we moved to Greene, Alabama, where I would be the rector of St. Thomas, a beautiful old parish on Main Street, two blocks from the courthouse square. Beulah got the water, electricity, and cable television connected while I connected with some of the members curious enough to come by and meet the new priest. Several members of the youth group came over to help us unpack; actually, they spent most of their time playing with Jude and our good dog, Jabbok.

One of the young people asked me if I'd met Miss Edith yet; when I asked her who Miss Edith was, she replied, "She's this old lady in the church." One of the guys added, "She's about a million years old." Another girl said, "If she likes you, you're okay. If she doesn't, you're not." The young man said, "She didn't like the last guy. He was here for about three years, but now they've moved to Florida."

When the senior warden of the parish came by to see how he could help, I asked him about Miss Edith. He said the young people were right and that it would be a good idea to pay her a visit. He warned me, "She will already know everything about you," which sounded ominous. He also told me that she was in her eighties, or maybe her nineties—nobody knew exactly how old Miss Edith was— and that she lived in a grand old home on Main Street, just three houses down from the church. She had grown up in that house where she had been born, and she had attended St. Thomas her whole life.

He said she had never married, but she had filled her life being a high school English teacher and then the school's principal, until her age forced her to retire.

He also told me that she had indeed not liked my predecessor, and he hinted that it would be best for me—and for the parish—if she liked me. I told him I'd do my best.

Later that afternoon, I called Miss Edith Frank's home and spoke to a younger woman who told me that Miss Edith had been expecting my call. She said that Miss Edith would be glad to receive me the next morning at eleven. And then she suggested, "It's best if you are not late."

The next morning at eleven sharp, I rang Miss Edith's doorbell, and in a moment a plumpish young African American woman with a sweet smile came to the door to let me in. She showed me into the parlor, a room clearly used for Miss Edith Frank to entertain her guests. She was waiting there, wearing a black dress, black heavy-duty sensible shoes, and a string of yellowed pearls. She might have been wearing that same dress, those same shoes and pearls, since before my parents were born; they looked like they'd been part of her since the Coolidge administration.

The lines of her face didn't suggest that she made a habit of smiling—her expression seemed to be set on scowl. She nodded at the settee on the other side of the coffee table, and I sat down. Abruptly, she said, "You like whiskey?"

I hadn't expected that. I was looking for something along the lines of "Hello" or "It's nice to meet you." I said, "Yes ma'am," and wondered if that was a test and whether I'd passed it. I wondered how the last rector of St. Thomas had responded.

She had a little silver bell that she rang, and the young woman who'd answered the door stepped into the room.

"Yes ma'am?"

"Pearlie, bring us a little something to drink, please."

Pearlie didn't ask what she might want, whether she might have tea or coffee, water or a soft drink in mind. A few minutes later, Pearlie brought a silver tray with two glasses of brown liquid, no ice. Miss Edith took hers and held it up, waiting for me to take mine and lift it, which I did. She said, "Cheers" and I "Cheersed" her back; she took a large swallow while I took a cautionary sip. I'm sure it was good Scotch, but it was still Scotch, which has always tasted like medicine to me. Still, I was trying to pass tests I couldn't even see, so I bluffed, "Oh, that's wonderful!" and downed the rest in one big gulp, fighting the impulse to gag, grimace, or cough.

She responded, "I'm glad you like it," and then she said, "Pearlie?" Pearlie took both of our empty glasses and brought them back full, still with no ice.

I took a polite sip this time, and Miss Edith declared, "Pearlie makes the best fried chicken in Alabama. Do you like fried chicken?"

I answered with complete honesty, "Yes ma'am—we love fried chicken."

She nodded approvingly, and after a quick glance to Pearlie she said, "I'll send some home with you. Well, Father—may I ask you a few questions?"

"Yes ma'am." I figured my options were fairly limited.

She went on to invite my opinions on a range of topics that were important to her. We talked for a long time; the questions I remember had to do with the new prayer book, the ordination of women, the 1992 presidential election, civil rights, and whether the AIDS epidemic was a punishment from God.

I told her that I grew up with the old prayer book and still loved it, but that I liked all the options in the new one; that when I was in seminary, I looked at some of the women there and thought I was opposed to women's ordination until I looked at some of the men and thought I'd have to be opposed to the ordination of men, too; that I had hoped the Democrats were going to nominate Tom Harkin from Iowa but that I was happy to vote for Bill Clinton instead; that we'd come a long way in civil rights but still had a long way to go; and that the ideas that AIDS was a punishment from God was clearly and ridiculously absurd.

After I said all that, I wondered if I'd gone beyond Beulah's limit of being who we are, but by then it was too late—either she liked me or she didn't.

Miss Edith studied me for a moment and then lifted her glass again, though there was almost nothing left in it, and I raised mine as well. We both said "Cheers," and I gulped down my Scotch and realized the interview was over. Whether I'd passed the test or failed it, now it felt like it was time to leave. I stood as she held out her hand, either to be kissed or shaken. I chose to shake it, and we said our goodbyes. Emboldened by relief that the interrogation was complete—and quite likely somewhat liberated by two shots of Scotch before lunch—I turned at the door and said, "Will I see you Sunday morning?" She answered, "Young man, you will see me *every* Sunday morning." And then she smiled, a big warm smile that even she seemed unable to prevent.

I wobbled home with a head full of whiskey and a paper bag full of fried chicken, and I told Beulah I thought we were going to be okay.

After most of the boxes were unpacked, the senior warden suggested that I should also go see Miss Frankie, not because she was feared but because she was loved. Frankie Claiborne was in her eighties, but she was still at St. Thomas for every service and every Bible study—every time the church doors opened. She always wore white gloves and a hat to church, with a little veil covering her eyes because that's how her mama had taught her, and, as I soon learned, she always said the same thing after every service: "Enjoyed the preachin', Father."

Everybody loved Miss Frankie: she was the sweet woman who brings irresistible cheese straws to every reception, mouth-watering potato salad to every potluck, a warm hug and a genuine smile to every gathering. It seems like every parish has someone like this; I hope you know who I'm talking about in your own congregation.

She was married to Mr. Lonny, who'd started a small chain of gas stations and coin-operated laundromats. He prided himself in being a good businessman; he was tight with his money, sparing in his affections, and always kept his eye on the bottom line. He came to church when he had to: Christmas and Easter and funerals he thought he had to attend so that people in town wouldn't talk about him. Every time I saw him at church, it looked like he'd taken a bite out of a sour lemon, as if he was there against his will.

Other people told me that he was most comfortable when he had something to be unhappy about, that he was easily offended and not someone to let go of a good grudge. Several people wondered why she had ever married him, something I had to wonder as well. Everybody understood that you had to meet him on his terms or not at all—and I have to admit, not at all was how I preferred it. That first time I went to visit Miss Frankie at her home, he shook my hand and sat awkwardly with us for a few minutes, and then he left. After that, every time I came to visit, he made it a point to be somewhere else, which was just as well with me.

I went to see Miss Frankie almost every week after that, and we became good friends. She had great stories to tell—about her childhood that was marked by the 1927 flood and the Great Depression, and about life in the town and the parish. She had organized drives to collect rubber and scrap metal during World War Two, taught English and dance at Greene High for nearly three decades, helped to start the local Little Theatre, and was the volunteer head coach for the 1972 girls' basketball team that was the runner-up in the state tournament. She was an incredible woman, and it was an honor to know her.

The congregation had more than our fair share of engineers because Greene is close to Huntsville, where Werner von Braun had settled after World War II to work on rockets for the American government. NASA had their rocket propulsion labs there. The town had been diversifying since the 1950s, but there were still a disproportionate number of left-brained people: computer engineers, systems analysts, and bona fide rocket scientists.

My father had been an engineer, working at the Waterways' Experiment Station in Vicksburg, Mississippi, and I knew a little bit about how engineers think—life is a problem to be solved. If something can't be solved, the best thing for an engineer is to ignore it altogether.

At first I was frustrated with the engineer's way of thinking: making sure that all the details were clearly defined before agreeing that we could decide whether we were going to do whatever we were talking about, arguing about the best way to define the question to the point of ignoring the answer. But almost every time, we would figure it out after lengthy discussions, often involving organizational charts and spreadsheets.

Because of that propensity to discuss and analyze, working with one engineer was usually helpful, working with two could be more of a challenge, and working with three or more could often be downright difficult. When we'd lived in West Branch, there were several years when we had three lawyers on the Vestry, and I'd asked the Lord to deliver me from attorneys. After several Vestry meetings at St. Thomas in Greene, there were a couple of times I found myself wishing I was in a room full of lawyers again.

Then I figured out that if I told one of the engineers about a problem I thought we needed to solve, or about an opportunity for ministry that the parish had, they would often suggest a solution or an idea to make it work—better, more easily, more efficiently than I would have known how to do it.

The engineer mindset was that we could do it. Whatever it was, we could do it. After a while, I believed it, too. I wrote in the weekly parish newsletter that St. Thomas was like a bumblebee. I told my readers I wasn't sure if this were true or not, but somewhere along the way I'd heard that someone had scientifically proven that a bumblebee is not able to fly. Of course, they do fly, but it doesn't seem likely if you look at one—that's a lot of weight for those little wings to carry. I told them I guess a bumblebee doesn't know it can't fly, so it just does it anyway. I wrote that we were like a bumblebee parish, and that we could do whatever we decided to do.

George, one of the especially left-brained engineers, told me that he'd looked into this some years before when he felt a need to defend science, and there had never been any scientific papers or lectures suggesting that bumblebees can't fly. I thanked him and told him he'd messed up a perfectly good simile, but my point was still valid: that we could do anything we could imagine.

He said, "As long as we keep our hearts right."

Wow—just when I thought I had engineers all figured out. This conversation led to one of those things that I said over and over at St. Thomas: "There is no limit to what people of good will can do together, in the power of the Holy Spirit."

THE THEOLOGY OF GUMBO

Our sweet baby girl Anna Grace Hinton was born the following February. It was more diapers, bassinets, and car seats, again regular and routine on the surface but also wonderful and extraordinary every day. Lost in the wonder of it, I told Beulah, "Babies are just everyday miracles!" Jude had been a cute baby; Gracie was simply beautiful. I was amazed at how fundamentally different two children born of the same parents and being raised in the same household could be; from the very beginning, she was going to do things her way, on her schedule, when she got ready.

JoJo called us once a week, every Sunday afternoon. He was doing well back in West Branch, but he missed us. In all honesty, we missed him, too. He'd started a yard care business, working there and at the Piggly Wiggly until his outdoor job became full-time year-round. People liked him and trusted him with their lawns and hedges and vegetable gardens. He was saving up money to buy a truck; until he got it, he would walk to different yards, pushing his mower loaded up with rakes and weed eaters and bags of fertilizer.

He always wanted to talk to Jude when he called, and he really wanted to meet baby Gracie. Every time we talked, he told us how much he missed us. We invited him to come visit, but he said he didn't want to bother us and didn't want to ride the bus over to Greene. That went on for a few months, until Beulah told him she had an all-day in-service training in Starkville, which was close enough to West Branch that she could go and pick him up on her way home. She told him she would bring him to Greene on Friday, and I could take him back the following Monday.

That Friday afternoon when Beulah came home from her conference, Jude and I were kicking a soccer ball in the front yard, with Gracie napping in her bassinet and our good dog Jabbok nearby, guarding her just as she had guarded Jude when he was our baby.

Jude was five now and played on a five-and-six-year-old soccer team. I was the coach of the Silver Snakes because none of the other parents would volunteer, even after I told everybody I'd never played soccer and didn't even know all the rules. As it turned out, the rules didn't matter all that much in five-and-six-year-old soccer, and neither did the score. Only a couple of kids on any of the teams had an idea about what they were doing—the ones with the most competitive parents. The main thing the rest of them seemed interested in were the orange slices at halftime. I was just glad to have a good reason to be outside.

Jude seemed to have gotten the idea that the point of the whole thing was to kick the ball very hard, which is good some of the time but not all of the time. It was especially not a good idea when he kicked it the wrong way.

We were working on kicking it more gently when Beulah drove up, with JoJo beaming his beautiful grin in the front seat. Jude had gotten quite bored with kicking the ball softly and was delighted that his mama was home. When JoJo got out of the car, Jude wasn't sure at first, and I worried it would break poor JoJo's heart, but then Jude remembered him and yelled "Uncle Joe!" as he ran into his arms. JoJo picked him up and spun around, holding him tightly.

I was afraid JoJo would get dizzy spinning, but he stopped and put Jude down. He said, "Now, let me look at you, just let me look a minute here." He walked all the way around him as Jude stood still, and then he asked, "How old are you now—seven? Eight?"

Jude swelled up with pride, stood as tall as he could get, and declared, "I'm five."

"Five? No, that ain't right. You got to be six, at least!"

"No sir, I'm just five."

"Well, it look like you've grown all up. You be drivin' a car pretty soon, now."

His mother stepped in and picked her little boy up. He hugged her tightly, and then squirmed to get away. She acknowledged, "He'll be driving before we know it." She stepped over to kiss me and murmured, "And way before we're ready."

Jabbok was standing at her post, still on duty close by Gracie, but she really wanted to come and smell her old friend JoJo. Her tail was wagging so hard I thought she'd capsize the bassinet, so I walked over to relieve her of her duty. She ran to JoJo, who knelt down and scratched her ears. "Hey, Jabbok—hey, old girl. It's good to see you."

Then JoJo came over to me. I was thinking about teasing him that I was third on his list of friends to greet, but he ignored me altogether and looked down at baby Gracie, which put me down to fourth. "Well now, ain't you just the sweetest thing I ever saw!" Turning to Beulah, he gushed, "She look just like you, Beulah!" Then, seeming almost afraid to say it, he asked Beulah, "Can I pick her up?"

She smiled and answered, "Of course you can, Uncle Joe."

I took the moment to look at him closely as he held our baby girl. There was no trace of the Special Session camper I'd known years before. He was sure of himself—not at all cocky, but confident. I was proud of him, proud of the progress he'd made, and proud of my little part in that. He looked up at me and said, "Oh, hey—Buddy. I didn't see you there." Then with his free arm he embraced me, and we laughed.

It felt good to have JoJo with us, a distinct part of our growing family. We caught up on some of the news about West Branch and the Church of the Holy Incarnation, but JoJo was much more interested in finding out about Greene and St. Thomas. Beulah suggested that he should think about moving over to Greene, too. "We've got lawns and hedges and gardens over here in Alabama, too, you know."

He considered the idea for a long moment and then asked, "Y'all got a Piggly Wiggly?" I told him we did, and other grocery stores as well, and that he should think about it. He assured us that he would, but I got the idea that there was something else keeping him from thinking about it too much, something Beulah and I didn't know.

We had a big supper of pork chops and mashed potatoes. Beulah made biscuits from scratch and JoJo surprised us by making some deliciously unhealthy gravy from the pork fat. Little Gracie was put to bed, and Jude stayed up as long as he could, sitting as close to JoJo as possible until he fell asleep leaning against him. The adults stayed up late, glad for the chance to catch up.

JoJo and Jude and I spent a lot of the next day in our yard, with JoJo either doing things that needed to be done for the grass or a bush or a tree, or telling me what I needed to get or do. Around lunchtime, he and I went to the Greene Lawn and Garden Store to get stuff to curtail the relentless invasion of weeds in our yard and help the grass take over, and we got two impressively expensive lawn sprinklers.

Apparently, I'd met the pretty young lady at the cash register before; she asked JoJo, "You workin' for the preacher?" I laughed and told her it was the other way around—I was working for him. I caught the appraising smile she gave him, but JoJo missed it. I also caught the young woman's name from her name tag: Joy.

The next afternoon, as Beulah was making hot dogs and macaroni and cheese for lunch—Jude's favorite—JoJo started cooking a pot of gumbo for us, the way his grandmother had taught his mother. JoJo's Granny was from Metairie, Louisiana; he'd put her gumbo pot in his suitcase to make it in, a large, heavy cast iron black Dutch oven.

After we'd admired the pot, Beulah asked JoJo what he needed to put in the gumbo. He smiled and asked her what she had in the freezer. He said you could put whatever you had or whatever you wanted in it. We had some chicken, but they decided that I needed to go to the store to get a pint jar of oysters, some crabmeat, and some okra. This was my cue to confess that I wasn't real sure about gumbo, although I had eaten it before. JoJo asked how I had lived my whole life without loving gumbo, and I told him the problem was that I don't like okra. When I suggested we might leave the okra out, JoJo was firm. "Oh, no—the only thing you *got* to have in gumbo is okra."

"But you said you could put chicken or oysters or crab meat or sausage, or whatever you want."

"That's right. You can put any of that in there, or all of it. It don't matter. But if it don't have okra, it ain't gumbo. It's just soup if it don't have okra."

By the time I got back with the necessaries, the whole house was filled with a glorious smell of chicken and sausage simmering in onion, celery, and bell pepper. JoJo and Beulah cut up the okra and put it into the big black pot with the crabmeat and oysters. Every time I went in the kitchen that day, my mouth watered. I wasn't enthusiastic about the idea of picking out the okra and the oysters, but I had to admit it smelled wonderful.

We spent most of that afternoon kicking the soccer ball with Jude and working a bit more in the yard. JoJo said that what we really needed was to put some lime on the yard so the grass would grow and the weeds would not. I told him I'd get some the next week, but he insisted that we needed to go back to the Greene Lawn and Garden Store so he could put it out that day. "You'd just mess it all up," he said. "You better leave this to somebody who knows what to do."

So JoJo and I went back to the Greene Lawn and Garden Store. I was thinking we could just duck in and get what we needed and head back home, but JoJo didn't seem like he was in much of a hurry. He dawdled at the front of the store, looking around and picking at the clearance aisle items without really seeming to look at them. I asked him if he was okay, and he nodded that he was, but he didn't seem like he was in any hurry to find the lime and go back to our house. I told him I'd get the lime and meet him where he was, and he nodded again, in a way that made me wonder if he'd heard what I'd said.

I spent a few minutes wandering around, hoping to demonstrate to an employee how completely bewildered I was, but apparently that was too subtle, so finally I had to chase somebody down to ask for help in finding the lime. It seemed like the man working there was more than willing to let me know I was bothering him and that he had more important things to do than to help a customer, but he did allow my interruption long enough to tell me to "look on aisle twenty-four," which was about twenty-three aisles away. I found the aisle, and, finding the lime in several forms, I put three samples in my cart.

When I got back to the front of the store, I found out the real reason we were there: JoJo was talking to Joy, the young cashier who'd helped us the day before. She was obviously flirting with him, and he was doing his best to hold up his end of things. I watched for a few minutes, partially concealed behind a display of paintbrushes and masking tape. She was listening to JoJo talk and laughing about something he'd said. Again, I was impressed by how much JoJo had changed in the years I'd known him. He'd lived so much of his life as Bobbo's brother, being treated as someone with intellectual disabilities, and now he was chatting up a young woman who seemed interested in him!

When I rolled the cart over to where JoJo and Joy were, she excused herself, saying she had to get back to work. When she was too far away to hear me, I whispered, "She's cute."

JoJo answered, "Yeah."

"So?"

"So what?"

"So, you gonna ask her out?"

"No!"

"Why not? You could ask her to come to supper tonight."

He was very serious when he answered, "I ain't gonna. That's all they is to that. You get the lime?" But I could tell there was more to it, and I thought that maybe he was trying the idea on for size.

I couldn't wait to tell Beulah. When we got back home, JoJo stirred the gumbo and added some hot sauce, and then he and Jude went out into the backyard. I told Beulah about JoJo talking to Joy.

She was just as excited as I was and wanted to know all about her: where she was from, how long she'd worked at the Greene Lawn and Garden Store, did JoJo get her phone number, did I even know her last name. The more questions she asked me, the more inadequate I was revealed to be, and the more exasperated she became, until finally she told me she'd go to the Greene Lawn and Garden Store the next day when I was taking JoJo back to West Branch and talk to Joy herself.

Finally, it was time for supper. Beulah had baked a beautiful loaf of bread, golden brown and fresh from the oven. And she'd made banana pudding with too many vanilla wafers—JoJo's favorite—for dessert. We all sat at the table in the kitchen, Jude in his big boy chair and baby Gracie in her bassinet, and I invited JoJo to say the blessing. He held out his big calloused hands for us to take, and we did. JoJo sat quiet a moment and breathed a deep, contented sigh.

"Lord Jesus, come sit with us a while, and help us know you're at this table with us. Thank you for this food, and for this home, and for this family." I almost said "Amen" then, thinking he'd pretty well covered it, but he hadn't looked up, and after a few seconds he continued.

"Thank you for Miss Beulah, for liftin' me up, for her honesty, and for her love. Thank you for Father Buddy, for havin' faith in me and you, for all his help, and for his respect. Thank you for Mr. Jude, for lettin' me be his friend, for his smile, and for his hugs. And thank you for Baby Gracie. She ain't much yet, but you can tell she gonna be sweet and tough, just like her mama."

I took a peek to see if he was finished and saw that he still had more to say, but I could tell he was struggling with what he wanted to say next. Another deep breath, and he continued: "And thank you for sweet Jabbok, about the best dog in the whole wide world. Lord, I just wish we could all be more like her, and love each other like you do, no matter what."

I heard Jabbok's tail thump on the floor when JoJo said her name, and I felt the tears come to my closed eyes. I thought, "Wow. The unassailable truth: God loves us no matter what. That will preach." And it has, for years.

It was a perfect moment. I sat there squeezing Beulah's hand in my right and Jude's in my left, both of them holding JoJo's hands to complete the circle, and I knew we were all wagging our tails with the joy of it. We sat in holy silence for at least five seconds, until Jude said, "Amen! Let's eat!"

We all laughed, and the moment became a feast. We passed our bowls to Beulah, who put rice in them and passed them to JoJo, who filled them with dark, mysterious gumbo. Then we passed the bread around, steaming and fluffy white.

At first I looked for okra and oysters to eat around or pick out, but after a few bites I gave myself permission to just relish every spoonful without trying to figure out what was in it. When I asked if I could have a second bowl, JoJo nodded his approval. He asked, "You want me to leave out the okra and the oysters?"

I said, "No, thanks. I guess I like them in gumbo."

JoJo put gumbo into my bowl and said, "Y'know—I believe gumbo is like livin'. You have to have some parts in it that you don't much like, and it turns out they's what makes the whole thing so good. You have to have some folks you don't much care for, but that's what brings everybody all together. The okra is what holds it all together, just like . . ."

He stopped, having realized that we were really listening to him, and became completely flustered and bashful. He muttered, "Oh, I don't know . . . don't pay me no mind."

Beulah replied, "No, JoJo—we have to live our whole lives, the good and the bad. Those things we might want to pick out just make us stronger in the end."

JoJo nodded. "Like when terrible bad things happen."

I realized he was thinking about his mother, his aunt, and his brother Bobbo, who'd died in an accident a few years before. I ventured, "I think you're right: you can't have gumbo without okra. You can't live without pain and loss, without losing people you love. It's just part of it." Then I added, "I think it's just what you said, JoJo—God loves us all the time, no matter what—even when we're okra and oysters. No matter what."

JoJo nodded and affirmed, "All the time, no matter what."

Then, to lighten the mood, I pontificated, "If you were some kind of professor, you could write this up into a dissertation or something."

Beulah added, "You could call it The Theology of Gumbo: Taking the Bad Parts with the Good."

JoJo wiped his eyes with his paper napkin. "It ain't my favorite part, though."

Beulah had teared up by now, and so had I. She put her hand over his and said, "No, it's not my favorite part, either."

JoJo looked up at me with a big grin on his face. "But we know that everybody we lost we gonna see again. We got hope for somethin' better comin'. Like banana puddin'!"

And really and truly, the banana pudding that night was heavenly.

Later, when Jude and Gracie were asleep, Beulah asked JoJo to write down his grandmother's recipe. She had taught him how to read when we lived in West Branch, and he was proud to share. He told us he didn't think the recipe had ever been written down before, but he worked on it when he went to bed and gave it to her in the morning.

Get you a great big heavy pot,
like the one my granny gave my mama.
In a skillet, or that big pot, fry up some bacon
or sausage or fatback, whatever one you have.
Bacon is best.
Take the meat out of the pot and put it off to the side.
Melt some butter in the bottom of the pot.
Not too much so it don't get oily.
Put some white flower in and stir it up real good
until it's about as dark as the back of my hand.
It should be the color of a chocolate candy bar.
Now you got the roo.
That's the most important part.
If it taste oily dump it out and start over.
You can't make no good gumbo with oily roo.
Now you put in some onion
and some bell pepper
and some celery
and your chopped okra.
Chop it up fine so Buddy can't pick it all out.
Stir it up a good long time.
Put in some red Cayenne pepper.
Be careful not to put too much.
I just add a little bit and taste it
and keep putting more in there until it is enough.
Add some water when the celery is soft
and the onion is almost clear.
Then you can add some water

and put that meat you just cooked back in there
and heat it all up slow.
Let that come up a boil for two minutes
and then turn the heat way down.
Now you can add in some garlic however much you want.
When that is cooled down enough
you can add in whatever else you want in your gumbo.
Some people put chicken in or sausage or fish.
I think the best gumbo has oysters and some crab meat.
It will need to cook a long time real slow.
The more it cook the better it will be.
You got to stir it a lot.
Just let it steam out so it will get real thick.
If you have a bay leaf or two you best put that in there
about a half hour before you want to eat.
Remember to pick it back out before you serve it up.
You can't eat no bay leafs.
My mama put Tabasco sauce in hers
but some people don't like that much
so I just put a little.
If I'm cooking it just for me I put more Tabasco in it.
But not as much as Mama did.
I like a little file spice, but you have to wait until the gumbo
is starting to cool so it don't get all clotted up.
Then stir it in real good.
Put some rice in a bowl and put the gumbo on top of it.
Some good bread and good friends make it a very good meal.
Good banana pudding make it perfect.

4

NUNYA

On Monday morning, as JoJo and I drove back to Mississippi, we had a lot to talk about. He told me he hadn't wanted to upset Beulah, but the Church of the Holy Incarnation wasn't the same anymore. He told me they'd hired an older priest to be their new rector, and that he was okay but didn't have much energy or any new ideas. JoJo said a lot of the people there thought that was just fine. I asked about Chuck and Kate, and he said they seemed to be doing okay, but they still didn't have much to do with him. He said the church didn't feel so much like home as it used to, and that he stopped going for a little while, until Sally the organist told him they really missed him in the choir.

He told me that his lawncare business was doing well and that he was probably going to quit his job at the Piggly Wiggly as soon as he could buy a truck. He told me he knew a man who had a 1972 Chevy pickup he wasn't using, and he'd told JoJo he could buy it at a good price.

I was concerned that this man was going to take advantage of JoJo's trusting nature, but the man had told him that JoJo had helped grow the best tomatoes in the county, and he wanted to give him the truck because none of his children wanted it. JoJo said the man loved that old truck, and he wanted to sell it to somebody who'd take care of it, but JoJo couldn't let him give it to him; he didn't want to take his charity. So they agreed on a selling price of one thousand dollars. I don't know much about cars, and I know even less about trucks, but I know a twenty-year-old Chevy pickup in good shape is worth a lot more than a thousand bucks.

I asked him if he'd ever thought about moving to Greene. He was quiet for a half a mile and then said, "Well, yeah—I have. But . . ."

"But what?"

"Well, I guess I just ain't ready. I got some unfinished business back in West Branch."

"The pickup truck?"

"Well, yeah."

"And?"

"Well, that'll be Nunya."

"Nunya?"

JoJo chuckled to himself. "You ain't never heard of Nunya?"

"No. Who's Nunya?"

"Oh," said JoJo, clearly enjoying himself. "Nunya is strong and powerful."

"Is Nunya a friend of yours?"

"Oh, yeah—Nunya's a friend. The mighty Nunya, that's what I say."

"What's Nunya's last name?"

"Binness."

"Nunya Binness?" I asked, still not catching on.

He laughed, delighted at the knowledge that I was in the dark. He said, "What all else I got goin' is Nunya Binness." Then he dragged it for me, slowly: "None . . . of . . . your . . . binness."

I thought about letting it hurt my feelings that I was being told to butt out, but he was laughing so hard I couldn't help but laugh, too. It's hard to be mad when you're laughing. We laughed for a mile or two, and then when I thought it was over, he said, "Y'know, for such an educated man you ain't always all that bright," and we had to laugh some more.

Somewhere around Decatur, I asked him about Joy. He said, "Who?"

"The young lady at the Greene Lawn and Garden Store. She's pretty cute."

I don't think I'd ever seen that expression on his face when he said, "Yeah, pretty cute."

"She seems to have taken a shine to you, JoJo."

"A shine?"

"Um, she likes you."

"You think?"

"Yeah, I do. She looked like she might want to go out with you."

"Oh. Well, I like her, too. But she ain't gonna go out with me. She just messin' around."

"Why? Why wouldn't she go out with you?" I thought I knew where this was going, but we had to talk about it.

"'Cause—you know. 'Cause I'm like the way I am, Buddy. Ain't no woman gonna be interested in me. That's just the way it is."

"That's not true, JoJo."

"That's what my mama said. She tol' us both, me and Bobbo, she said, 'Ain't no woman ever gonna want to fool with either one of you, so you better just leave 'em alone.'" He looked down at his knees, hard, and continued, "She said that's just the way it is, and I don't need to worry about it."

I didn't want to contradict JoJo's mother, but I couldn't let that stand. "JoJo, that was a long time ago. You've changed a lot since then, grown into a fine man. I think Joy would be lucky to have you."

He looked up and smiled. "You do?"

"Yes sir—I do."

We rode a few miles more, and then he said, "You think I'd be a good, a good—you know—a good boyfriend?"

"Of course. You're kind, you're polite, you've got a good job, you care about other people, you're not going to hurt anybody or lie or cheat. I think you'd be a very good boyfriend. And when the time comes, you'll be a good husband."

I looked over to see my friend JoJo in deep thought, working on something. I let him work on it, and eventually he said, "Well, all right then. There's this other girl, too. You know Wanda from back home, right?"

"Wanda? Do I know her?"

"Yeah. You remember her—you and her drove all the way down to Hattiesburg that time with that crazy John the Baptist. You bought her supper at the Western Sizzlin' and y'all talked all about God and the church and all. After that, she started comin' to church and we just started talking. I think she might be shinin' on me a little bit, too."

I remembered Wanda now. She was the deputy sheriff who had not been very happy about having to drive a crazy man and a preacher all the way down to Hattiesburg in south Mississippi. I remembered that we talked on the way back, and she was concerned about her recently deceased mother's salvation and skeptical about whether I was really a preacher at all after I told her that God loves her mother no matter how hard she was. I remembered she was pretty intimidating at first but that she softened up on our drive back to West Branch.

"Is Wanda that Nunya you were talking about?"

"Yeah."

"And you think she's interested in you?"

"Interested?"

"You know, like she wants to go out on a date with you."

"Oh. Yeah, I think so."

"Why do you think that?"

"'Cause she told me."

"What did she say?"

"She said, 'JoJo, we ought to go out sometime.'"

"And what did you say?"

"I said, 'Okay.'"

"So have you asked her out?"

"No!" I waited, and he continued, "'Cause of what my mama said, 'bout no woman ever gonna want to fool with me. 'Cause of, you know, 'cause of how I am."

It felt like a critical moment, and I wanted to be careful. I said, "JoJo, listen to me. I'm sure your mother was a fine woman and that she loved you and Bobbo and wanted to protect you. She didn't want anybody to hurt either one of you. But listen"—I took a deep breath—"you know I loved Bobbo, too."

"Yeah?"

"You and Bobbo were treated the same way, but you were never the same. Bobbo was not smart, and they treated you like you weren't, either—but you are. You're just as smart as anybody."

He murmured, "Yeah," but without conviction.

I pulled into a gas station parking lot and turned off the car. I said, "JoJo, look at me." When he did, I saw his eyes watering. I said, "It's got to be hard to realize that you're not who you thought you were for most of your life. But you have to believe me: you are a smart man. You're not like Bobbo."

He replied, "No, I ain't. I ain't like Bobbo."

"But you've been treated like you were not smart for such a long time, I think you believed it, too. And you wanted to stay close to Bobbo, to take care of him, so you let people think you weren't smart. But now it's time."

"Time for what?"

"It's time for you to be who God made you to be, JoJo."

"You tellin' me that God want me to ask Wanda out on a date?"

"I'm telling you God wants you to love and be loved. I'm telling you God wants you to enjoy your life. If a woman is interested in you, and you're interested in her, you ought to see how things might go. Ask her out. What's the worst thing that could happen?"

"She could laugh at me."

His pain was so deep I could feel it in my stomach. "She could, JoJo, but she won't. There's no reason for anybody to laugh at you, ever again."

"Well . . ."

"Well, what?"

"Well, we'll see."

"Well, all right!"

"I ain't sayin' I'm gonna ask her out on a date or anything."

"No, but you know you can. And you know she'd go out with you if you do ask her."

"Well, yeah, I guess."

"So it's your choice." I put the car back into drive and we headed on, toward Sulligent, back toward Mississippi. After a few miles I asked, "So if you did ask her out, where would y'all go?"

"Out on a date?"

"Yeah."

"With Wanda?"

"Yeah."

"Well, Buddy, that's some more of that Nunya, ain't it?"

And of course it was.

5

Two Boxers Nose to Nose

There's a story in almost every sermon I preach; it's just the way I talk. There's something powerful about stories.

When I was fifteen, a friend of mine talked me into going to be a counselor for the Episcopal Church summer camp, and I started to become who I am. A pretty girl talked me into coming back for a session for people with a variety of abilities and disabilities, and it changed me forever. I was asked to direct one of the two Special Sessions two years after I was ordained, and directed eleven sessions before we moved to Alabama.

One Sunday after a service in which I preached a sermon using a Special Session story, Gail, a nurse in the congregation, asked me, "Do you just want to talk about camp sessions for people with mental and physical challenges all the time, or are you going to do something about it?" There's something powerful about stories.

Truthfully, I didn't think it was a good idea at first. Camp McDowell, the Episcopal Church camp and conference center in Alabama is a wonderful place, but it wasn't well suited for this group: most of the campers are adults, some in wheelchairs, many with mobility issues, most living sedentary lives. There wasn't much flat ground, the bathrooms weren't accessible, and the sidewalks were too narrow.

I happened to know the executive director; Mark had been in the class before me in seminary. I also knew how tight camp schedules were during the summer, and I felt sure that if I talked to him about starting a Special Session at Camp McDowell, he would politely tell me that it was impossible. So I could say I tried, but Mark said we couldn't do it. I told Nurse Gail that I would talk to the camp director about it.

By the time I met with Mark, I'd had time to remember what a significant part of my life these camp sessions had been. It would be something important, not just for the parish but also for the diocese. I wanted Jude and Gracie to grow up in that loving, inclusive environment, and I had to admit that I missed being part of a community that offered such unconditional love.

When I presented the idea to Mark, I was surprised and gratified that he said he would consider it. It turned out that he'd worked with people with disabilities somewhere along the line. He'd heard about the Special Session at Camp Bratton-Green in Mississippi and knew how an important it was—not only for the campers but also for the counselors. The more we talked about it, the more he seemed willing to make room for it. He thought he could cut a day from one session and move another session a day or two later, and that we could use the mid-summer break over the Fourth of July to do the Special Session. And so it came to pass that the first Special Session at Camp McDowell was in the middle of the summer of 1998.

I contacted two centers in Central Alabama for people with disabilities to tell them what we were going to do and started trying to find people to serve on a staff. When I'd started doing Special Sessions in 1971, they had already been doing them for three years, and everybody knew what to expect. Now, starting a new session among people who'd never heard of such a thing, it was difficult to get people to commit. As always, the most difficult positions to fill were the camp nurses. Nurse Gail was committed, but we would need another—there's an awful lot of medication to be distributed to this population of people with a wide range of special needs.

We had a relatively new family in the church: Richard and Candy Chambliss, their daughter Noelle, and their son Belk. Rich was an ambitious attorney who prided himself on being tough and aggressive, but Candy was a nurse who had worked with a physician in private practice until he'd sold his practice. It seemed perfect, but I felt there was a significant problem: Candy was strikingly beautiful.

She had grown up in Winona, Mississippi, and been Miss Ole Miss a decade before and then the runner-up to Miss Mississippi. Now, years later, she still looked like she could be walking the pageant runway. Tall, blonde, graceful, elegant—I had a hard time imagining her at summer camp. I asked several other people, but I didn't ask her. She heard that I was looking for a nurse, and she asked me about it. When I asked her if she'd be interested, she asked if her children could come to the session. I told her our kids were coming and that we'd love to have Belk and Noelle—and Richard, too, if he could come.

A young man named Riley heard that we were starting a Special Session in Alabama and called to ask if he could come. I'd known him when he was a counselor at the camp in Mississippi; now he'd graduated from Mississippi State and lived in Birmingham. I told him it would be good to have somebody else who knew what I was talking about. Beulah had been trained in special education and was on the Special Session staff in Mississippi, but this time she was concerned that she would have to spend most of her time looking after Jude and Gracie, and she didn't know how helpful she could be.

The other big problem was that we didn't know the campers, not a single one. Some homes and centers were willing to send their charges, but they tended to fill out the applications in one extreme or the other: either making sure that we were aware of the worst possibilities they could imagine or minimizing the individuals' issues and challenges so we would accept them as campers. This had probably happened in Mississippi as well, but I knew most of the campers there before I became the session director, and we didn't have to rely on the applications as much.

Eighteen brave young people volunteered to serve as counselors, without any real idea of what they were getting into. Nineteen other people were on staff, including Beulah, Jude and Gracie, Nurse Gail, and Nurse Candy and her two children. Noelle was thirteen, and we trusted her to ride herd over her brother and Jude and Gracie; actually, the four of them did pretty well together. Richard had planned to come, but he couldn't at the last minute . . . something about a big case that he had coming up.

We had the training session and prepared as best we could to be ready to welcome twenty-three campers. They arrived two days later, many of them quite different from what the applications had led us to expect.

One of our campers was a "large" muscular man whose application described him as "emotionally disabled." The memorable sentence from the application was that "Eric has the potential to exhibit aggressive and occasionally violent behavior." Eric was in his thirties, always ready to fight, not likely to try anything new. He didn't sing along, didn't want to get up, didn't want to go to bed. When the campers arrived, I suspected we'd made a mistake in accepting him, and I asked Riley to keep his eye on him. Eric's counselor was a seventeen-year-old kid from Tuscaloosa named Jeremy who loved Jesus and wanted to do the right thing, but he was not equipped to deal with Eric.

I don't think any of us were equipped to deal with Eric; I know I wasn't.

The week went well enough for most of the campers and most of the staff. Each of the campers—and all of the staff—had their own particularities that had to be learned and accounted for. There were several seizures, some obsessive-compulsive behaviors, and several homesick campers and counselors. All in all, it was a pretty good experience, and I knew the problems could have been much worse.

One of the highlights of every Special Session is the Talent Show: every camper is given the opportunity to perform for the rest of the camp. When I mentioned the Talent Show during the training session before the campers arrived, one of the counselors laughed, thinking that I was making a joke. I said, "You will be surprised at the talents you'll see."

I went on to tell the counselors that the whole thing succeeded or failed because of them—them finding the campers' talents and then receiving whatever they did on stage with wild enthusiasm.

I asked Riley to cue the music backstage and told him that I would be the Talent Show host, congratulating the performers and introducing the next act. I asked Riley because he knew how these things went; if a camper is out there lip-syncing along with the Backstreet Boys or belting it out with Shania Twain, sometimes you need to cut them off, and sometimes you need to let it run, and you just have to have a feel for it. Riley and I talked about this, and he said he understood. I told him if I thought somebody would need to be cut short, if they looked like they were ready to leave the stage, I would pull on my ear a la Carol Burnett. I told him since we only had twenty-three campers, we would have a lot of time for the Talent Show and wouldn't need to cut anybody off for the sake of time. He said he understood.

Toward the end of the show, Eric took the stage to MC Hammer's "U Can't Touch This" to wild and energetic acclaim. It was one of those moments when it felt like the whole camp was together, all of us hollering and clapping and encouraging Eric, who seemed to be enjoying himself for the first time that week. He was singing and dancing, and most of the rest of us were singing and dancing along with him, and then, just before Hammer says, "Stop—Hammer Time," Riley stopped the music.

Sometimes at the Special Sessions in Mississippi, we'd had to stop the song before it was over, but when a performance was generating that sort of magic, it was understood that we could let it run. Later, Riley told me he thought he'd already let it run too long, and he told Eric he was sorry. Eric's counselor Jeremy led the counselors in their righteous booing, and we thought about starting the song over, but the damage was done. The moment died, and Eric was furious.

During chapel that evening, Jeremy and Riley took Eric out of the chapel and tried to talk to him. Whatever they'd tried didn't work, apparently: before the last prayer I saw the counselor in the back of the chapel desperately trying to get my attention. When he did, he motioned frantically for me to come and help. I brought the prayers to an end, reminded everybody about milk and cookies and night medicines, and hurried out to find Eric threatening to leave.

Eric was extremely agitated, in a "potential to exhibit aggressive and occasionally violent behavior" sort of way. He told us he hated Jeremy, calling him "that little white boy," and kept pointing to Riley and referring to him as "that fool." I tried to keep everybody calm, which worked pretty well on Riley and Jeremy but didn't do anything at all for Eric. I asked him what he wanted to do, and he told me he was going home. I asked him how he was going to get there, and he told me he was going to walk. I asked him where he lived, and he said it was on Third Avenue. I asked him what town he lived in and he told me it was across the street from the high school. His counselor, completely undone by the whole thing, told me Eric lived in Birmingham. I told Eric that Birmingham was about sixty miles away, and he said he didn't care. I told him it would take about thirty hours to walk that far, and he said he didn't care.

I tried to call his bluff. "Well, all right—go. Which way are you going to turn at the end of this road?"

He hesitated. "Right."

I asked, "Are you sure? Are we north of Birmingham, or south of it?"

"I don't care."

"What if you go the wrong way?"

"I don't care."

"I tell you what, Eric. Let's wait until after breakfast, and then we'll take you home in a car."

"I ain't stayin'."

"We can take you in the morning."

"I ain't stayin'."

I took a moment to look at Riley and Jeremy to see if they had any ideas, and Eric started walking down the road. I jogged ahead of him and stood right in front of him so he'd have to either stop or go around me. He came up and stood so close I could smell his breath; I'm sure we looked like two boxers nose to nose after the weigh-in, both trying to intimidate the other.

I am a large man, at least three inches taller than Eric. But I have a lot of built-in fluff, while he is mostly muscle; his effort to intimidate me was more successful than my effort to intimidate him. But I couldn't just let a camper walk down the road and into the dark, and I wasn't sure that I was able to stop him. Eric glared at me, a tactic I'm sure he had often used to great advantage. He was used to people being scared, and maybe he could tell I was scared, too. But I wouldn't get out of his way.

After a long, tense moment, he asked, "After breakfast?"

I answered, "Yes sir." We both relaxed. As we walked back toward Riley and Jeremy, I suggested, "Or tomorrow night, if you stay, during the dance you could do '2 Legit 2 Quit.'"

He stopped, seeming surprised that I knew an MC Hammer song, and looked at me like he expected a trick. I told him, "We shouldn't have stopped your song, man. I'm sorry. But tomorrow night, it could be . . . Hammer Time!"

He stayed, decided that he was better with "U Can't Touch This," and this time Riley played it all the way through, to thunderous applause and my great relief.

Our children and Nurse Candy's children stayed together, most often with Beulah watching over them and Noelle assisting. They swam in the pool, enjoyed the activities, and ate in the dining hall. They were afraid of the campers at first but relaxed as the week went along. We all agreed that this was a wonderful experience for them.

On the last full day of the session, Nurse Candy's husband Richard came and had lunch with us. It was always loud and chaotic in the dining hall; it's just the nature of the place. He was clearly uncomfortable—with the noise and with the campers and counselors who were making it. I'd seen similar reactions from visitors before; the environment is not something most folks can slip into easily.

Richard sat with his family and seemed nervous about being there among all the odd people. His children looked happy to see him, but he and Candy were having what looked like an unpleasant conversation before she had to go distribute lunchtime medications.

One of our campers that first year was a man named Tommy. He was in his mid-fifties and had lived with his mother in the same house his whole life. We were concerned that he'd never been away from home for even a single night; I told his counselor that he might be homesick or afraid, but I think the separation was harder on his mother than it was on him. Tommy had a good time most of the week, but his counselor told me he was slowing down some, getting tired and grouchy from all the heat and activity. Like a lot of our campers, Tommy was fairly dramatic, not one to keep any discomfort to himself.

After lunch that day, Tommy was trying to help clean up. The plates, cups, and forks all went into gray tubs that were carried to one window where they were collected and taken to be washed, but everything else had to be brought to the big window where the cooks put the food for us to come and get. Tommy was trying to carry too much—a platter, a bowl, a pitcher, a bottle of ketchup—and he was having a hard time balancing it all.

Richard saw him as he was walking past him toward the big window, got up, and offered to take something for him. Tommy had been proud that he was helping, and it looked like he would refuse Richard's help. But Richard said something that made Tommy smile, and Tommy let him take one or two things; they walked up to the window together. It wasn't a big thing, and it didn't take long, but it was an act of kindness that I was glad to see.

Later that afternoon, Beulah told me she'd heard Richard telling Candy that he didn't want his children exposed to this. She told me they'd argued about it in the cabin during the rest time after lunch and that Richard was so angry, she thought she was going to have to come and get me.

I asked, "To calm him down?"

She answered, "To make sure I didn't slap the smirk off his arrogant face." Beulah has never been one to back away from a confrontation.

I checked in with Candy that evening and told her I was sorry the session had caused a family problem; she replied that the session wasn't the problem, that Richard was the one with a problem. She told me she thought it was wonderful for her children to be there at the Special Session, that she was hoping they could come back next summer. She assured me she would work it out with Richard.

At that first Special Session at Camp McDowell, we made a lot of mistakes, we learned a lot, we had a lot of fun, and we began to gather a remarkable community whose primary goal is to celebrate who we are rather than who somebody else says we should be. It was difficult, it smelled bad, it was hot, and it was magic. Well before the session was over, we were talking about how we could do it better the following summer. The closing service was filled with tears and promises to "See you next year."

When we got home, I had a note to call Miss Frankie, whose husband Lonny was dying in the hospital.

WEIGHED DOWN BY WHAT COULD HAVE BEEN

I went to the hospital, and as terrible as it sounds, I have to confess that I was relieved that Lonny was not conscious and I didn't have to talk to him. At the nurses' station, I was told it was just a matter of time. The nurse also told me that nobody had come to visit—not even his sons, both of whom lived there in town.

I went to visit with Miss Frankie, who was not able to go to the hospital because of the arthritis in her hip. She was kind to me, as she always was, but I got the sense that there was no great love story coming to an end with Lonny's death. We talked about the funeral, which hymns to sing and what readings to use, and then we had a prayer and I left. The next day, Miss Frankie called to tell me that he had died. Her sons were working with the funeral home, and she wanted to know when we could have the service at the church.

The funeral was crowded, filled with members of the parish and people around town. Their two sons sat on the front row with their mother, clearly uncomfortable at the prospect of being in church and just as clearly determined that nothing I said or did was going to be of any significance to them at all; I expect they were probably right about that. The readings were read and the hymns were sung, but it was all somehow lacking something, as if we were just keeping up appearances, going through the motions.

I've been to some boring church services, but nothing is worse than going through the motions. I wondered about the two sons on the front pew and about all the people who were clearly not buying in to the idea of "hope in resurrection." What do you do? I wondered. How can you live your life if you have no hope, no faith?

At the graveside, after we offered our prayers, I went and hugged Miss Frankie under the funeral home tent. There were no tears, but when she said, "Enjoyed the preachin', Father," I could sense her relief that it was all over. I shook hands with both sons, both of them looking away as if it was somehow distasteful to take my hand, and we were done.

I asked Miss Frankie when a good time might be for me to come for a visit, and she said she'd love to see me, and why didn't I just come by that afternoon. Someone had given her a bottle of sherry, she said, and we might have a little taste. I didn't tell her, but I'd never had sherry. Still, it had to be better than Miss Edith's lukewarm Scotch.

By the time I got there, I saw that she'd started on the sherry without me. I sat down and began to say the things you say: that I was sad for her loss and sorry that her husband was gone. She started to cry a little and told me she knew she ought to feel that way, too, but she just couldn't. She leaned toward me and whispered, "I shouldn't say this, but just between you and me, I'm glad the son of a bitch is dead."

I'm sure my face registered the surprise I felt: Miss Frankie was one of the sweetest people I'd ever met, and now she was telling me that she was glad her husband had died. And not only that, but she'd called him a son of a bitch in front of her priest. I glanced over and saw that her head start on the sherry was nearly half the bottle.

She told me that he was mean to her and to their sons, that he drank too much, that they went for days, weeks sometimes, without ever saying a word to each other. She whispered that those were the best times, when he just ignored her.

She told me how they'd met at a dance in the first months of our involvement in World War II. He had just enlisted in the army; she thought he was brave, handsome, and dashing. She remembered that her mother had begged her not to marry him—"Mama said he was too rough." She told me her mother's disapproval made it seem even more romantic. They were married the day before he shipped off overseas.

She told me that before she met him, she'd had an offer to study dance at The School of American Ballet in New York City under George Balanchine, the famous Russian teacher and choreographer. In her youth she'd been a gifted dancer who loved ballet. Her mother had wanted her to go to New York and dance in the ballet . . . it was the great dream of her life. But instead she'd married Lonny, she said, and regretted it, and resented him, every day since.

She started crying now, and she sobbed, "Father Buddy, I could really dance. But I was just too scared to chase my dream."

She sighed, a great burden not relieved but at least shared, and poured us both another sherry before I could stop her. Then she declared, "Life is a long hard walk when you're weighed down by what could have been."

Two months after that conversation, Miss Frankie abruptly died as well. Some of the people of the parish speculated that she didn't have any reason to live now that Lonny was gone, but I suspected she'd just achieved her goal of outliving him. I was gratified to see that her funeral was even more crowded and that the people sang the hymns with enthusiasm, attending not because they had to but because they wanted to. Her sons sat in the same pew with the same sour expressions on their faces. She had picked her hymns as well, and we ended with an Easter hymn: "The strife is o'er, the battle done, the victory of life is won; the song of triumph has begun. Alleluia!"

A few weeks after Miss Frankie's funeral, I got a call from her attorney, who told me he wanted to talk to me about her will. I had known that she wanted to leave some money to the church and was concerned that her sons might be causing some legal difficulty, so I went to see the attorney that afternoon.

It turns out that they had all been surprised, at the reading of the will, to find that she had left two hundred and fifty thousand dollars to the parish, to be used to start an endowment for outreach ministries. I'd wondered if that was what the attorney had called me in to tell me, and I told him that was wonderful news. I asked if the sons were okay with it, and he told me they weren't happy about it but that Miss Frankie and Lonny had a lot more money than anybody had ever known about, and the sons were well taken care of.

Then he told me that Miss Frankie had left forty acres of land to me personally. He gave me an indistinct map of the area, with the property lines of a forty-acre section of land highlighted in yellow. He said, "It's about twelve miles out of town, out on County Road 14, off Mockingbird Road."

A codicil explained that this was land her mother had left to her, and she'd forgotten she had owned it at all. A note written in her own careful handwriting and attached to the will described the land as worthless, just wilderness, but she said that every man ought to own some land, and she knew that clergy lived in homes that the churches owned. She wrote that it was another gift to the parish, because she hoped if I owned land there, I would be more likely to stay a while. And she wrote, "Father Buddy showed me more kindness than my husband or my sons or any other man I've ever met, and I want him to have this land."

I looked at the lawyer and worried. "I don't think I can keep it."

He answered, "Yeah, she told me you'd say that. There's another note that says she's written a letter to your bishop that purportedly explains all of this, which was to be sent upon the opening of the will, and that I was to wait and call you the following week, which I have now done."

I asked if the sons were okay with this, too, and the lawyer replied, "What they said to me was that the land couldn't be used or sold, and they'd rather you pay taxes on it than them."

I called Ward, my attorney friend back in West Branch, Mississippi, and he told me that it seemed completely legal to him. He admitted that he didn't know the policies in the church but said he would argue that since the provisions of Miss Frankie's will hadn't caused me to show her any special treatment or favoritism, there shouldn't be a problem.

Then I called the bishop, left a message, and waited for him to return my call. When he did, he told me that he'd gotten Miss Frankie's letter, and he assured me that it would be okay to keep the land. He suggested, though, that I might not have a lot of time to do anything with worthless land, and his advice was that I wait a while and then sell it. He went on to suggest that it would be appropriate and a good example for the members of the congregation for me to give ten percent of the proceeds to the parish as a tithe.

When I told Beulah about it, she was excited. I told her it was worthless land, out in the wilderness, and I didn't even know where it was. I told her the bishop had said we should sell it and give some of the money to the parish. She looked at me levelly and answered, "We haven't even seen it, and you're talking about selling it? Somebody's trying to do something nice for you. Do you think you can stand it for just a few minutes?"

She told me she was going to call her friend Charlie, who'd grown up out in the county, and ask her if she knew anything about the land. We'd met Charlie and Polk Guthrie when Polk signed up to be the veterinarian on our parish's medical mission to Honduras; their little boy Gideon was about the same age as Jude, and the two were fast friends. Charlie told Beulah she knew County Road 14, and she knew where Mockingbird Road was, but she didn't know anything was out there. With Beulah on the phone, she asked Polk if he knew what property Miss Frankie had out there, but he did not. Still, he suggested, we ought to go out there and look at it.

So, on Saturday morning, Polk and I went out to see my land. Polk knew about the land around there, knew who owned what and how it was used; his father's property was not far from there. He had taken my little smudged map and compared it to some better maps in the county land office. He'd looked through some land records and found that it was an undeveloped parcel, and it looked like it had belonged to Miss Frankie's mother's family for generations. He said there might be a stream on the property, or some of it might be marshy. As far as he could tell, nobody had ever done anything with it.

He told me I ought to wear heavy jeans and boots, and I told him I didn't have any boots. He told me we could expect stickers and mud and uneven terrain, that the land Miss Frankie had left me could not be reached by any road. On the way out there in his old Ford pickup, he did his best to prepare me for what was surely waiting for us: "It probably ain't gonna be worth nothin', Buddy. It's gonna be a chore for us to even get out there and see it."

He was right about the last part. There was a lot of mud, and stickers, and scrub trees and vines tightly interlocked with each other that seemed to reach out and snag at my jeans and jacket. It was slow going, and we were both scratched up pretty well before we got there.

Finally, Polk stopped. Pointing at a map in his hand, he declared, "I guess we're about right here." It didn't seem any different from any other point in our painful journey—underbrush and sticker bushes, vines growing up into the trees, soft squelchy ground.

"Well," I observed, "you were right. Not much here." And then, hoping only to be able to tell Beulah that we'd made a fairly complete survey of the property, I asked, "Would you say this is about the middle of the property?"

He looked at his map again, calculated our location as best he could, and answered, "Well, no. The middle of the property should be over that way, maybe a hundred yards. Is that where you want to go?"

I was pretty satisfied that the worthless land was indeed worthless, but I sure didn't want to go back and tell Beulah that I hadn't given it a thorough look, only to have her tell me I'd have to come back and look again. I replied, "Yeah, let's go over there."

We came over a slight rise and were surprised to see a tiny pond or pool of some sort and, on the far side of the pond, a little lean-to shack that, judging by the wisp of smoke coming out of the roof, was occupied.

1

Ain't Worthless at All

Polk and I stood there for a while trying to reconcile ourselves with a reality we had not expected and could not have foreseen: there was somebody living on my land! We talked about it for a minute, and then I called out, "Hello!" There was no answer. I called out again, "Hey! Is anybody there?" Again, no answer. Polk suggested that we ought to go over and knock on the door. I told him I wasn't sure there was a door, and he told me we ought to go knock on something.

As we approached the shed, a dog barked from the surrounding woods, until it sounded like someone clamped a hand over the dog's mouth. I called out, "Who's here? We just want to talk!" There was no answer, and we stood there for a few minutes, not knowing what to do. Polk whispered, "Best thing is for us to go back into town and call Sheriff Burrell." When I objected, he continued, "We don't really know what we're gettin' into here, Boudreaux." Boudreaux was his playful rendition of Buddy, owing to my having grown up near the Mississippi River, which made me almost a Cajun in his mind.

I called out, "We need to talk. If you don't come out, I'm going to have to call the sheriff!"

A shot rang out, and something struck the ground between Polk's right foot and my left as we stood together, less than a yard apart. Then I noticed a bright red dot, a small, intense spot of red light, dancing in a tight little pattern on Polk's chest. Polk whispered, "Don't move."

"Somebody's shootin' at us!"

"If he'd wanted to hit us, he would've. He's got his laser sight trained on me right now. Don't move." Then he yelled out, "All right, all right now. No need for anybody to get hurt out here. My name's Polk Guthrie. My daddy Dunn has the Guthrie place 'round here. Just come on out and let's talk. We don't want anybody to get hurt."

Now a male voice sounded out: "Leave us alone!"

I yelled, "Just come out and we can talk. We just want—"

The red laser dot was playing on my chest now, as the man in the woods yelled, "No! Go away!"

Polk yelled, "Don't shoot!"

Now the man spoke again, still loudly but with a deadly calm: "You got 'til three. One . . . two . . ."

A woman's voice called out, "Oh, Sutty, stop your foolishness. These boys ain't gonna hurt us." Then she stepped out into the little clearing around the shed and added, "Are you, boys?" She was dressed in dirty old jeans and a ragged T-shirt, her long brown hair tied up in a bun. Behind her were two children, a girl of eleven or twelve and a boy of about seven.

She walked up to us and took a deep breath before saying, "My name's Sarah Jo McCaskill, and these are my children." I knelt down and held my hand out to the boy, who was closest, and said, "Hi. What's your name?"

He moved behind his mother and looked at me from behind her, distrustful. But the girl stepped up and spoke clearly, "Hey. My name is Mary Grace. This here's my brother Wil."

I answered, "My daughter's name is Grace, too; we call her Gracie. She's four."

The girl smiled then, but it was a smile full of sadness and loss. I got the idea that here was a girl who'd seen too much in her short life, whose innocence had been stolen and taken over by something tragic. "I hope you can meet her someday," I said.

She whispered, "Me, too."

I stood up and said, "Ms. McCaskill, it's very nice to meet you."

She murmured, "Nice to meet you."

I asked, "You don't think our friend with the shotgun is gonna shoot me, do you?"

"No, you're safe." I felt better about that until she continued, "He ain't gonna chance hittin' me or the kids." I looked for the red laser dot, but it was gone.

"Is he Mr. McCaskill?"

Without a trace of emotion, she answered, "No," but Mary Grace added, "Mr. McCaskill's dead."

I said, with my best and most sincere pastoral tones, "Oh, I'm so sorry." And then, still wondering about the man with the gun, I began, "So is the man with the shotgun—"

"It ain't no shotgun, mister," the boy declared. "It's an M-21."

Polk whispered, "A sniper's rifle, Vietnam."

I asked, "So who's the guy with the M-21?"

Sullenly, the mother responded, "Sutty." Again Mary Grace was more helpful: "He was my daddy's friend in Vietnam. They came home together. Daddy got him a job at Mr. Claiborne's . . ."

Now Sarah Jo showed some emotion, fierce and protective— "Hush, sister." There was an awkward moment, and then she nodded toward me and said to her daughter, "We don't know these men."

I offered, "My name is Buddy—Buddy Hinton."

Sarah Jo replied, with more courtesy than conviction, "It's nice to meet you, Mr. Hinton."

Things were okay until Polk added, to establish my credentials, "He's the minister at the Episcopal Church here."

I watched the woman's eyes narrow with suspicion, which I had come to expect when being introduced to somebody who didn't already know that I was a member of the clergy. A lot of people feel like they've been pushed away from the church and resent having it shoved back in their faces. It changes how people regard you, and rarely for the better. There was no way I could dismiss it or make it unimportant—Polk had let it out of the bag; I was and am an ordained minister in the church.

I suggested, "Just call me Buddy," but I knew it was already too late.

Mary Grace asked, "You're a preacher?"

I answered, "Yes ma'am. In the Episcopal Church."

Now her eyes narrowed, too—most people in Alabama have never heard of the Episcopal Church and assume it must be some sort of new denomination. But it wasn't the time for a church history lesson, and I was wishing Polk hadn't interjected any of this into the conversation.

Now the dog limped up, a thin, malnourished hound with bloody scabs at the base of its tail. Mary Grace snapped, "Get back, Maggie!" I wondered if the dog had rabies or was an attack dog, but Polk knelt down and took the dog's head in both of his hands, looking at her teeth and eyes. He looked at Ms. McCaskill and told her, "This dog has mange and needs some food and vitamins."

She replied, "That ain't your business."

I said, "This is Polk Guthrie. He's a veterinarian in Greene."

Now the suspicion was relieved, and the daughter asked, "Can you help Maggie?"

Polk stood and answered, "Yes ma'am—I'd like to. But I'm not coming back out here until the man with the sniper rifle tells me he won't shoot."

There was a long pause in which the daughter silently sent messages with her eyes, imploring the mother to do the right thing. Finally, Mrs. McCaskill called out, "Sutty!"

The voice from the woods rang back, "Yes ma'am?"

"Come on out and meet these two men. This man"—she nodded at Polk—"is a veterinarian and says he can help Maggie." A pause, and then she added, nodding at me, "And he is a preacher of some sort."

The man called out, "What do they want?"

The mother asked us, "What do you want?"

It didn't seem like the best time for me to tell them they were living on my land, so I replied, "We just want to help you, if you'll let us."

"You ain't gonna preach, are you?"

I meant to say, trying to lighten the mood, "Not unless you ask me to," but instead I said, "Not until you ask me to."

She laughed at that. "Then we won't need to worry about that." She called out to the man in the woods and told him, "They're all right. C'mon out, Sutty."

Sutty stepped out of a war movie: dressed in camo from head to Army-booted toe. He had a deadly-looking rifle in one hand and a dead rabbit in the other. He wore a camouflaged floppy hat, under which I could see that he was bearded and that his eyes were intense.

I held out my hand, which he ignored, and I told him, "My name is Buddy, and this is my friend Polk." The man said to Polk, "You Guthrie's boy?"

Polk drawled, "Yes sir. This dog needs some medicine for mange, and some vitamins. Has she had her rabies shots?" Sarah Jo shook her head, and Polk continued, "We can bring all that, and some dog food that'll help her coat, but we're not coming back until we have your word that you're not going to shoot either one of us."

"All right."

In the Hinton household, Beulah had planted the notion in our children's heads that if you crossed your heart, you had to tell the absolute truth. Now we used it between us, and with our friends, as an absolute guarantee that what was said was true, and not just somebody trying to spare the other's feelings. Somewhere along the line, I think Beulah had suggested to Polk and his wife Charlie that if they lied to me after they'd crossed their hearts, they'd go to hell.

It had become almost automatic, but still I was surprised to hear myself say it in this context: "Cross your heart."

"What?"

I repeated, "Cross your heart that you're not gonna shoot us."

While Sutty was considering it, Polk added, "If you cross your heart on a lie to a preacher, you're going to hell." It didn't seem like the right moment for a lecture on soteriology, either.

Sutty looked at me as if I were a puzzle to be solved, and then he crossed his heart and solemnly promised, "I ain't gonna shoot."

I held out my hand again, and this time he took it. The eyes looking out from under the brim of the floppy hat were the eyes of a caged animal. It seemed to me that he was determined that he was not going to be fooled or controlled.

Polk told Sarah Jo we'd come back the next afternoon, after church. I asked her what else we might bring them, and she told me they didn't need anything.

On our way back to Polk's truck, following the trail we'd left in broken twigs, Polk drawled, "Well, Boudreaux, I guess this land ain't worthless at all. Not to everybody, anyways."

A Story Too Terrible to Tell

My wife, Beulah, the social worker, had a million questions, only a few of which I could answer. She asked me how old the children were, what size clothes each of them wore, and, failing any intelligent answers from me, how tall they were and if they were skinny or fat. She asked about their teeth. She asked where they went to the bathroom, if the water was good to drink, and if they had a garden. She asked if the kids could read and if they were in school. Finally, I told her that she could come with us the next day and ask them all these questions herself.

She told me that she was going to Walmart, and she needed for me to either come with her or give her a signed check from the Rector's Discretionary Fund. We came home with a carful of necessaries.

The next day after church, we took Jude and Gracie to stay with Charlie and picked up Polk to go with us out to the land. He carried a machete he'd brought back from Honduras and used it to cut through some of the more belligerent underbrush. Beulah and I followed behind, lugging a bag from Polk's veterinary office as well as at least twenty bags from Walmart: toilet paper, toothbrushes and toothpaste, bags of dried beans and rice, underwear and clothing for all of them.

I introduced Beulah to Sarah Jo McCaskill, who was cool but not unfriendly. Polk called the dog Maggie over, put some sort of cream on the mange, and fed her a can of Vienna sausages spiked with various pills and vitamins. Then I held her as Polk gave her two different injections. The poor dog stood perfectly still; I imagine she was hoping for more sausages.

It was then that I noticed the water in the little pond. It was not much more than a pool, really, eighteen or twenty feet across and shaped like a jellybean. The water seemed to be moving, rippling out in the middle. I looked around and saw that the pond didn't have a stream coming into it or going out from it. Polk told me it must be a spring, that the water must be coming up between layers of rock and then going back underground somehow. It seemed odd to me that water could come burbling up out of the ground and then go back down in almost the same place, but he said the jumbled layers of rock did all sorts of quirky things like that. I put my hand in the water; it was colder than I thought it would be.

Polk asked Sarah Jo, "Y'all drink this water?"

"Yeah—that's why we're here. It's good water, clear and cool all year-round."

I asked, "Where's our friend Mr. Sutty?"

"Mr. Sutter. Jimmy Sutter. We just call him Sutty. He's out there somewhere . . . he doesn't come around much, just when he has some meat for us."

Beulah asked, "What else do y'all eat?" Sarah Jo talked for a while about catching fish in a larger lake a few hundred yards distant and working a vegetable garden, and then she mentioned that sometimes Sutty would bring them groceries. Beulah wondered, "Where does he get them?"

"At the Walmart."

"Where does he get money for groceries?"

Sarah Jo told us Sutty received a check from the Veterans Administration. "It ain't much," she concluded, "but we're doin' all right."

"Why don't you live in town," Beulah asked as gently as possible, "where you'd have electricity and your kids could go to school?"

There was no place to sit, so we were all just standing there awkwardly. Polk told us he was going to walk around a little; later he told me that three of us interrogating her seemed like too much, and I think he was probably right. When Sarah Jo McCaskill told us her story, I had the sense that it was the most she had said at one stretch for years.

"My husband and Sutty were over in Vietnam together," she explained. "Both of them were drafted and they met at Fort Dix when they went to training. That's up in New Jersey. Sutty and Lamar, that was my man, him and Sutty were over in Vietnam together," she explained. "Both of them were drafted and they met at Fort Dix when they went to training. That's up in New Jersey. They sort of found each other because they were both from Alabama, and everybody else was from New York and California and Chicago and places like that, and they all thought Lamar and Sutty were stupid because they talked like they were from the South. Those other guys called 'em rednecks, and after a while that's what they called themselves, too. When they got to Vietnam, they met another guy from Georgia and they made him a redneck, too.

"Lamar was a good shot before he went into the Army, and he and Sutty were both snipers. Neither one of 'em told me much about it, but I think they both killed a lot of those Vietnam people."

She leaned in confidentially and murmured, "I think it messed up their heads a little." There was a wistful pause, and then she continued, "I know Lamar was different when he got back—tougher, meaner. He always had a bad temper, but he never hit me until . . ."

She seemed to realize then that she was getting too close to something she didn't want to talk about, and she changed course. "When they came back, they came here to this little pond. Lamar grew up out here in the county, and him and his brother used to come swimmin' here. He said it was the only place he'd ever been happy. He thought nobody else knew about it out here. He told me he didn't want to be around anybody right then, when he got back from Vietnam. Me and Lamar had dated in high school, and I guess I sort of waited for him to come back from war—like it was all in a movie or something, so stupid."

We waited for a minute, not knowing whether she was through, and then she gathered herself and went on. "He told me he didn't want to see me, either, that he couldn't trust himself. I thought I could help him. I thought he loved me, too. But he said he didn't want to leave this place. He said he wasn't nothin' but a killer now, so he would stay out here and eat what he killed." She paused for a moment and added, "He always did like huntin'.

"After a while I gave up on him, and I didn't see him anymore after that, for some years. I still thought about him, but I just didn't see him. Then there was another man chasin' after me, and I gave him a little . . . encouragement, 'til he asked me to marry him. He had a good job, workin' for a plumber. So we got married, and a few months after that, my Mary Grace was born."

I realized we didn't need to look too closely at the math there, and we waited again for Sarah Jo to go on.

"We were livin' in a trailer, but we were going to buy a house. Jackie—that's M.G.'s daddy—Jackie told me he was going to do something and be somebody. When he wasn't drinkin', he was good to us, wasn't he, M.G.?" Mary Grace nodded dutifully, and I wondered where Jackie was now, and how he could let his wife and daughter live out here in the woods by themselves.

"But then, when M.G. was about four, Lamar came back around. I didn't ever know where he'd gone, or if he'd ever really gone anywhere at all—I just knew he came back. When he found out that I was married and had a kid, he was . . . he was furious. Him and me had talked about gettin' married and all, and I guess he thought I was promised to him. But I didn't never make no promises, and he didn't either.

"When he came back and he was all mad and everything, he told me he was gonna kill me, gonna kill all of us: me, Jackie, and M.G., and then he was gonna kill himself. I told him I was gonna call the police, but he didn't leave me alone. Then one day he came around talkin' all crazy, and I did call the police, but he was gone before they ever got there. They asked me where I thought Lamar might be, and I knew where he would be—right out here at this little pond, but . . . I didn't tell 'em. I told 'em I didn't know."

Beulah and I looked at each other; neither one of us liked the direction this story was taking.

"Then me and Jackie had this big fight. We had fights before, but nothin' like this. We never had much money, and a little girl needs shoes and dresses and bows in her hair. I guess Jackie thought he needed his Pabst Blue Ribbon beer more than that, even more than we needed to pay the rent, I guess. Well, I'd figured up the bills and we didn't have enough money to pay what we owed, and we yelled and fussed and cussed like fools, until the police came out there and hauled him off.

"I thought I wasn't ever gonna see Jackie again, and I didn't want to. I fooled myself into thinkin' that a little girl needs a daddy, so the next day I came out here to find Lamar, to tell him I'm sorry, and to see if maybe he'd take me back.

"He was real sweet to me then, sweeter than I ever thought he could be. We fixed up this little place enough so me and M.G. could stay out here with him, and he promised that he was gonna get a job and take care of us. He promised he would."

"But he never did," ventured Beulah.

"No ma'am, he never did."

Beulah asked, "How long have you been out here?"

"Well, I came out here when M.G. was just about to turn five. Then the twins were born, and I've been here ever since."

I asked, "Twins?"

There was a silence, until Wil whispered, "Orville died."

There was a heavy pause when nobody knew what to say, and then Beulah asked, "When was the last time you went to town?"

"I've never been back to town since I come out here." We waited, and after a moment Sarah Jo continued. "It's a long way and all, and I ain't got a car. At first, Lamar told me he'd smack me if I went to town. He told me he'd hunt me down if I left." Then, in a whisper, "He told me he'd kill M.G. or one of the boys if I went to town, and . . . I believed him.

"And then after that, after Lamar and Orville died . . . I just couldn't. I guess I was too ashamed to go 'round town people after that."

There was a tragic mystery here, a story too terrible to tell, that had trapped this woman and her children in a prison of stickers and shame. I put my hand on her arm and coaxed as gently as I could, "Sarah Jo, you need to tell us what happened."

"Why, so you can call the police?"

"No, so you can get past this. Whatever happened out here is still eating at you—you know that. It's time to let it go."

She thought about it, and I think she wanted to tell us, but she just couldn't bear it. "No," she breathed, "I can't." She put on her bravest face then and begged, "Please leave it alone for now. Please."

I was still wondering what we should do when Beulah asked, "What about Mr. Sutter?"

"What about him?"

"Well, does he live with y'all? Are you and he . . . ?"

"No. He was a friend of Lamar's, and he stayed out here with him until I came. Now he lives out there somewhere"—she motioned to the woods around the pond—"and hunts for deer and rabbits. He gets a check from the government every month, and when he goes to town to pick it up, he buys us some groceries."

I wondered, "How does he get to town and back? Does he have a car or a truck or something?"

Wil said, "He's got him a old Harley."

"Why does he bring you things from town?" asked Beulah.

Sarah Jo replied, "I guess he feels guilty."

We waited for her to say more, but she didn't, and I was about to say something just because I thought somebody ought to when Wil flatly said, "'Cause he killed my daddy."

9

CROSS MY HEART

Then the whole story had to come out, all the way. Beulah told Sarah Jo that because she was a social worker and I was a member of the clergy, we were both bound by the laws of Alabama to report a crime when we heard about it. Sarah Jo collapsed into a sitting position on the ground, and Beulah and I sat down with her. It took us a long time, and there were a lot of questions and answers, but eventually we got at least the bones of the story straight.

Lamar McCaskill may have had issues before he went to Vietnam; he certainly had some problems when he came back. Beulah thought he was probably suffering from post-traumatic stress disorder. He was abusive and controlling of Sarah Jo, whom he never married but who had taken his name. She named their twins Wilbur and Orville because she knew they were smart and because she wanted them to fly. She wanted them to be free.

One afternoon, Jackie Ludden, who had heard that his wife Sarah Jo had gone back to Lamar and who knew that Jimmy Sutter was a friend of Lamar's, saw Sutty at the bank, cashing his check. Jackie had lost his job with the plumber and had a lot of time to kill, so he followed Sutty to the Walmart, where he picked up a couple six-packs of Pabst Blue Ribbon to bolster his courage. Then Jackie followed Sutty out of town, out on County Road 14, and down Mockingbird Road, careful to keep his distance until he saw Sutty's motorcycle leaning against a tree. He pulled his truck over and set out into the woods on foot.

Jackie always carried a little .410 shotgun in his truck, for snakes and rats; he took it with him as he followed Sutty through the brush.

When Jackie came to the little pond with its lean-to shed, he saw Sarah Jo washing out some clothes in the pool, and he called out to her. Lamar stormed out of the little shack with a rifle in his hands and aimed it at Jackie. When Jackie raised his shotgun in defense, Lamar raised his rifle and shot him just under his left eye. Sarah Jo told us M.G.'s daddy was dead before he hit the ground.

She said something must've rattled loose in Lamar's head after that: he was wild with anger and seemed confused about where he was. She said he was looking into the woods, as if there might be more enemies trying to shoot him. When Sarah Jo tried to calm him down, he pointed the gun at her and the children, and Mary Grace stepped in to take the gun away from him. It turned into a struggle, which Lamar won as he pushed Mary Grace away. In that horrible moment, with Lamar wielding his sniper's rifle like a baseball bat, he struck his son Orville in the temple, killing him instantly. Sarah Jo said she thought it was an accident, but when I asked Mary Grace about it, she said she didn't know.

Sarah Jo sobbed and explained that she couldn't stop screaming— her husband and her son killed in less than a minute. Then Lamar was yelling that he was going to kill them all, a threat he had made before. It looked like he would follow through, until she heard a single shot fired from the woods and saw a little trickle of blood start to flow from the middle of Lamar's forehead. He fell forward and died without another word.

When her story was finished, we sat there in silence for a while, respecting her agony and anguish and also her courage in telling us. Mary Grace and Wil both came and sat beside their mother without saying a word, just touching her.

I said, "So Sutty shot Lamar."

"Yeah," said Mary Grace. "He saved our lives."

Beulah said, "Oh, Sarah Jo, I'm so sorry. You deserve better. Your children deserve better."

Sarah Jo replied, "I never told anybody because I didn't want Sutty to go to jail. He was just tryin' to take care of us. He killed his best friend to take care of us."

Sarah Jo told us she had to go pee, and she walked off into the woods, answering one of Beulah's unasked questions. Both of her children went with her. "What can we do to help?" I asked. "How can we help?"

"Well," suggested Beulah, "there are several things we have to do. We have to report these deaths to the proper authorities, who will have to investigate them fully. The children will have to go to school, or be home-schooled, or something. All of them will need to see doctors and dentists. We need to find them a place to live. We need to figure out a source of income for Sarah Jo, and we need to reintegrate them into society."

She thought about it for a while and continued, "Maybe we can get some sort of probation and counseling for Sutty. You'll need to talk to him about that."

"Me?"

"Well, sure," she continued. "You're the preacher. He'll trust you as much as anybody." I didn't know what to say, and she declared, "Look, Buddy—if Sheriff Burrell and his deputies come out here and try to arrest him, we don't know how many of them will get shot. He's like a wild animal out there, and he is not going to want to go into a cage. It's going to be much better if we can get him to turn himself in. I'll help him as much as I can, and we can get an attorney to argue his case, but he's going to have to surrender voluntarily."

She was right, of course, but that didn't make it any easier. When Sarah Jo got back, we told her what would need to happen, for her and her kids and for Sutty. She said, "He ain't gonna like that."

"No, he won't," I responded. "But it'll be best for everybody, including him."

"At least we know he won't shoot you," replied Beulah. I looked at her in amazement, and she reminded me, "He crossed his heart."

Sarah Jo said she should be the one to talk to Sutty and that I could come back for him the next day. She and Beulah talked for a bit about where Sarah Jo's family was and where she'd grown up; I decided it would be best if I gave them a little time and space to say things they might not want to say with me sitting there.

I saw that Wil was watching me from behind the shed he lived in. I took a few steps toward him and knelt down on the ground to be a little less intimidating, and he took a step toward me. He muttered something I couldn't understand, and I answered, "I can't hear you—I'm old, y'know. Come a little closer. I promise I won't hurt you. I don't want anybody to ever hurt you again."

He took a couple more steps then, holding something behind his back. It didn't look like he was going to say anything, so I asked, "Whatcha got there?"

He held it out for me to see. It was a sort of plate made out of white clay from the spring, with four human-shaped figures lying on it: a big one holding a straight stick in his hand, another one, smaller and wearing what might be a dress, and two small ones close to that one. When I looked more closely, I saw that what I had assumed was a tree stump was another smallish person, the only one of them who was standing.

It was a family portrait, I realized: his family, the only family he'd ever known. He put it into my hands, and murmured, "For you."

I thanked him and told him it was wonderful and then, pointing at the big one, I asked, "That's your daddy?" He kept his eyes down and shook his head and said, "Sutty." When I pointed at the other large figure and raised my eyebrows questioningly, he said, "Mama." I pointed at the two others and asked, "You and M.G.?" and he nodded again. I pointed at the stick and he responded, "That's the M-21."

I thought I already knew, but I pointed at the standing figure and asked, "Who's that?" He sat still for a long time, and finally he said, "That's Orville." Then he added, "He's gone."

I tried to give it back to him, but he repeated, "I made it for you."

I said, "Thank you very much."

He nodded, and answered, "Yes sir."

The next day I came out with Polk's machete and Jude's Radio Flyer wagon to carry whatever they wanted to bring with them. It took me a while to get the wagon down to the pool, and I was sweating by the time I got there. Sutty was there, waiting for me and watching the Radio Flyer creaking toward the shed.

He didn't say anything, so I said, "I always wanted one of these when I was a kid, so I got my son one before he was born."

"You a good daddy?"

"I try to be. I hope I am."

"And a preacher?"

"Yes sir. In the Episcopal Church."

"You takin' me to jail?"

"Well, I'm going to take you to the police station. My wife is a social worker, and she knows a lot of people in the system. We're going to try to get you some counseling so you can be free and get a job and live wherever you want."

"Counselin'?"

"Yes sir." He didn't know what to ask about that, so I said, "We'll get you set up with somebody who understands about being in Vietnam, who knows some of the scars you're still carrying." I'd worked on that idea and was glad I could insert it into the conversation.

"They healed."

"I mean scars in your mind, scars on your heart. Most everybody who came back from Vietnam has all kinds of scars. You don't need to carry them all by yourself."

He paused, weighing it out, wondering if I could be trusted, and I offered, "I'll go with you, Sutty. They don't want to hurt you, I promise."

He asked, "Cross your heart?"

I crossed my heart and promised, "Cross my heart."

Sarah Jo and her children came out of their little shed, and we put a few things in the wagon: a cast iron skillet, a few plastic plates and cups, a bag of clothing. Sutty pulled the wagon to Beulah's minivan on the side of the road, and we all got in. I took Sarah Jo, Mary Grace, Wil, and their dog Maggie to our house, where Beulah was ready to welcome them with iced tea and an invitation to hot baths and showers, clean towels and fresh clothes. Her friend Tanya, who cut our hair, had agreed to come by that afternoon and give them all a haircut "on the house."

We introduced Maggie to Jabbok; they sniffed each other and were immediately fast friends. Well, fast for two old dogs.

I took Jimmy Sutter to the Waffle House and bought us both breakfast with waffles, eggs, hash browns, and lots of coffee. I tried to get him to tell me about his time in Vietnam, but he clearly didn't want to talk about any of that. I asked him about his rifle, and he told me he'd hidden it away where nobody would find it, someplace dry. We finished our breakfast and I took him to the police station.

Beulah had gotten to know Officer Meigs at the police station when he'd helped her with taking a child out of an abusive home, and she trusted him. She had already talked to him that morning and told him the story, making sure he knew Mr. Sutter was a Vietnam veteran and stressing that he was giving himself up voluntarily.

When Sutty and I got to the station, Officer Meigs was respectful and relatively gentle with him. I stayed with him through the fingerprinting and as he told them the story of the deaths of Jackie Ludden, Orville McCaskill, and Lamar McCaskill. Sutty was not accustomed to talking, and it took a while to tell the story; I tried to help out, asking questions to clarify some of the details. Officer Meigs seemed grateful for my help; mostly I tried to support Sutty and stay quiet.

The policeman listened and wrote it all down on a legal pad, asking questions that were meant to get the facts, not to badger or accuse. I wanted to go with Sutty when they took him back into the jail, at least until I could tell Sarah Jo and Beulah that he was settled, but they wouldn't let me. I started to argue, but Sutty nodded to me gravely and said, "I'm okay." I hesitated, and he continued, "Cross my heart."

By the time I got home, Sarah Jo, her children, and their dog were all clean and dry, and all four of them were sleeping on our guest room bed. They would stay with us for the next three weeks, taking it slowly but reestablishing contact with family, interviewing for jobs, and finally finding an apartment. Sarah Jo was hired to work in the Lincoln Elementary School kitchen, and teachers from that school volunteered to work with Mary Grace and Wil to bring them to the academic levels appropriate to their ages.

They were with us for the holidays that year, one of the most magical Christmases ever. Christmas is a swirl of poignance and irreverence every year, profoundly sacred and harshly secular, fictional and factual blended almost indistinguishably together, but this time as we tried to negotiate Santa and the Incarnation, it all seemed that much more miraculous.

We had two services on Christmas Eve, an early service for children and families and a later service with a big crowd and a full choir, incense, sanctus bells, and chanting—pulling out all the stops.

By the time I got home, Beulah had hung nine stockings on the mantel: four for the Hintons, three for the McCaskills, and two for the dogs. Santa had filled the stockings with candy and useful items, and the tree was floating atop what looked like a flood of gifts, some wrapped while others were not.

Nobody got anything really expensive, but Beulah had negotiated with one of the local merchants to buy each of the kids a bicycle, two of them at a generous discount.

On the afternoon of Christmas Day, after we'd eaten all we needed and then kept on eating, as we all played with new toys or tried on new clothes or looked at new books, or just tried to recuperate from eating way too much turkey and dressing and chocolate pie, Wil came up to me with something to say. He wouldn't just come out and say it; he had to be encouraged. I coaxed, "Yes sir—what can I do for you?"

He replied, "I don't have nothin' for you."

I had been expecting this—they didn't have any gifts for us. "It's okay."

"No sir. I don't have no gift for you. I don't have no way to thank you."

I stood up and went to the bookshelves by our fireplace and picked up the clay representation of his family he'd given me. I brought it to him and said, "This is my Christmas present from you, Wil. You've helped me remember how important our families are. I bet it sounds weird to you, but sometimes I forget that. I'm the one who should be thanking you."

He took a step toward me, awkwardly. I leaned over and hugged him, and he hugged me back as hard as he could. It was the best Christmas present I could have imagined.

10

SILOAM

After the new year, I took some of my Christmas loot to the office: a new desk calendar featuring a daily quote from William Shakespeare—the year before, the desk calendar had been "365 All-New Church Bulletin Bloopers," and I hadn't made it past February—a Fantastic Four coffee mug, and a Calvin and Hobbes coffee table book. I put Wil's clay family portrait on a shelf in my office.

A few weeks later, Judy Monroe, a sweet member of the parish and a regular at the Wednesday morning Bible study, came into my office to ask a question. She wanted to know what we thought about abortion; it seems that a woman she played tennis with was all worked up about it and had announced to the whole tennis group that Episcopalians were all liberals who supported abortion and didn't care for the lives of unborn children. Judy said she hadn't known what to say.

Sometimes it's hard to find a good answer to questions that begin with "What do Episcopalians believe" about various things, because we don't always agree, and people from other parts of God's one holy Church seem to have a hard time with the idea that we have different opinions about some things. For the most part, Episcopalians agree about the big stuff: God created the universe, Jesus became human by the agency of God to redeem the world, Jesus died on the cross and rose from death, and the Holy Spirit of God came to inspire and transform and challenge and guide Jesus' followers to be the Body of Christ in the world. But how God created the world; how long it took or is still taking; how long Mary was a virgin; how salvation was or is being achieved and the workings of the mysterious Third Person of the Trinity are things you might expect an energetic conversation about, at least among Episcopalians.

I told her that I thought the official position of the Episcopal Church was that abortion should only be allowed in cases of rape or incest or if the child to be born would be "a monster." I'd remembered that phrase from the language in a resolution at the General Convention of the Episcopal Church, and I told her that I'd had a hard time with the idea of people being born "monsters." She asked, "So we're not encouraging women to have abortions?"

"No, of course not. But Judy, it's much more complicated than a system of easy answers will allow. These are real people we're talking about, with real lives and real pain." I did not tell her that I'd spoken to several women about their own stories, either before or after having abortions. "It's a terrible thing to have an abortion," I said, "but it's the woman's choice. And sometimes it's the lesser of evils."

That seemed to satisfy her, and we chatted a bit. That would have been the end of it, but she happened to see Wil's family portrait on my shelf and seemed interested. She asked with what seemed like unwarranted enthusiasm, "Where did you get this?"

As it turned out, Judy was very interested in pottery. She had been taking pottery classes at the local community college and had been trying to convince her husband to help her set up a wheel and kiln at their home. I told her that a little boy made this *objet d'art* from clay he dug out of the land Miss Frankie had left me. I told her it represented his family and that I called it "Hope Beyond Tragedy." (I was stretching it a little there, but she seemed interested; call it a preacher's prerogative.)

Actually, what she was most interested in was not the sculpture but the clay. She was quite excited that this pure white clay was found near a spring out in the county. Her pottery teacher had lectured at some length about native clays, and she told me that she thought this clay might be something fine and rare. I looked at it again and didn't see anything I hadn't seen before; I wondered if she was stretching things, too. Maybe potters also have prerogatives.

A week later I took Judy Monroe and her friend Allie out on County Road 14, down Mockingbird Road, and into the woods. I invited Wil to come with us so he could show us where the clay was, and his mother and sister came, too—just to be sure that Wil was okay.

There was a sort of path now, thanks to Polk's machete and a few trips back and forth; it wasn't quite so impassible as it had been. Sarah Jo was embarrassed that these women saw how her family had lived, but I told her they didn't know that her family had ever lived out there, only that Wil had found this white clay by the little pond.

Wil showed them where he'd dug up the clay, and both of the pottery students were delighted. They went on and on about texture and color, trying to remember from the notes they'd taken in class the different classifications of clay occurring in north Alabama, using words in Latin that I didn't know and suspected were not actually pronounced the way they said them.

After the scholarly moment passed, Judy asked if she could take a sample to her professor. I told her that would be great, and they put some clay in a Tupperware bowl and snapped the lid shut. As we were turning to go back to the car, Allie wondered, "What is this place?"

I answered, "It's just a little spring that comes up here and goes back down here."

She walked to the edge of the water and looked down into it. "How deep does it go?"

Wil declared, "It's real deep. Cold, too."

Mary Grace continued, "We used to swim here sometimes in the summer."

Judy, not especially interested but trying to be nice, asked, "Oh, do you live around here?"

Sarah Jo replied, "We used to live around here, but now we live in town." Her tone was so defensive that I wondered if Judy and Allie might catch on that something wasn't quite as it seemed. But the moment passed, and we took the trail back to the car.

The following week, I received a call from a Professor Hawkins who taught ceramics arts at the junior college. He was proud of his students for recognizing what he referred to as "an unusual clay," and he asked if he could come and see the site. I took him out there the following Saturday, and after looking at the clay he wanted to know if I was interested in selling the property. I told him I'd thought about it but didn't have any plans. He offered me $10,000 for the plot of land, and I told him I'd have to talk to my wife about it. It was what the bishop had suggested, after all.

Beulah told me the land must be worth a lot if a college professor wanted to buy it. We took our kids out there the next day after church, and Beulah brought two lawn chairs and a quilt for the kids so we could sit and soak the place in. She told me to be quiet and listen to the silence of the place, and she was the one who floated the idea that it could be a spot for us to retire, that we could build a little cabin out there. I told her it would be nice, in the same way people say it would be nice to have a million dollars or go to Paris or cure cancer. Still, we sat there until the sun was dipping toward the western horizon, enjoying the calm quiet. Gracie explored, and Jude played in the remarkable mud, wallowing in the birthright of every little boy.

That afternoon, I called the number the professor left with me and told him we were not interested in selling the property.

The next Wednesday, Judy brought her friend Allie to the weekly Bible study. Allie sat quietly through the Bible study and came to the healing service that followed. She didn't come up for healing or to receive Communion—she didn't seem hostile to any of it, but she didn't seem interested in any of it, either.

When everybody else had left, Judy told me she and Allie had a proposition for me. We sat down in my office, and she said that she and Allie had been talking with their husbands, and they wanted to build a pottery studio by the spring on my land. They both wanted a pottery studio, and both of their husbands were willing to go in together to pay for it, but the husbands didn't want it in their homes.

Judy's husband Drew had done well in banking and investments before his retirement, and now he spent his time doing woodwork.

Allie was married to an optometrist named Gerald, and she drove a Jaguar. The four of them had discussed it, and the husbands agreed they would be willing to widen the little path and make it into a gravel driveway. They would tear down the little shed and build a log cabin studio, running electricity for the pottery wheels and the kiln. They would put in a septic tank for the necessaries, well away from the clear spring.

I decided to let them use the land, with its wonderful pure white clay. Beulah and I would hold the titles for the buildings they would build and use without payment for as long as they wanted. When they were done with the studio, it would belong to me and Beulah. I would pay all the taxes, and, of vital importance to the husbands, I would find someone they could pay to live there and maintain the property.

I knew just the man.

In the spring of 1998, Mr. JoJo McCain moved to Greene, Alabama. He had gotten a driver's license, and he drove over in his "brand new" 1972 Chevy pickup truck, with all his worldly possessions in an old suitcase and a garbage bag, along with my old lawn mower, a blower, and some rakes and shovels and other yard tools. It was a glorious reunion. He was amazed at how much Jude and Gracie had grown. Jabbok, our good dog, was getting old and frail, but she was glad to see her friend JoJo again and thumped her tail in greeting.

The next morning, I took JoJo out to the land. He stepped into the little clearing and took a deep breath. He knelt beside the water in the pool and scooped up a handful, tasting it carefully at first, and then using both hands. When he turned his face to me, I saw the tears running down his cheeks, and he declared, "Now I am home."

He took another deep breath, breathing the place in, and continued, "That's good, sweet water." I had never tasted it, having been taught from an early age that you never drank water that hadn't gone through some purification process, but he insisted until I had to try it, and I agreed that it tasted wonderful. He wondered, "What do you call this place?"

"Um, I don't know. We haven't thought about calling it anything."

"Oh, no, now. A beautiful place like this ought to have a name."

"What would you call it?"

He thought a moment and said, "If it was me, I believe I'd call it Siloam."

I knew the word and recognized it as a name in the Bible, but I couldn't remember where it was from. I asked him, "Why Siloam?"

"My granny used to take us to her church sometimes—it was called the Church at Siloam Pool. They was a spring there, and a little pond—not as big as this one—and that water was always so clear and cool. Granny said that little spring had always been there since God made the world, and that they made them a little pool there to catch the water, and named the church after that pool in the Bible, Siloam Pool." I still hadn't made any connection, so he said, "Like in that story about Jesus healing on the Sabbath day."

I was beginning to put things together, but I was still missing some pieces. When I told him I didn't remember the story he was talking about, he explained.

"Well, one day Jesus and his friends was just walkin' along, and they see this blind man. One of the disciples asked Jesus why he was blind, was he bein' punished for somethin' he done. But Jesus said no, that he was born blind so they could all see the power of God!

"Then Jesus spit on some dirt and made mud out of spittle to put on the man's eyes, and told him to go wash his face. You know where Jesus told him to go?"

I guessed, "Siloam?"

JoJo said, "Yes sir. The Bible verse up over the pulpit in Granny's church said, 'Jesus anointed mine eyes and said unto me, Go to the pool of Siloam and wash.' The man went and washed the mud off his eyes, and he could see! Granny's preacher said that must be some pretty powerful water in Siloam Pool." Then JoJo added, "That's where me and Bobbo was baptized, out at Granny's church, in that Siloam Pool."

He looked up at me and said, "If I was namin' this place, I'd call it Siloam. This right here is powerful water, and it's a place for healin', too.'"

I knew it was perfect, and we've called the place Siloam ever since.

11

JoJo's Tale, Reprised

JoJo stayed with us for a few weeks but soon moved out to Siloam, even before they finished building the cabin studio. Drew and Gerald, the optometrist, let me know that they weren't pleased that they would be paying a Black man to stay out there where their wives would be spending so much time, and they told me they'd be keeping their eyes on him. But after they got to know him, they let all of that go.

Gerald knew a man named Pete who'd been something of a free spirit after dropping out of high school in the sixties. Pete had lots of stories to tell, but the ones that fit into this story involve traveling around building log cabins when that was in vogue in the late seventies. Now he was a carpenter in town, and he agreed to work with them in building the cabin. As it turns out, and as no surprise to anyone, the two husbands "supervised," which mostly meant they stood around, got in the way, and second-guessed whatever Pete the carpenter said or did.

JoJo helped to build the cabin, which included a bedroom for him, and he also built a neat new shed for his tools from discarded materials that were left lying around. He kept a little fire smoldering almost all the time, burning brush and dead trees; after a couple of weeks of him living there, I barely recognized the place. He planted jonquils, daylilies, and plum trees; he built birdfeeders and bluebird houses and benches to sit on by the water. The place bloomed, and so did he.

Beulah and I agreed not to tell anyone that JoJo had been treated like a person with mental deficiencies most of his life; nobody needed to know, and this was a clean start for him. She was the one who figured out that he'd been labeled early on because he followed his brother Bobbo's lead. This was his chance to break out of the mold others had made for him. So, for Judy and Allie, and the people at the parish where he joined the choir, JoJo was just a large, sweet, gentle African American man with a remarkably green thumb whom the Hintons had known back in Mississippi.

It had taken several attempts, but JoJo had finally asked Wanda Stovall out on a date, and they'd been spending a lot of time together until he'd moved to Greene. It was a difficult decision for him; he'd never had a woman interested in him before, and he didn't know what to do. Beulah—Cupid's assistant—told him he could come to our house whenever he wanted to call Wanda on the phone and said we would love to give her a place to stay any time she came to visit.

They finished the cabin and studio, and it was rustic but beautiful, with a wonderful, roomy front porch. JoJo made four wide rocking chairs for the porch, using bodark wood for the frames and rockers, and Judy's husband Drew got someone he knew to cane them—they were instant masterpieces. It was a peaceful place, a place for creativity and quiet, a place to be still and know that God is not far away. There was no cell phone signal, which was fine with me, but Judy and Allie said their husbands thought they needed to be able to call them, so they said they'd work on it.

One day when I went out to the cabin, JoJo showed me an ancient cast iron wood-burning stove he'd rescued from a junk yard. It was rusty and dirty and missing one leg, but he assured me he could fix it up to keep the cabin warm in the winter. When I noticed a cat hanging around the porch, he said two cats just came up and made themselves at home. "They both gray, they look just alike, I s'pose they're brothers." I asked him what their names were, and he said, "Tom and Bob."

"Are they both male cats?"

"I don't know. They just looked like they ought to be Tom Cat and Bob Cat."

"Oh. Well, which one's which?"

"It don't matter—they don't know their names, anyway. Mostly they just come runnin' when I put food in their bowls." They were both scared of me, but they tolerated JoJo, who loved them.

It was Beulah who suggested that I invite JoJo to come to our camp Special Session as a member of the staff. And that reminded me of an idea I'd given up on.

My contrary friend Kyle and I had done several Special Sessions together in Mississippi, and for years he'd been saying that when we got old, we ought to come to a Special Session as campers. "We could just do and say whatever the hell we want, and get all these kids to take care of us," he imagined.

When Beulah and I moved to Alabama and started a Special Session there, Kyle and I came up with a plan. He would apply to come as a camper, invent some sort of disability he could fake—"I could be hyperactive, with OCD and Tourette syndrome!" The idea was that he would spend one night in the cabin as a camper, and then the next night, at the first staff meeting, he would reveal that he wasn't a camper at all and would talk to us about how he'd been treated. Then he'd be on staff for the rest of the week.

We'd never put it all together before, and eventually he accepted a call to a nice parish in Florida, so I forgot about it until JoJo McCain moved to Alabama and Beulah suggested he should be on the Special Session staff. The last few years when I'd directed the Special Session in Mississippi, JoJo had attended as a sort of blur on the line between camper and staff, and it occurred to me that Kyle's scheme might actually work this time. Beulah said, "That's sounds like Kyle—some combination of crazy and brilliant."

So I told JoJo about it. At first, he was apprehensive, reluctant to reprise his role as a camper, but the more we talked about it, the more he thought it was a great idea. We filled out an application for him, using information from an old application from when he was a camper in Mississippi. We answered the question, "Describe in your own words this person's disability," using the same words his mother had written back in 1984: "He just not smart."

The staff arrived, and I told the story of my first Special Session back in 1971, when I was fifteen years old and scared to death, and how much it had meant to me. We talked about seizures and respect, about schedules, activities, cabin duty, and looking for the kingdom of God. We sang songs and we played games, and several people told stories about campers and counselors, and by the time the campers arrived we were about as ready as we were going to be.

In all the chaos of the campers arriving, Polk and Charlie Guthrie brought a new camper: JoJo McCain. He acted just like he did when I had first met him—I hadn't realized how much he'd changed and grown until I saw him playing his old role. I went up to him and held out my hand; he held his hand out as if it didn't have a muscle in it, in stark contrast to the strong grip he shook hands with now. I said, "I'm glad to meet you," just like I had fifteen years earlier when I'd met him, and he answered, "Yes sir" with the same quiet, scared little voice I hadn't heard for many years.

We gave JoJo his name tag and a water bottle, and Polk and Charlie took him to his cabin. His counselor was a boy I thought was the most frightened among the male counselors, a skinny kid named Bailey, on the young side of fifteen; his hair flopped over his eyes so you couldn't see them at all. He didn't understand why all the adults called him Beetle, which made it even funnier.

When most of the campers had arrived, we rang the big bell for the first time, signaling the counselors to go to the Rec Hall for the ice cream social, our first event together as a community. JoJo sat down at the edge of the group and wouldn't move; I watched as Beetle Bailey cajoled and coaxed and tried to be firm with him, and I had to laugh as JoJo just sat there while his counselor finally went to get him some ice cream.

We had supper, and then came the evening activity—some sort of scavenger hunt by cabins around our theme for the session, "Wild, Wild West," which culminated in two of the counselors in a cap gun shoot-out, with the hero Dirk Dogood saving Missy Prissy Pureheart from the devious Dick Dalton. Everybody cheered, dastardly Dick had a lengthy death scene, and Dirk and Prissy chastely kissed and rode off into the sunset, which in this case was behind the canteen.

We had chapel, and after milk and cookies, all the campers and all the counselors went to the cabins to rest up for the next day. The established norm is that there's no staff meeting the first night because we need all the counselors to be in the cabins. The first night is full of new excitement and trepidation for most of the campers and for many of the counselors. Usually by that point, the counselors are tired of hearing me talk anyway.

The next day I was busy making whatever shifts and switches I needed to make, moving campers into different cabins, swapping campers and counselors around if a counselor had more than she or he could deal with (or not enough). I saw JoJo at meals and in the pool; he seemed to be playing his part convincingly.

After supper on the second night of the session, we had the evening program, chapel, and milk and cookies, and after the campers were quiet in the cabins, the staff started to gather for the staff meeting in the Rec Hall, sitting on old benches we dragged into something like a circle. I went to get JoJo, telling the counselor who'd been left behind in his cabin that I needed him and that I would bring him back. We waited until Beulah signaled me that most of the counselors were there, and then JoJo and I walked in together.

Bailey was a sweet kid; when he saw me with JoJo, he was afraid that he'd done something wrong. I motioned for him to come over and whispered, "Look, Bailey—I have to tell you something."

"Okay," he replied.

I went on, "You're okay. You're doing fine. JoJo's okay. But he's not a camper. He's a friend of ours. He was just pretending to be a camper, to see how we're doing. It's not anything directed at you, all right?"

He wanted to understand but couldn't quite fit it all into his head, not sure what to believe. JoJo held out his hand and took Bailey's in such a firm grip that he had to wince, and said, "Hello, Bailey, I'm JoJo McCain," in such a strong sure voice that even Bailey couldn't miss the difference. Beetle Bailey put both of his hands through his hair and opened his eyes and mouth wide, but he didn't make a sound. I told him, "Go sit down, and we'll explain everything."

Then, before Beetle Bailey had time to mess it all up, I called the staff together. "Hey, y'all—I want to introduce you to another member of our staff, Mr. JoJo McCain." They clapped tentatively, not sure what response might be appropriate, and Whitney, one of the more experienced counselors, asked, "Hey, wait a minute—isn't he a camper?"

JoJo looked at me, and I nodded. He said, "Well, I was. My brother Bobbo and me came to the Special Session in Mississippi back in '84." He told them about being treated like he was stupid most of his life and shared a short version of the story of how Bobbo had wandered off when I'd taken the camp into Jackson to see a minor league baseball game, how I'd said in my sermon the next morning that we can't throw anybody out of God's family, that we're all God's children forever, no matter what. Then he told them about Bobbo's death, and coming to find me and Beulah in West Branch, and getting a job at the Piggly Wiggly.

"And then people started treating me like I had some sense, 'til I started to believe it, too. People didn't think I was stupid, didn't treat me like I was stupid, 'til I thought, well, maybe I'm not stupid after all." Whitney started clapping then, and we all clapped with him, until I became afraid we would wake the campers up and shushed everybody.

JoJo concluded, "Then I started my own business, cutting yards and all, 'til a few months ago Buddy called and wanted me to manage some property for him up in Greene. Then he told me about this idea, that I could come as a camper again, just for one night, so I could tell you how this looks from a camper's way of seein' it."

He let that soak in for a minute, and I asked, "So how are we doing, JoJo?"

"Pretty good. That Bailey"—he paused for dramatic effect—"he's all right. He don't know what he's doin', but he got a good heart, and that's the main thing." Several of the other counselors called out, "Beetle!" and when Bailey asked, "What does that even mean?" we all had to laugh.

JoJo talked to the staff about treating people with disabilities like they're people instead of labels. He told them that the girl counselors need to be nice to the male campers without flirting with them. He smiled and added, "Most of these guys don't never see girls as pretty as you, 'less they on the television, and they don't always know what to do with it."

He told us that when he had been "treated like somebody who didn't have no sense, they wasn't nobody who invited him to do much more than I done ever' day. They wasn't no new ideas, they wasn't no new songs, they wasn't no new peoples. Then them campers come here. Y'all need to know that all this bein' new and different is kinda excitin', but it's kinda scary, too. You get used to everything bein' the same ever' day."

He told us that most of the campers were used to being ignored, and "they ain't gonna say nothin' about it. But that's what makes this so powerful, y'all payin' some real attention, carin' what they say and what they want. Y'all don't know . . ." He had to clear his throat. "Y'all don't know how good that feels to somebody who been looked over they whole lives."

He pointed out that most of the campers were adults and that most adults don't want kids telling them what to do. He said, "Some of the campers think this is your world, and they're just trying to fit into it. You need to do whatever you can to show 'em this their world, too—*our* world." He thought about it for a second, and corrected, "No, that ain't right. You need to do what you can to make sure they know they have a place in God's world."

I said, "Amen," and then everybody joined in: "Amen."

12

ALL YOU'VE GOT IS THIS GUY

That same session we actually did have a new camper, whose name is Edward. Edward is as intelligent as the next guy, assuming the next guy is pretty bright, but he was born without optic nerves. Like the man in the story of Siloam, he was born blind: he has never been able to see anything at all.

We learned from his application that he had never been away from home, even though he was twenty-seven years old, that he could read and write Braille, that he could play the piano, and that he was completely and irretrievably blind. His mother wrote a note and attached it to the application: "Edward is a very nice young man and will be no trouble at all. He needs to go have a good time without his mother hovering over him all the time."

Part of the purpose of staff training is for the director and some of the adults on staff to figure out who the counselors are so we can assign them to the right campers. The afternoon before the campers arrived, I met with a few of the people who'd been doing the session for a while to decide which counselors to put with which camper or campers: the most challenging campers get the most experienced and capable counselors, while the weakest or most frightened counselors get the easiest or least demanding campers.

When we started considering which counselor to pair with Edward, we agreed that he would likely not be difficult or demanding but would need someone who could stay with him all the time, at least until he knew the lay of the land. I didn't want to assign him to a rookie counselor, but our most experienced counselors were all needed to work with campers we knew could be more challenging.

One of the other people on the staff suggested that Edward's counselor could be Zach, a sweet kid from the parish I was serving and whose parents I knew. He wasn't a kid who went looking for trouble, but when it came looking for him, he wouldn't put up much of a fight. He had been a counselor the year before, assigned to two easy campers who were no challenge at all, which left his mind with plenty of time to wander. Somewhere in that wandering, one of the girl counselors must have batted her long eyelashes at him, and he got lost in that starry-eyed yearning that only a fifteen-year-old boy can generate.

It got so bad I had to sit him down and tell him that if he didn't pay his campers some attention, I would have to send him home. He got a little better, at least enough to get him to the end of the week, but then he and some others snuck out after curfew on the last night, and he was worried that I'd tell his parents when I caught a bunch of them. I was content to let him worry about it, and I'd been surprised that he had applied to come back again.

When somebody suggested we put Zach with Edward, I replied, "No—Zach's a knucklehead!"

But the person who'd suggested it persisted. "Zach was a knucklehead last year because he didn't have enough to do to keep him out of trouble. If we put him with Edward, he'll have to stay with him." I didn't think it was a good idea, but I didn't have any better ideas, so we assigned Zach to Edward. It's amazing how often I've had to be talked into good ideas.

The campers arrived and I introduced myself to Edward; somebody took him to his cabin to meet Zach the Knucklehead, we had the ice cream social, supper, and the Wild Wild West Scavenger Hunt and Shoot-Out, and I started focusing on problems to solve. The next morning, I saw Zach at breakfast and asked him if he was doing okay, if Edward was okay, and Zach declared, "He's awesome!" I decided I didn't need to worry about them, freeing my mind to focus on other assignments we'd made and situations we hadn't been able to anticipate.

A few days went by and everything seemed to be going pretty well. JoJo the camper became JoJo the member of the staff without any complications. In the middle of the session, I tend to give most of my attention to the campers who are either having a lot of difficulty or are having a spectacular time, and to the counselors who aren't doing their jobs. So I didn't see it, but Edward and Zach the Knucklehead were having a great week. Both of them were coming into their own, and I almost missed it.

The last full day of the session, one of the younger female counselors came running down to the dining hall to find me. "Buddy," she panted, "Edward's about to go off the diving board!"

"Okay," I responded, thinking these young counselors get so excited about such little things. "Remain calm. It's okay—he can swim better than I can."

"The high dive!" she continued.

I've never been tempted to go up there to the high dive, but a lot of the counselors love it: it's quite a popular feature of the camp pool. I think it's probably about seventeen or eighteen feet above the surface of the water if you measure with a tape measure, but if I could measure emotionally, it would be closer to seventy.

It had become a big deal for some of the campers to go off the high dive. Our idea was that anybody should be able to do it if they wanted to, but nobody had to. So even campers who couldn't swim would let us put a life jacket on them and, after some coaxing from whoever was at the pool, jump in. There were always lots of people treading water in the pool around where the camper would land, and I was assured that there was no danger at all, but it still terrified me.

Now Edward the blind camper was going off the high dive. I hurried up the little hill to the pool to see it.

By the time I got there, Edward was halfway up the ladder, with Zach the Knucklehead right behind him. It seemed like the whole camp was at the pool to watch, and most of them were chanting, "Ed-ward, Ed-ward, Ed-ward!" Edward smiled to hear it, and he took his hand off the rail to wave to us; I yelled, "Put your hand back on the rail!" I don't think they could have heard me, but I was glad to see Zach calmly help guide Edward's hand back to the rail, talking to him the whole time.

I couldn't hear what Zach was saying because everybody was chanting Edward's name, but in my imagination, it must have been something like, "Okay, Edward, you're doing great. Now take another step up, that's good, now another step—hold on to the rail, good— now step up on the platform, there you go, now the other foot, good, good—now step up on the diving board, that's good, you got this, hold on to the rail, good, good. You've got about three steps to go, just walk straight, that's it—hold on to the rail, okay, keep going, just one more step. Now, you have to let go of the rail, all right? Okay, now your other hand. You've got about three more feet to the end of the board, just walk straight, I'm right behind you—are you okay?—okay, good, one more step, okay, now stop, stop. You feel the end of the board with your toes? Okay, great—now when you ready, just jump in."

I couldn't hear any of that, but I bet Zach was telling Edward something pretty close to it. Everybody was still hollering, "Ed-ward, Ed-ward, Ed-ward!" and I was yelling too: "Ed-ward, Ed-ward, Ed-ward!" He jumped out into the darkness, trusting his counselor, who jumped in right after him, off to the side, just like we always tell all the counselors *not* to do.

Edward came spluttering out of the water and waved. The crowd went wild: "Yeah! Edward!"

I saw Zach, formerly a knucklehead, later that day and told him he was doing a great job. I told him that if he came back the next year, he would have a more difficult camper. He replied, "Aw, man—I'll be here! Thank you for letting me come back. This is awesome! Edward is completely frickin' awesome!"

That night, as we were waiting for everyone to arrive for the staff meeting, Beulah and I talked about Edward and Zach. She'd already heard about what had happened, but when I was telling her how I saw it, we were both surprised when I got so choked up so that I couldn't talk for a bit. She asked me why it made me cry, and I had to think about it before answering.

"I think it's the trust."

I told her I had always thought that faith was about figuring God out, but it turns out it's really about trust. "Can you imagine standing up there, and you can't see a thing? And all you've got is this guy who's been there before, and he tells you that you have to let go of the rail? And then he tells you you're going to be okay, and when you're ready, to jump in? And you trust him enough so that on his word and assurance, you jump. You jump out, into the darkness. I had tears running down my face when he came back up out of the water. I think that's about the best example of faith I've ever seen."

I was preaching then, but Beulah nodded for me to continue. "We all have moments in our lives when we're standing in a scary place and we can't see where we have to go or what's going to happen next, and all we can do is trust the guy that's been there before. You have to have Good Friday so you can have Easter. The faith has never been about the facts, or about making things make sense—it's always been about who you're going to trust."

Beulah has built up a sort of immunity to my preaching after enduring so many sermons for all these years, but there were tears in her eyes when she said, "I'll hear that story a few times from the pulpit."

"Yes ma'am."

She nodded and suggested, "Now maybe now you can give some of those other stories I've heard a hundred times a rest."

13

Axes to Grind

Months went by, marking the seasons of the church year: Pentecost, Advent, Christmas, Epiphany, Lent, and Easter—a full liturgical year. Mary Grace and Wil were enrolled in the public school in the fall of 1998, and our little Gracie went to kindergarten. Beulah saw wonders and horrors as a social worker. She helped those who could be helped to navigate a social system that often seemed like it was designed to keep them down rather than trying to lift them up.

Our good dog Jabbok died when she was seventeen, a good long life for one of the best friends I've ever had. She'd been a trusted companion through happy times and sad—always faithful, never complaining. Whatever else was going on, whatever joys or frustrations, whatever complications or successes, Jabbok met me at the door with her tail wagging, happy to see me. And no matter what, I was just as glad to see her: love beyond words.

For months she had been slowing down, moving less, eating less. She peed on the old quilt we folded up for her to lie on, and it embarrassed her. Her eyes were not so bright as they'd always been, and her breath had started smelling sour.

My friend Polk the veterinarian could see that she was dying. He ran some tests and told us that her kidneys and liver were both under-functioning; "The only thing keeping her alive is her heart," he told me. A few days later, knowing that it was the right thing to do and desperately wishing we could do something else, I held Jabbok's sweet head as Polk gave her a shot and she went to sleep, resting forever in peace. We buried her out at Siloam. There's a whole lot of love in a dog; I'm not sure the hole left by her passing has ever been filled.

One of the questions I have been asked most frequently—and most fervently—is whether I think dogs go to heaven. I thought people were kidding at first; it took me some time to recognize that this is not just theological frippery. When your dog dies, she takes part of your heart with her, and the person asking the question genuinely wants to know, "Where is my sweet dog now?"

I believe the part of us that is reunited with our loving God is our soul. I believe dogs definitely have souls; that's why we love them so much. I believe it wouldn't really be heaven without my friend Jabbok. Therefore, yes—I believe dogs go to heaven.

And cats, being cats, can go to heaven if they choose to.

For the most part, it was a good chapter in the life of St. Thomas, though not without its frustrations. It was a good fit for me as a priest and for us as a family. But there was some friction. There's always friction: church people are just mostly people after all.

It seemed that the Episcopal Church as a whole was becoming more progressive, although it could also be argued that the rest of the culture in which we were set was becoming more conservative. Fundamentalism, that pernicious virus in the Body of Christ, seemed to be reaching epidemic proportions.

In my lifetime, the Episcopal Church had worked our way through disputes about civil rights, the revision of the Book of Common Prayer, and the ordination of women, and we lost some membership by individuals or families and, in some cases, entire congregations. St. Thomas Episcopal Church in Greene, Alabama, had ridden those waves with the rest of the denomination, remaining mostly unscathed.

I agreed with most of these changes, but I did have some concerns: not that the more progressive elements were wrong but that they were often pushy and—that most grievous of Episcopal sins—they were sometimes tacky. As a rule, Episcopalians don't really get upset about sin, but we have a hard time with tacky.

Nobody likes to be pushed, and usually, when people are pushed enough, they will start pushing back. I think some of the struggle the church has been through was made more complicated and more difficult than it needed to be by some people pushing and other people inevitably pushing back.

At the 1999 Diocesan Convention, some of my fellow clergy in the diocese wanted to nominate me to be a deputy to the 2000 General Convention of the Episcopal Church in Denver. I was flattered, but I didn't let them nominate me. I didn't actually think I'd be elected, but I didn't want to run the risk that I might. I told them I thought the General Convention was where people in the Episcopal Church with an axe to grind went to grind it, and I couldn't see the appeal of being in the same room with so many angry people wielding sharp axes.

The axe being ground most sharply just then was about homosexuality, a controversy that we had been struggling with for years and would continue to wrestle with for many more to come. What should God's church do with people who are attracted to people of the same sex? Is this lifestyle something homosexual people choose, or are they born that way? Do the few references to homosexuality in Scripture apply to consenting and committed couples, or are the authors of the Bible addressing homosexual rape or prostitution or pederasty? Is sin a condition of human existence, or is it the choices we make? These were some of the questions being asked by many in the Episcopal Church in 1999.

It was and is an important issue with the potential to tear the Episcopal Church, along with every other denomination, apart. I was content to be a parish priest and let other people work their way through it. My concerns were more tightly focused: my family, the parish I was serving, Siloam. Things were going well; I didn't need to borrow trouble. I was content to let the axe grinders grind their axes, far away from me and mine.

At St. Thomas in Greene, we had an early service at eight o'clock, then some time for Sunday school and coffee, and then the late service at eleven. The Rector's Forum was a discussion I led in the parish hall, which was also the location of the coffee. People were always coming and going; some stayed and listened to the conversation, and some just got their coffee and slipped out. There was always a little bit of chaos in the Rector's Forum, which I suppose must be how I liked it.

Our class was dutifully working our way through a tape series on Karen Armstrong's *A History of God*, which I'd read and greatly appreciated. The tape series was wonderful and thought-provoking in some spots but somewhat tedious in others; the class had started off with about thirty people and had now winnowed itself down to the dozen or so who were really interested or just too stubborn to give up.

One Sunday morning, as we were chewing on Ms. Armstrong's assertion that Islam is the third of the Abrahamic faiths and that it should therefore be considered on equal standing with Judaism and Christianity, I noticed a new face. It belonged to a thin young man standing outside the circle, staring at me intently. It was clearly a face that didn't belong in that particular circle, but there was something familiar in his eyes.

I could tell he knew me, and I had to assume I knew him, too, so I looked more closely. There was something I almost remembered about him, maybe, but surely I would not have forgotten somebody who looked like this.

He was alarmingly thin, nearly skeletal. His long, not-quite-naturally reddish hair fell over his eyes, and he nervously pushed it back behind his ears. Over a canary-yellow undershirt, he wore a loose, brightly flowered shirt tied in a knot below his navel. He had on an old pair of loose-fitting jeans, with patches holding other patches together; over one knee I'm pretty sure he had a patch made of leather. One Converse All Star tennis shoe was green with red shoelaces, and the other was red with green laces. I had to assume he must have had another pair at home almost exactly like them. His rainbow-striped suspenders completed the effect. He looked like he'd stepped out of the cast of *Godspell*.

I thought I had seen him before and could almost revive a dim recollection of the two of us talking about important and difficult things, but I had no idea who he was or where we'd known each other. When he looked at me, I caught his eye and nodded slightly, trying to send him a message that I recognized him and that we'd talk later. He nodded and moved toward the coffee pot.

Looking around the circle of chairs we'd set in the corner for our discussion, I saw the other people in the group relax a little when he moved away. His appearance, carefully chosen to be unique and provocative, had been very effective: most of us don't like what we don't understand.

The conversation in the class moved from Abraham to Judaism to Christianity to Islam, and then to the regrettable but inevitable cataloguing of atrocities committed by Islamic extremists, and we were just about to have a head-on collision with some of the atrocities of the Christian Crusades and contemporary Christian extremists when we were all saved at about ten to eleven by the Sunday school bell. I told the class we'd pick it up here next Sunday, although I could not have said with any integrity that I was looking forward to it.

Every Sunday, that bell signaled the start of a hectic race for me to make it through the members of the class, some of whom had just one more point to make or a question they didn't want to ask in front of the whole class, through the Parish Hall filled with people milling around, some of whom wanted to exchange pleasantries with the priest before the service, and into the vesting room where I needed to put on my vestments while making sure that all the readers, acolytes, and ushers had shown up that day, that the acolytes all put on robes that were approximately appropriate to their bodies, and that their cinctures were tired so the robes or ropes wouldn't drag on the floor. The complexity of the challenge was somewhat like trying to make sense of the previous sentence.

Somewhere in that mad rush, the colorful visitor grabbed me by the shirtsleeve, and I turned to face him. I thought, "Who is this guy?" but what I said was, "It's good to see you. I've gotta get dressed for the service. Can you hang around after?"

There was a hint of long-suffering tragedy in his disappointment as he answered, "Of course—the show must go on!" Then he added, in a voice that suggested he was talking to himself but was pitched so I would be sure to hear, "It's not like I have anyplace else to go." I saw something in his eyes just then, something familiar; it didn't feel like a happy memory.

We started the service with the procession singing "There's a wideness in God's mercy, like the wideness of the sea." The psalm appointed for that day was Psalm 23, and when we read the fourth verse of that most familiar psalm—"Though I walk through the valley of the shadow of death, I shall fear no evil; for you are with me; your rod and your staff, they comfort me"—I realized who the guest was.

And I knew that the axe of controversy had found its way to St. Thomas Episcopal Church in Greene, Alabama.

14

NOTHING LOATHSOME LURKING IN THE PASTA

When I was a sophomore at Mississippi State, I met a young woman named Eleanor. I'd been sitting in the Student Union, working a crossword puzzle, and a young woman I'd noticed in our Comparative Religion class came and sat beside me. She told me she'd read my aura. I didn't know what an aura was, and when she told me, it scared me. She scared me.

Even so, I thought Eleanor was smart and friendly, and I was flattered that a graduate student was interested in me. We had a pleasant conversation and she figured out that we had the same gap in our schedules on Tuesday and Thursday afternoons. We agreed to meet at the union on those days, and we forged an odd friendship based on the idea that each of us could learn from the other. I thought she was an attractive older woman (at twenty-four, she was six years older than I); I fantasized that she might be interested in having a relationship with me, and that scared me, too, but not as much as it intrigued me. We worked our way through auras and several other bits of paranormal phenomenology, touched on a bit of sacramental theology, and spent an entire afternoon discussing Edgar Cayce and the idea of reincarnation. Week after week we met and talked, each of us easy in the other's company, with our free and challenging conversations covering a wide array of topics, including everything from heaven and hell and the writings of C. S. Lewis to Haile Selassie and the Rastafarians.

Eleanor said that every two thousand years or so, at the change of each zodiacal age, the world is given a Messiah. She said that nearly two thousand years before, Jesus of Nazareth was born. Two thousand years before that, it was Zoroaster, also known as Zarathustra. In a desperate attempt to be part of the conversation I was sitting in, I told her I'd seen *2001: A Space Odyssey*, which I thought featured a song about Zarathustra. She gently but distinctly ignored that and told me some interesting things about Zoroaster, repeating her conviction that he had been a Messiah like Jesus. She said that the wise men who visited the newborn Jesus were Zoroastrians, followers of Zoroaster, and that after they saw Jesus and gave him their costly gifts, they worshiped him because they were satisfied with what they saw in him.

Then she informed me that after reading my aura, she believed that I could be a Master Soul, and that she was hoping I might be the Master Soul of the Age of Aquarius, which in 1974 was still dawning, even though the song by The Fifth Dimension was five years old by then. I figured maybe zodiacal ages take a long time to dawn, but I kept that observation to myself.

I told her I was pretty sure I wasn't a Master Soul, and that for sure I was nowhere near perfect. She told me that's just what a Master Soul would say. I told her I didn't believe in reincarnation, and she told me that Jesus and Zoroaster hadn't, either. I told her it made me feel uncomfortable to talk about her thinking I was a Master Soul, and before she could tell me that Jesus and Zoroaster would have said the same thing, I continued, "So let's talk about something else."

Then one day she mentioned that she'd worked in an Italian restaurant in her undergraduate days. The restaurant had eventually failed, but she assured me it had nothing to do with her and said that she was more than competent with pasta and sauces.

I told her that the only Italian food I'd ever had was either spaghetti and meatballs or pizza. She described a bunch of dishes I'd never heard of, some of them with eggplants, clams, or calamari, which turned out, much to my amazement and revulsion, to be squid. I told her I'd fished using squid as bait a couple of times in the Gulf of Mexico, and putting it on a hook was a nasty enough experience to know I didn't want to eat any of it. I couldn't imagine how hungry someone would have to be to eat squid; I also wondered if this might have been why the restaurant had gone under. She told me that people in this town only wanted burgers and pizza, that someday she'd cook me some real Italian food to broaden my horizons.

I told her I didn't want my horizons broadened to the point of including eggplant, squid, clams, or any other slimy thing. I also told her my mom cooked the best spaghetti in the world. She told me I was being provincial, and after she explained what that meant, I had to plead guilty. She also told me that she was a vegetarian, so I wouldn't have to worry about eating squid. I didn't know what to make of that, and while I was still wondering how people survived without eating burgers and pizza, she told me she didn't eat meat because she believed in reincarnation. Seeing that this idea left me completely bewildered, she said, "You never can tell who that cow might have been in a previous life." If I'd ever been tempted to consider believing in reincarnation, the idea that I could never again eat another cheeseburger was enough to pull me back.

One morning a few days after that conversation, she invited me to dinner. She said she had been wanting to introduce me to her housemate, and she offered to cook spaghetti, something she thought was not too adventurous for me. After she gave her solemn oath that there would be nothing loathsome lurking in the pasta, we arranged the time and she gave me directions to their house.

I rode my ten-speed out to their little place, about three miles out of town, through pastures and soybean fields, down Stark Road. It was a little white-frame house with an inviting front porch. They had planted a garden behind it: lots of tomatoes, squash and okra, even some eggplant. Who needed clams and squid for slime content when you could grow your own slimy things in the backyard?

I walked across the porch and knocked, surprised when a young man opened the door. As provincial as I was, I'd assumed Eleanor's housemate would be female. Now I had to assume she was romantically entwined with this guy, and the last vestiges of the illusion that she might be interested in an amorous relationship with me were extinguished like a candle that had never actually been lit, except in my starry-eyed imagination.

Her housemate was tall and thin, with dark, reddish-brown hair tied back into a ponytail. He looked like the kind of guy you might want your sister to go out with. He asked, "You're Buddy?"

I nodded, and he introduced himself as Michael. Eleanor came out of the kitchen and said, "I see you've met my housemate, Michael. Michael Graham, this is Buddy Hinton, the possible Tuesday and Thursday Master Soul of the Student Union." She looked at me and explained, "I've told Michael a little about you."

I laughed and held out my hand. "Eleanor sees more in me than I do. It's nice to meet you, Michael."

He shook my hand. "My pleasure."

As I went in the house, I said, "Kind of disappointing, isn't it? I'm not even glowing or anything."

Behind me I heard Eleanor murmur, "Yes, you are."

Eleanor brought out a bottle of red wine and a glass for each of us. I'd never had wine other than a sip of the strong port at Communion; this was much lighter and not so sweet.

We all sat down while the noodles cooked, and Michael told me he was from Jackson and was a senior majoring in English lit, which is how he'd met Eleanor. Michael was a poet who'd been published in the *Reflector*, the university newspaper. When he went to get some of his better work to read to me, I asked Eleanor if she and Michael were . . . romantic.

She laughed and answered, "No. I'm not his type."

The pasta was something like spaghetti, with thicker noodles. It was the first time I'd ever eaten black olives or mushrooms—olives because it was the first time I'd ever encountered them in a dish, and mushrooms because I'd always picked them out before. I was surprised to find that they were actually very tasty. Eleanor was not afraid of garlic, or oregano, or basil; the result was delightful. I told her it was all delicious and thanked her for expanding my horizons a little.

After Michael and I had taken the dishes to the sink, Eleanor dismissed us to the front porch. I sat in the hanging swing, and Michael sat in one of the rocking chairs. He pulled a pack of cigarettes out of his shirt pocket and offered me one. My primary experience with cigarettes had been watching my parents quit after I'd described how a lung looked in a fifth-grade anti-smoking film; I declined his offer. He lit one for himself. He leaned back, took a deep puff, and closed his eyes. I watched the smoke slowly leak out of his nose.

He began, "Buddy, the reason Eleanor invited you to dinner is so that I could talk to you. I'm not in the habit of making my business anyone else's business, but she assures me you're someone I could talk to, you know, about . . ."

I didn't know what to say or do, so I just nodded my encouragement for him to continue. When he did, he said, "She says you have a wisdom in you that . . . well, you know, she told me you were born with an old soul."

I protested, "I don't know about that."

He waved me off and said, "No, I can see it, too. I just need somebody to talk to, and well . . . I can't talk to my parents anymore, or a professor, or a preacher. Eleanor said I could, you know, talk to you."

"Michael, I will be glad to listen. But I can't promise that I'll be able to say anything that'll help, okay?"

He took a deep breath, nodded, and pulled his knees up into the rocking chair, hugging them to his chest. He had a desperate, lonely look on his face, as if he wished he could be anywhere other than right where he was, as if he was struggling to find a way to say something he didn't want to speak aloud. There was an awkward pause, and, trying to help, I assured him, "Whatever it is, it'll be all right."

He smiled sadly and whispered, "No, it's a long way from all right. It's not all right now, and it won't ever, you know, I don't think it ever will be . . . all right. I'm not going to pretend that it is; I can't."

"What's not all right?"

"Me. I'm not all right. Well, at least to my family, I'm . . . I guess they would say I'm all wrong."

"What's wrong with you?"

He looked like the poem he'd shared with me before dinner: full of despair, loneliness, and pain. There was another graceless interlude, and again, trying to make things easier, I asked, "You're not sick, are you?"

"My parents think I am."

"Do you think you are?"

"No, I'm fine—no, I don't know. Physically I'm fine, well . . . I don't know. That's what I wanted to talk to you about."

By this time, I was frustrated and feeling completely inadequate. I didn't have any idea what we were trying to talk about or how to steer us into actually talking about it. While I was trying to sort it all out, he just dove in. Actually, it was more of a belly buster than a dive.

"I'm a homosexual."

15

THE SEX LIVES OF AMPHIBIANS

"Oh," was all I could think to say. I knew a little about homosexuality, mostly from watching how maliciously some of the other guys treated a kid named Jimmy in high school. Jimmy's primary offense was a severe lack of interest in or aptitude for anything athletic and a tendency to be visibly cleaner than any of the rest of us, which I expect was probably not all that difficult to achieve. The rumor was that he was a homosexual, but I figured it wasn't any of my business, so I stayed out of it. It hadn't seemed like a big deal when I was in high school, and I was consumed with my own issues.

I looked up to see Michael watching me, expecting a response of some sort, maybe wisdom and guidance from a potential Messiah.

Instead, I disappointed both of us by asking, "How do you know?"

"I know because it's . . . you know, it's how I am, who I am. How do you know you're not?"

"Because I like being with girls. Or I would like to be with girls, anyway."

He nodded. "Exactly. But I don't. I'd like to be with . . . with other men."

Again I said, "Oh." Then it occurred to me that mine might not the only sexual fantasies at work here, and I was distracted by the fearful possibility that he might be attracted to me. It was bad enough to be suspected of being Spiritually Advanced without potentially having to be a sex object, too. I was terribly aware that he and I were alone together at night, drinking wine. I repeated, this time at a higher pitch, "*Oh.*"

He saw my discomfort and offered a sad smile. "No, not you. I'm sure you're a very nice guy, but I'd prefer someone a little . . . well, let's just say you're not my type."

When Eleanor had told me she wasn't his type, it had been a relief; when he told me I wasn't his type either, it was a very different sort of relief. Then I saw his shoulders slump. He nestled his head between his knees, and I knew that I was failing him. I fussed at myself: it wasn't helping either one of us for me to be scared of his sexuality; I'd been too worried about my own self and not concerned enough about him. I stopped trying to find the right thing to say and just said the thing that was on my heart.

"How can I help you, Michael?"

"I just want to know if God . . . hates me."

It had never occurred to me that God would hate him. I took his hand in mine, which surprised us both, and waited until he looked up at me. I looked into his eyes and resisted the impulse to look away. What little wisdom I had to give would have to be the best I could do: "Michael, God made you who you are. Of course God loves you."

When I was much younger, I'd met a remarkable man named Jake Jefferson, who'd taught me a lot about life and love and God. He'd been a tent preacher for years before becoming an alcoholic and going to prison. I'd met him down in the woods behind our house, and we'd been friends ever since. I remembered one of my favorite things Jake used to say, and I shared it with Michael: "God loves you more than your mama does."

It had always been a marvel to me to think that God could love me more than my mother did, but it had a different effect on Michael. His head went back down. "My mother isn't speaking to me. My father says . . . well, he says he doesn't want me to come back home. It wouldn't take much for God to love me . . . you know, to love me more than that."

I slogged on. "I believe God loves us perfectly, all the time—not because we're perfect but because He is. Surely you can't actually think God is going to stop loving you because you are who He made you to be."

He looked up now, trying to decide if I knew what I was talking about. I was beginning to wonder about that myself. He asked, "Do you think God made me . . . a homosexual?"

I asked him, "Did you choose to be a homosexual?"

"Are you kidding? Who the hell would choose to grow up homosexual in Mississippi? Did you choose to be a heterosexual?"

I'd never thought about it that way. I told him I didn't think it was something I'd ever decided on; it was just assumed; I was just always that way. He said, "Exactly. I was always just like this. But Mom and Dad . . . well, you know, my whole family has thrown me out, and my church, my church has condemned me. They want me to live a lie, but I . . . I just can't. I've prayed that I could be normal, you know, like Mom and Dad want me to be. But it's just not me. Some guys I know are, you know, homosexual, and they just pretend they're not. They get married and have children and everything. It just seems like . . . it just seems like such a lie."

"If you didn't choose this, how could it be your fault?"

"But the Bible says . . . well, the Bible says it's a sin to be homosexual."

That took me aback. I didn't think I'd ever seen that part of the Bible; it hadn't been in the Sunday morning readings at church as far as I could remember. Michael continued, "The Bible says it's . . . you know, the Bible says it's an abomination."

"An abomination?"

"Yeah. Our preacher told my parents that it's an abomination, that if a man lies with another man they shall surely be put to death."

"Oh, good Lord." I was ambushed by an image of waves of good Christian souls with their Bibles in one hand and stones in the other, lining up to execute people accused of homosexuality, all in the name of Jesus. How far could a Christian take a literal, inerrant approach to reading the Bible?

"Okay, Michael, listen," I said. "Do you really think God wants you to be put to death because you are the way you are, even though you didn't choose to be that way? Is God that mean?"

He shuddered a sob. "I hope not."

I replied, "No, of course not."

He was stunned. He'd been expecting a religious conversation with a semi-holy man, and here I was questioning the Scriptures. He asked, "You don't believe in the Bible?"

I answered, "I do. I believe it's a remarkable book, a collection of stories and ideas that have been passed down for generations. But I think it was written by people, not dictated by God. It's a wonderful source for what we believe, but I don't believe the Bible is divine or without error."

"Don't you believe the Bible is . . . well, you know, that the Bible is inspired?"

"Sure. I guess so. Maybe. But I guess Beethoven was inspired, too. I think Shakespeare and Mark Twain were probably inspired from time to time, but that doesn't mean everything they ever wrote is the absolute truth."

Now it was his turn to be taken aback. "What?"

"You know the Twenty-Third Psalm?" I asked.

"'The Lord is my shepherd,' that one?"

"Yeah. It says the Lord is your shepherd, too—not just the preacher's or the people who think they're not doing anything wrong. *Your* shepherd. Surely that part of the Bible had to be inspired—the Spirit of God had to have helped whoever wrote that, right? And it says, 'Yea, though I walk through the valley of the shadow of death, I shall fear no evil; thy rod and thy staff, they comfort me.' That's talking about you, too."

Michael repeated, "Though I walk through the valley of the shadow of death . . ." He was deep in his own thoughts.

"But listen," I insisted. "Later, in another psalm, the psalmist wrote about the people who took the Jews into captivity, and it says 'Blessed shall he be that taketh thy children, and throweth them against the stones.'"

Michael said, "That's horrible!" and I agreed.

"Completely horrible." I told him I'd found that passage when I was an acolyte sitting through church one day during a sermon I wasn't listening to, thumbing through the Book of Common Prayer for any sort of distraction.

At first I'd been excited to realized that Psalm 137 was what the clowns in *Godspell* were singing about, and then I was horrified by the last two verses, which weren't included in the song. I said, "I don't think the Spirit of God had anything to do with writing that, do you?" Michael sobbed then, with a deep shudder that seemed to take over his whole body.

"Look," I continued, "I'm not pretending that I know all this stuff, all right? All I know is that we have to trust what Jesus said, that God our Father loves us. All of us. We have to trust that. That's the whole thing about sheep—they trust their shepherd."

He nodded and murmured, "Through the valley of the shadow of death."

I realized there was a lot going on that I didn't know anything about. We sat quietly for a few seconds, until I asked, "In the Bible, what does it say a homosexual should do?"

"Oh. I don't think it talks about . . . you know, it doesn't talk about that. It doesn't offer any help to the homosexual. Well, at least I haven't heard any. It just says it's wrong."

"Maybe the writers of the Bible were caught up in the way people thought back then. Maybe people think different now, or we should."

"So where it says that homosexuality is a sin, and an abomination . . . ?" He waited, hopefully.

"Then I guess we need to read that part carefully. Things are almost always more complicated than people want them to be." He took that in for a moment, and I continued, "All that stuff was written a long time ago; now it's a different world. But once an idea is written down, it gets sort of set in stone." He nodded, trying to make it make sense, and I went on. "There are all sorts of rules and commandments in the Bible. A lot of them are about greed or envy or anger. People break those all the time, right? But God still loves us—it's who God is."

"You think?"

"Of course."

I looked up to see Eleanor standing at the screen door. She echoed, "Of course."

Michael smiled a little then, and he looked at me with a respect that hadn't been there before. He nodded to Eleanor, but then a sudden grief flashed across his face. "But what about . . . my mom and dad?"

Eleanor answered, "They'll either come around, or they won't. Don't give up on them, Michael. But you have to live your life who you are, whether they like it or not."

I nodded. "That can't be easy, but I think she's right. Give them some time, and don't ever give up on them. I guess this has to be hard on them, too."

Eleanor sat beside me on the porch swing, and we rocked for a while, each of us lost in our own thoughts. It was early spring, warm enough to sit outside but before the mosquitoes were out in force. We listened to the sounds of the night, and after a while I mused, "Listen to those tree frogs."

Michael said, "They're all trying to attract their mates. All that noise—it's all about sex."

Eleanor said, "Leave it to Michael to bring up the sex lives of amphibians."

We all laughed at that, and as we sat there contentedly, I said, "I'm glad I'm not a frog."

Eleanor said, "Not in this life, anyway."

16

WONDER OF WONDERS

At Mississippi State in the mid-1970s, Michael Graham and I continued to talk from time to time, usually over a cup of coffee in the union. Sometimes Eleanor was there, but sometimes it was just the two of us. He told me that his mother used to play the piano for a little church south of Jackson and had insisted that he learn to play as well. She'd suspected and feared that her son was homosexual for years, well before he knew what it meant and long before either one of them were willing to address it.

When he was about to turn sixteen, Mrs. Graham had taken it upon herself to talk to their new preacher about her son's "condition," desperate for some comfort that, as it turned out, she would not find in Brother Jimmy. He was a fiery young man in his first pulpit, full of righteous certainty. He piously told Michael's mother that her son would have to repent from what he declared "a pernicious, perilous sin," and she'd left his office in tears.

Brother Jimmy made the sin of homosexuality the focus of a sermon soon after that, and even though he didn't mention Michael by name, the Grahams felt like they were in the crosshairs of his homiletical sights. The board of deacons, proven heterosexuals all, encouraged their young preacher to pull no punches, delighted that he'd found something to talk about that didn't put any of them on the defensive. It seems that in his first few months there, he'd already preached about cigarettes and alcohol, which a few of the deacons had taken personally, and he had come disturbingly close to suggesting that racism was a sin, which had seemed awfully close to being some kind of liberal conspiracy, and which moreover they thought could be bad for business.

All in all, with his sermon on homosexuality, they were just relieved he'd moved on to somebody else.

Michael's father had been an usher and a Sunday school teacher; when he learned that Brother Jimmy was going to expand the sermon about homosexuality into a series, he threatened to withdraw his pledge. When he heard that Brother Jimmy, swept up with the deacons' newfound enthusiasm, was making arrangements to spell out "HOMOS ARE ABOMINATIONS" on the sign in the holly hedge by the church's front door, he turned in his resignation.

Michael had told me his story in bits and pieces as we sat there in the Student Union. He said, "They tried to get me to repent, and well . . . I tried, I really did. I almost asked a girl out . . . to go out on a date, see a movie or something . . . but well, you know, it was . . . well, it was scary."

He had tried to be heterosexual. He had gone to counselors and to a Christian psychiatric center. He had prayed, looked at the girls in *Playboy* and *Penthouse*, thwacked himself with a rubber band around his wrist when he had impure thoughts about men. "I didn't get any help. All I got was condemnation." When he went off to college, his parents moved to another little town in south Mississippi and made it clear to him that they were making a fresh start without him.

Mostly all I could do was listen, the whole time thinking that if I really was an Advanced Soul, I'd have something intelligent to say.

When he left Mississippi State, I thought I'd never see him again. But now here he was, looking thin and fragile but quite flamboyant, sitting in the congregation of St. Thomas Episcopal Church in Greene, Alabama, where I was about to deliver a sermon.

I had planned what I wanted to say in the sermon the night before, using the Gospel lesson for the Fourth Sunday of Lent. Just by coincidence, if you believe in that sort of thing, the Gospel reading for the day was John 9:1-38, the healing of the man born blind, at the pool of Siloam.

It's a long, wonderful story, and I encourage you to read it for yourself. The part that I was most interested in for the purpose of that sermon was that the religious people of the day, the Pharisees, were not concerned about the man or his healing; they were mostly concerned that Jesus had broken their laws by healing the man on the Sabbath day. As St. John told the story, "Some of the Pharisees said, 'This man is not from God, for he does not observe the sabbath.' But others said, 'How can a man who is a sinner perform such signs?' And they were divided."

I had thought that the theme of the sermon was going to be "How can we serve God and God's people, as imperfect as we are?" But Michael Graham was in the congregation, and I knew that wouldn't do.

I read the Gospel text, and the people were all seated, and I began by repeating what the Pharisees had declared: "'This man—Jesus—is not from God, for he does not observe the sabbath.' That's what the church people of the day said. And they were right.

I let that sink in for a moment before continuing, "Very clearly one of the Ten Commandments says that God's people are to do no work on the Sabbath day. Jesus violated the Law of his people, the Law of the Torah. The Pharisees believed that their religion was about keeping the Law. Jesus broke the Law—no doubt about it—so therefore they reasoned he could not from God."

I paused for a bit, wondering what to say next that would offer good news about Jesus, that would build up the community of faith I served, and that would offer a message of hope to the parish and to Michael.

In that pregnant moment, I remembered what the camper named Glenn had said at camp in Mississippi when I told him he couldn't smooch with his girl: "You could be wrong."

I told that story, not really caring whether I'd already told it to these people, and the words came smoothly to me, as if I was listening to myself while I talked. I shared that one of the campers, an intellectually challenged man at the Special Session in Mississippi, had wanted to smooch with his girlfriend. When I told him he couldn't because it was against the rules (rules I was making up on the spot), he said something that has been precious to me ever since: "You could be wrong."

Faithful people need to know we could be wrong so we don't get trapped by our own ideas, so we'll keep looking for God in other people with different ideas and assumptions.

At the end of the story ("I told him they could smooch: 'All right, you've got ten minutes, and keep all your clothes on.'"), I made my point: "The Pharisees wanted more than anything to be right, to be correct. God save us from being Pharisees. God deliver us from valuing being right more than we value compassion. Deliver us from the presumption of thinking we've got it all figured out."

It was pretty short as sermons go, and I think I caught some of the folks off their guard, as we started saying the Nicene Creed together before they were ready. When it came time to receive the bread and wine, Michael knelt at the rail and crossed his arms over his chest, the signal that he wasn't going to receive the sacraments but wanted a blessing. I choked up a little as I made the sign of the cross on his forehead, saying, "Michael, the Lord bless you and keep you, and make his face shine upon you. Amen."

After the service, after the "Enjoyed your sermon" line, after making my way through the people and stopping to listen to the inevitable concerns that it's too hot in here, or the organist plays too slow, or we should have more children involved in the service, or it's too cold in there, or the organist needs to slow down, or the children are too fidgety, and after getting out of my vestments, I found Michael in the parish hall, talking to Beulah. They were standing with Charlie and Polk Guthrie.

Beulah exclaimed, "Buddy! Sinclair tells me you're an old friend?" Her face betrayed curiosity and some concern; Polk was looking especially amused.

I thought, "Who's Sinclair?" and then I took another look. Maybe it wasn't Michael after all! The Michael I'd known had nervous mannerisms; I didn't remember Michael being so skinny or so flashy, and this man was confident to the point of being smug. Maybe I had him confused him with somebody else. But he'd told Beulah that he was an old friend, and he had Michael's eyes. No, I decided. This was Michael.

I walked up to the four people standing together and surprised three of them by saying, "Hello, Michael."

Beulah, always the soul of composure, whispered to me, "It's Sinclair."

I answered, "I know. I know him. This is my friend Michael; we were in college together."

"Buddy, he just told us his name is Sinclair."

I was about to try to explain, even though I didn't really understand, when our flashy visitor exclaimed, "You're all right. The name I was given at birth is Michael Lewis Graham, okay? When I was in college, when Buddy and I met, people called me Michael. But now I am simply Sinclair, a new man." He said this last with a sort of theatrical flourish.

I held out my hand and said, "I'm glad to see you again . . . Sinclair."

He held out his hand for me to take and replied, "Hello, Buddy. Or should I say Father Buddy now?"

"No, just Buddy. I'm still just me."

"Yes," he gushed, "still you, but married to a gorgeous woman and the father of two adorable children, the minister of your own delightful little church. It's so good to see you!"

Polk and Charlie left, and Beulah and I took Sinclair and our two adorable, delightful, fabulous children to lunch at the Golden Palace, the best and only Chinese buffet in all of Greene, Alabama. The kids were about as well-behaved as you could expect from a ten-year-old boy and a five-year-old girl; still, we ran out of their relatively good behavior long before we ran out of conversation, so we adjourned to our house for coffee, where we could let the kids run wild. Sinclair had known me for years but was not quite at ease with me; I wondered if he still thought I was a Master Soul. Beulah he trusted instantly; there is something magical about that woman.

He talked almost nonstop from egg rolls to fortune cookies, and then through coffee later. I noticed with some relief that his hesitant, fearful speech pattern was gone and that he was much more confident than I remembered him. He told us he had just accepted a job as the Program Director of the Greene Little Theatre, had come to look for an apartment, and was surprised to see my name on the sign in front of the Episcopal parish.

I asked about his parents and regretted it immediately. He answered, darkly, that he hadn't spoken to them or heard from them since his college days and was determined that the next move would have to be theirs. "I don't think about them or talk about them, Buddy. And I'm sure they don't think or talk about me."

He told us that after graduating from Mississippi State, he'd thought about graduate school but didn't have the funds or the energy. He drifted his way up to New York City and had several different jobs and adventures before being hired as a stagehand at the George Gershwin Theater on West 44th Street. He'd worked there for a few months when they took on a new play, a revival of *Fiddler on the Roof*. Mostly he helped with the sets, he said, but he did get to sing in the ensemble from time to time. And one memorable evening, he played the role of Motel the Tailor when the actor cast for the role had a stomach bug and his understudy was in New Jersey with his sick mother. "Wonder of wonders, miracle of miracles," he sang.

After that, he went from theater to theater doing sets and makeup and hair, selling tickets or programs, whatever was required or available. "I just loved it! The people there are so free, free to be who they are, and it gave me permission to be me. In that freedom Michael Lewis Graham was laid to rest, and in his place I rose: Lewis Sinclair Graham."

"Wasn't there a writer by that name?" Beulah speculated.

Sinclair beamed. "That's the genius of it, don't you see? I adopted the name after the brilliant writer Sinclair Lewis."

I was lost but hoping to hide it, and Beulah tried to help: "He wrote *Elmer Gantry*."

I started to say that I'd seen most of the second half of the movie on late-night television once while rocking one of our children to sleep, but I was feeling distinctly uncultured just then, so I kept it to myself.

Sinclair added, "He also wrote *Main Street, Babbitt,* and *Arrowsmith,* and many others. He won the Nobel Prize for literature. He wrote short stories and plays, but did you know that his first published book was titled *Hike and the Aeroplane?* It was published in 1912, and he wrote it under the pseudonym Tom Graham! *Graham,* see? He used my name, so now I'm using his. It's all very tidy, don't you think?"

What I thought was that Greene, Alabama, was not prepared for Lewis Sinclair Graham.

17

A Beetle Up His Butt

Sinclair stayed in our guest room for nearly a month. He was great with the kids and a fantastic cook—we were almost sorry when he found an apartment and moved out. He was not particularly interested in religion, he told me, but he came to church almost every Sunday, always getting a blessing at Communion rather than receiving the bread and wine.

When I asked him about that, he said, "All that stuff about the bread and wine being the body and blood is just kinda creepy. I know it means something to y'all, but it gets in my way. I can't understand it the way y'all do. But the blessing of the priest and the church, that means a lot to me."

That was the year that Richard Chambliss was elected to serve on the Vestry. I'd always had the idea that he came to church on an as-needed basis, for Christmas or Easter or when one of his children were singing in the youth choir or serving as acolyte; I was surprised that he let himself be nominated. When I congratulated him, he looked at me coolly and replied, "Well, if Candy's going to insist that we give half of our money to the church, somebody with some sense ought to be looking out for how it's going to be spent." I did not miss the implication that I was not somebody he trusted to have sufficient sense.

We had a Vestry meeting the third Monday night of every month, starting with a prayer and moving through the agenda "without haste, but without rest," as the priest of my parish when I was growing up used to say. By this time I'd been there for almost six years, and I'd tried to make the Vestry meetings business-like but friendly, community-building but efficient. The mood and tone had been, for the most part, light, loving, and cooperative. I'd had the sense that we were playing on the same team.

All of that changed when Richard Chambliss joined the Vestry. In January he challenged how much money we were sending to the Diocese and suggested that we appoint a subcommittee to review the finances of the parish. No one volunteered to be on that committee with him, and I was glad to watch the idea die. In February he hinted that we were paying the rector too much and wondered if we needed to keep the church open as for as many hours a week as we did. At the March meeting he questioned whether we were doing the people of Honduras any good at all with our medical missions or were we just making them more dependent on us. In that same meeting he suggested that most of the campers at Special Session were living on welfare and Medicare and were "a drain on the government."

I'd just been sitting there, waiting for the other members of the Vestry to step up and challenge him, trying to preserve the harmony of the Vestry and watching it evaporate, trying to be patient, as I thought a good priest should be. When he pronounced judgment on the campers at Special Session, I couldn't take it anymore.

"Richard, what would you like—for these people to starve? Let them have no medical care? I promise none of these folks chose to be born with disabilities."

He was ready and waiting for me to say something. "Well, *Father*, it shouldn't be our responsibility to take care of all the strays in the whole world." He said "Father" with a sharpened point, coated in derision and injected with scorn. "I know you've got a tender liberal heart for misfits and freaks, with your black friend and your gay friend, but that's our money you're spending as you build up your . . ." He stopped, realizing that he was about to go too far.

My hands were trembling; I don't know if I've ever been that angry. "As I build up my . . . what, Richard? My résumé?"

The other eleven members of the Vestry sat in shocked silence, every one of them looking down at the financial statements we'd already gone over as if they'd suddenly found something interesting. Nothing like this had ever happened at a Vestry meeting before. Richard looked around the room for support, and seeing none, he retreated a little. "You said that, not me."

"No, you didn't say it, and I guess we'll never really know what you were going to say." I told myself I needed to calm down, and then I ignored myself. "If you want this Vestry to consider putting an end to our medical mission to Honduras, make a motion. If you want to cut back office hours at the church office, reduce our giving to the diocese, or eliminate our donation to the Special Session"—I took a breath—"if you want to reduce my compensation or run your priest off, make a motion."

I waited, with him staring me in the face and me glaring back, and then I continued, "I understand that our politics and our values are different. Feel free to disagree with me. But I assure you that what I do is about the good news of the love of God in Jesus Christ—and I don't give a *damn* about my résumé." He continued to stare but said nothing. I announced, "If there is no new business, we stand adjourned until next month. Thanks, everybody."

Richard Chambliss scowled at me, and then he stood abruptly and left without looking back. The other members of the Vestry milled around a little, not wanting to talk about what had just happened but not able to let it go, either. Thed, a big-boned man on the Vestry who liked to keep things simple, came over and put his large, calloused hand on my shoulder. "He'll be all right, though, you reckon?" he asked.

"Oh, sure," I answered, not believing myself for a moment.

Thed seemed reassured and replied, "He's sure got a beetle up his butt about somethin', though."

Later that night, when Beulah and I talked about it, I told her I was the aggrieved party, that Richard owed me an apology, but after some discussion she convinced me that I would need to call him the next day. I wasn't convinced until she agreed with me that he should be the one telling me he was sorry and then told me I needed to call him anyway, just to give him the chance—not for his sake but for mine. She knew him from the courtroom, where he had been an attorney in a few child custody cases she'd worked. She said, "I don't think he's the kind of guy who'll ever back down, but I know you're the kind of guy who needs to give him the chance."

I thought all night about what I was going to say, but in the end it didn't matter—his secretary told me he wasn't in, so I left a message and he didn't call me back. I called again that afternoon with the same results, and then even Beulah conceded that there was nothing else to do when he clearly did not want to talk to me.

He was talking to other people in the parish, though—anyone he thought would be sympathetic to his point of view. Thed called me the next night and told me Richard had called him.

"He's gonna try to stir up some trouble for you, Buddy."

"Yeah, I know."

"What're you gonna do?"

I'd been worrying about that for some time, but I didn't have any answers I liked. "I don't know, Thed. What can I do? What would you do?"

"I believe I might have to go over to his house, knock on his door, tip my cap to his beautiful wife, and punch him in the nose!"

I laughed. I had to admit there was something attractive about Thed's approach, but I said, "No, I probably better not do that. And that's the problem: I don't know if there's anything I really can do. He can fight as dirty as he wants, and I can't really fight back."

"You mean all that stuff about forgiveness and turning the other cheek and all that?"

"Yeah." All that stuff about forgiveness and turning the other cheek, all the stuff that Jesus said.

Thed said, "You know, I don't always tell you how good a preacher you are, but I do listen, most of the time, anyway—more than you might think. I remember one time you read us that part where Jesus tells his disciples that he's sending them out like sheep in the middle of wolves. I remember you sayin' that we have to either let the wolves chew on us or become wolves so we can fight back. I remember you said that if we was gonna follow Jesus we can't let ourselves become wolves. Maybe this right here is what you were talkin' about. If you can't fight back, how you gonna stop Richard from chewin' on you?"

I didn't want to say out loud the only answer I had just then: if I'm going to follow Jesus, all I can do is love, even those who are chewing on me. I believe that, but I don't always like it.

He said, "Well anyway, most folks ain't gonna listen to Richard. Hell, most of us don't even like him!"

I sat quiet for a moment, not knowing what I should say and not saying what I wanted to say. Then Thed said, "My daddy used to tell stories like you do. Well, not the preachin' part, but stories like that, stories that had a point to 'em."

"Yeah?"

"Yeah. So now I want to tell you a story. You got a minute?"

"I've always got time for a good story."

"I had an uncle named Ed, who sold insurance. Well, when he was a young man, he musta been pretty good at it, 'cause the people higher up in the insurance company gave him a big promotion and a raise and moved him up to Nashville. He married a woman from up there, who looked like she ought to be on some kind of magazine cover, just as pretty as she could be, and just as mean as a snake. Her name was Sylvia; me and my sister were scared of her. I guess Uncle Eddie did pretty good in Nashville, too, and they moved him and his wife up to New York City."

Thed paused for effect, I think, and it seemed to me like I ought to say something. I said, "Good for him. Well, not the part about being married to a woman who was mean as snake, but it's always good to hear a story about a local boy who makes it big."

"Yeah, well—he made a lot of money, a whole lot of money, all right? More money than he knew how to spend, I think. Aunt Sylvia was glad to help with that—the diamonds she wore just got bigger and bigger. In a few years they moved out of the insurance company's apartment in the city and bought a big ol' house on Long Island."

He paused again, and I said, "I'm thinking there's going to be more to this story."

"Well, yeah. The thing was, every time he came home, he told us all about how everything was better in Nashville, or in New York City, or on Long Island. They'd come back to Greene for Thanksgiving every year, and he'd tell us all about how he would take the subway to the Bronx to watch the Yankees, and how he would take his wife to Paris and Vienna and places I never even heard of, and how they would eat at swanky expensive restaurants and what all fancy stuff they eat up there, and his mama would just have to listen to all that and then serve him and his snooty-ass wife a plate of turkey and cornbread dressing with giblet gravy all on the top and sweet potato pie and homemade biscuits and pecan pie for dessert."

"That sounds good to me. I bet he was glad to be home."

"No sir. That's the thing—you'd think he would be, but he wasn't. And his wife thought she was too fancy and sophisticated for us, with all her diamonds and designer jeans and fancy-ass perfume. One year she brought a whole bunch of water from a spring in France or somewhere, said she could taste the difference between that water and our water! When I told her I couldn't tell the difference—it was all just water—it was like that just showed she was right about me all along, that I was ignorant and crude. It was like they thought they were swans and peacocks and all the rest of us were just blackbirds and crows."

"Oh, Thed. I'm sorry."

"Yeah, well. The next Thanksgiving after that, they took a trip to Milan to see a fashion show or somethin'. And then after that they just didn't come home at all. His mama was my grandmother; she called him and asked him about it. He said they just didn't feel like they were at home down here anymore."

This time as he paused, I stayed quiet, almost always the smart thing to do.

"Well, about eight or ten years ago Aunt Sylvia left Uncle Eddie for a millionaire who lives somewhere over there in Italy or someplace you see in the movies. He sold his big expensive house on Long Island and all his shares in the insurance company and came back down here and moved into Grandma's house. None of us ever saw him much, though—he just stayed in that house until he died in there."

Thed took a deep breath. "Some people thought he'd killed himself, all right? Mama said he died of a broken heart, but I told her she's been reading too many of them romance novels. I think he died because he just didn't know who he was or where he belonged anymore. I think that's what broke his heart—he just didn't know who he was."

He paused again. He'd told his story and was all set to make his point. "And that's the thing, Buddy—you got to know who you are, and where you belong, all right?"

"Yes sir."

"Don't let Richard or anybody else make you think you need to be somebody else. You didn't put that beetle up in there, all right? Just keep doin' what you're doin'. We got you, all right? We got you."

I was amazed once again at how powerful a story can be. "Thanks, Thed. I appreciate it."

"I guess that's what I wanted to say, y'know—you are where you belong—just be who you are. We got you."

It was a powerful moment for me, and I found I couldn't talk because my throat had tightened with emotion. All I could do was nod and hope that he could sense it over the phone. He seemed to understand. "We got you," he repeated.

18

Nothin' Good About This Morning

I suppose it is part of my nature to focus on what's going wrong, to make it better if I can and just worry about it if I can't. Richard was a pain in my neck just then, and he continued to be for a long time. Sometimes, as Beulah reminds me, I need to look at the larger picture and admit that, despite whatever problems are the moment's distractions, life is good for the most part.

In the spring of 1999, the Hinton family was doing well, things at the parish were hopping, JoJo was thriving along with Siloam, and Sinclair had added a new and different spice to our gumbo.

Then a little girl died, and I got lost.

Her name was Caroline, but everybody called her Callie. She had a dimple in her left cheek and a sparkle in her eyes that captured my heart the first time we met. She and her parents came to church a few minutes early most Sundays so she could get what she called her "Buddy hug." I told her I looked forward to my "Callie hug" every week, too.

She listened, she *really* listened to the sermon every week, even the ones I didn't think were much good. After a few months, I realized I was talking more and more to her, preaching in such a way a ten-year-old would understand. Nobody else seemed to notice or mind, and I felt pretty sure my old friend and teacher Preacher Jake would have approved.

She was a bit chubby, which can be tough on a little girl; she was self-conscious about that and her propensity to giggle even when she didn't want to or wasn't supposed to. I told her that sometimes I laughed when I wasn't supposed to, too. I told her I loved to hear her laugh, that maybe we laughed so much because we were just full of joy.

All that giggling stopped on a Thursday morning when I came into the office early and listened to the answering machine as it played her father's voice from the night before, full of hopeless heartbreak, telling me that Callie was dead and pleading with me to come as quick as I could.

Dead? I was stunned. I left the office and walked out to my car in a daze. How could Callie be dead? Why?

I'd parked in my spot on Elm Street, in front of St. Thomas. I sat there in the car for a minute or two, not wanting to make myself go to their house, not willing to become part of this new and terrible reality: no more giggling, no more of her sweet embodiment of love and joy and blossoming faith—no more Callie.

I'd buried people before; I'd been with parishioners when they died. I'd shared the Christian's hope of resurrection to eternal life with those who were about to die and with those left behind. I believe all this stuff, I reminded myself. I don't always understand it, but I do believe it. I hope it. I want it all to be true; I need it to be true.

But . . . Callie was dead? Sweet little giggling Callie was dead? "No," I thought, "that can't be right." I started the car and put it into drive, my foot firmly holding the brake in place. I knew what I was supposed to do; I just didn't want to do it. I didn't want to go and face her parents. I didn't want to tell them a bunch of stuff I wasn't sure I could believe right then.

Without prelude or warning, it was on me: a full-fledged, all-out crisis of faith.

Callie's parents were Drew and Tammy Compton, both in their mid-thirties, both shy and a little overweight. He was a computer engineer. I asked him about his job once, and he told me using a lot of words and acronyms I didn't understand, and I never asked again. She worked for an insurance agency, but I wasn't sure what she did, either. He'd grown up in Greene, in the Roman Catholic Church; she'd grown up in the town of Harmony in a Southern Baptist family. They were nice people. I couldn't imagine how devastated they had to be.

I sat there with the car running, trying to figure out who I was and what I was doing. I'd said all the words I knew I was supposed to say to other people in similar situations, but just then they all sounded hollow when I said them to myself. In that moment, sitting in that car with the engine running, I couldn't find or feel my faith. Callie was dead, and in that moment, it felt like God was nowhere to be found.

I called Beulah's office but didn't leave a message on the machine on her desk, and she didn't answer her cell phone.

With some effort I took my foot off the brake, took a right at the next corner onto Third Avenue, realized I had headed exactly the wrong way, then took another right at Walnut and another on Second, until I'd made the block onto Elm Street right back where I'd started. I pulled into the same parking spot I'd just left and put the car in park. But it wasn't the same place it had been when I'd parked there ten minutes earlier: this time Callie was dead.

This time St. Thomas was no longer a place of safety and sanity but a representation of an ancient, tattered remnant of a religion that seemed to be falling apart. In that moment, my faith seemed like a fragile balloon full of hopes and dreams that I'd held on to my whole life, a balloon that had now sprung a slow leak, the atmosphere of faith in God and the teachings of the church that I'd breathed in and out since childhood slowly escaping. Callie was dead, and I felt like I was gasping for reassurance.

I sat there unwilling to move, stuck in place. How could I tell Callie's parents about the love of God, the hope of resurrection in Jesus Christ, when all of a sudden I didn't know if I still believed any of it? I was stuck—stuck in my car, stuck in my faith, stuck in my soul.

Cars drove past as I sat there. Mrs. Carston who lived in the house next to the church walked Rudy, her nervous little yip-yap dog, dutifully picking up his tiny droppings in a blue Walmart bag, as if it mattered. People walked up or down the sidewalk. Life went on as life always does. As if any of it mattered. I felt like I had stepped aside, out of the stream of life, to let it pass me by on all sides.

A friend of mine, an older priest in the Diocese of Mississippi, told me once that when he felt like he was in trouble, when he didn't know what to do or say, when he was about to have to do or say something unpleasant or painful, he would make the sign of the cross on his forehead with his finger, just to remind himself that he was a child of God, a Christian for whom Jesus died. He told me that it reminded him of his own baptism. Even though he'd been baptized as an infant, he knew that the priest who'd baptized him had made the sign of the cross right there on his forehead, and he was retracing the sign that priest's finger had made all those years ago.

I'd borrowed the idea from him, and for years I'd made the sign of the cross on my forehead when I thought things were getting dicey, when I thought I was in over my head, or when I thought I was about to be. But this time, sitting in the car in front of the church, I stopped myself. Is that just a silly, superstitious thing to do, calling on an imaginary, mythical, fictional, nonexistent nothing? What if it's all just a lie?

How could I continue to believe in a God who would allow Callie to die? And if there is no God, what is life really about?

I'm pretty sure other people think these thoughts as well; I know we all have doubts. I'd talked to other people who were struggling with their faith, with their doubts, with making sense of it all. I'd told them that Christianity doesn't always make sense, that being faithful isn't about making it make sense. But right then I really needed something to make sense.

Maybe somebody had just come up with the idea of God because they needed something bigger than themselves, to believe they had some help when things were about to get difficult or dangerous. And maybe—and I regretted thinking about this because it seemed to stick in my thoughts—maybe people just need some sort of bogeyman, a threat to hold over people to make them do what they're supposed to do, the threat of everlasting hell to keep us all in line.

I remembered something that my friend Jake had said: "People are going to believe what they want to believe, most of the time." Maybe I had spent this much of my life agreeing with the silly myth of God not because God is actually up there but because I needed God to be real. What if God is just fiction?

My friend Jake—the Rev. Jacob Jefferson—had taught me a lot about God and the Christian faith, but even Preacher Jake had had doubts. When he found his wife in bed with a banker, he started drinking heavily but he kept on preaching. When his son was killed in the Battle of the Bulge, he lost his faith completely and could not preach anymore. He was the most faithful person I'd ever known, and even he had lost his faith. When I was young, he'd told me that he and God hadn't been on speaking terms for years. But even then, still angry with God about his son's death, I remember him saying, "I don't understand God, but I knows He up there."

It was good for me to remember Jake just then, good to remember his piercing eyes and soothing voice. When I was a kid, our priest's son had told me he didn't believe in God, that it was "all just mind-control crap." When I told Jake about it, he said, "We ain't s'posed to know ever'thing 'bout God. . . . ain't nobody got Him all figured out. But that don't mean He ain't there."

In the end, Preacher Jake's faith was restored, but it took years. I needed mine to be restored in the next few minutes so I could talk to Callie's parents, so I could say something I believed.

Sitting there with the car running, I prayed. I prayed the Lord's Prayer, just to get started, and realized I wasn't really paying attention to what I was saying, so I started over.

This time I made it all the way to "Lead us not into temptation, but deliver us from evil" and had to stop. Had I somehow been led into temptation, bringing this debilitating doubt into my head and heart? Or maybe I had been delivered to evil and this was this some sinister ploy of an evil force outside of myself, like one of Satan's sinister schemes. Was Screwtape or one of his nephews trying to lead me astray? Or was I just playing a mind game with myself and losing?

After some time sitting stupidly in my car, I told myself that I couldn't solve any of this in a few minutes, and that meanwhile I had work to do. I put the car back in gear and drove to Callie's house. The driveway was full of cars—family friends gathered to express their condolences. Before I could think too much about what I was about to do or say, I walked across the yard, stepped up on their porch, and rang the doorbell.

Drew's father answered the door. He had some sort of funny nickname from his Army days, but right then I couldn't remember what it was, so I said, "Good morning, Mr. Compton. I'm so sorry about Callie."

He made no indication that he wanted me to come into the house, but stood blocking the door. He said, "Ain't nothin' good about this morning, preacher."

"No sir. There's really not."

We stood there somewhat awkwardly, me waiting for an invitation to come in and him not showing any sign that he was going to make that possible, until both of us were saved by Callie's mother Tammy: "Cappy? Who's at the door?"

"It's that fancy preacher they been listenin' to, that Hinton fella."

"Well, let him in!"

Cappy stepped aside somewhat grudgingly, and I went into the house. There were lots of people there, some I recognized but most I didn't know. Drew's family was quite extensive, and most of them went to Sacred Heart, the old Roman Catholic parish in town.

The priest at Sacred Heart was Father Mullen, who gave the impression that he hadn't cracked a smile since Vatican II in the early 1960s. He still celebrated the Mass in Latin every day and had no interest in anything ecumenical, wanting nothing to do with the Protestants. He came to the ministerial association meetings because his bishop told him he had to, but he didn't have to like it, and he didn't. One of our Methodist colleagues called him Father Sullen, but not to his sullen face.

Tammy had grown up in a very Protestant Southern Baptist Church. It was a difficult transition for her to join the Catholic Church before she married Drew. It was their daughter Callie who'd led the family to St. Thomas and the Episcopal Church, after she'd come with a friend to our youth choir pool party. Tammy and Callie both loved St. Thomas. Tammy thought it was a compromise, somewhere between Protestant and Catholic; I didn't have to tell either of them that the Episcopal Church was much closer to Catholic than Baptist. But Drew was always torn between the Episcopal parish, which I think he felt a little guilty enjoying, and the Roman Catholic Church, which he felt he had deserted.

Father Mullen was already there that morning, sitting on the couch and wearing the same black suit and dark expression he always wore. It looked to me like he and Drew's mother Doris had their heads together and were making plans the rest of us would be told about later, when they decided we needed to know.

Tammy came over to me and gave me a tight hug. "She loved you, Father Buddy. She loved you so much."

"Yes ma'am—I loved her too." I wanted to say—I needed to know—"What happened?" But I didn't want to ask Tammy to relive whatever had happened so soon, so I didn't ask. Instead I said, "She was such a sweet little girl." Tammy didn't say anything, and, not willing to face the silence, I asked the stupidest question I could have thought of: "Are you okay?"

She lied, which I suppose is the expected response. "I'm fine, thanks."

And then she asked the inevitable question, the question I had been dreading, the question I needed an answer for and did not have: "Why, Buddy? Why did this have to happen?"

I felt like everybody was looking at me. All I could do was be honest. "I don't know, Tammy. I wish I had a better answer, but I don't. I'm so sorry." I wished I had something else to say. I wished I could believe the glib, pre-packaged theology others found comfort in. I wished I could bury this tragedy in layers of impressively impenetrable theology. I wished I could be a better priest. I wished I could tell her that I believe all this stuff. But right then I was lost.

She just nodded, like that was the answer she'd been expecting. She was expecting to be disappointed, and that was a whole new sting. I took her hand, hoping to transmit some comfort in my touch

since I had none in my words, and she nodded again. She knew I was
trying; I knew I was failing.

19

You've Got to Say Something

Tammy led me over to Drew, who was sitting at their kitchen table, looking down at the placemat in front of him, not seeing it, seemingly not aware of anything or anyone around him. Tammy said, "Drew—Father Buddy's here." He didn't show any sign of hearing her. If I hadn't seen his shoulders slowly rising and falling as he breathed, I might have thought he was dead. And I would have been partly right.

More often than I want to admit, I don't recognize how selfish I am, but this was one of those times that I did. I'd spent the last half-hour feeling sorry for myself, that my sweet little friend was dead. But Callie was this man's daughter. He and Tammy were the ones who needed comfort, not me. They were the ones who needed their faith to make sense right now. Whether it made any sense to me had nothing to do with it.

There are moments when you have to ignore your doubts and misgivings and either plunge ahead or retreat completely. You have to walk down the aisle at your wedding or call it off; you have to consent to the anesthesia or cancel the surgery; you have to sign the contract or leave the deal on the table. Whether I could explain it or not, whether I believed it or not, right now it was my job—my *privilege*—to offer hope to a man who desperately needed it.

I put my hand on his shoulder and said, "Drew." Again there was no response. I squeezed a little, just to let him know I was there with him, and said, "Hey, man." He didn't budge, didn't move a muscle. I leaned in closer, aware that everyone else in the house was watching. I heard myself thinking, "Oh, please Lord," and smiled inwardly. Still praying: sometimes it's good that old habits are hard to break.

Neither Drew nor the Lord God made any response that I could detect. If anything good was going to happen, it seemed like was up to me. I sat down in the chair at the end of the table. Not for the first time, I thought about my own children. What if this was me? What if it had been Jude or Gracie who'd died? What would I want, what would I need? I wouldn't want some damn faithless priest intruding on me, that's for sure. I'd want . . . I'd want to scream; I'd want to hit somebody. I might want to hit that damn faithless priest sitting at my kitchen table, just looking at me with nothing to say.

There was another knock at the front door, and Cappy got up to answer it. I heard him say, "Yes?" and then I heard Beulah's voice saying "Hi, Mr. Compton. I'm Beulah Hinton from St. Thomas. I'm so sorry to hear about Callie."

Cappy mumbled, "Yes ma'am."

She said, "I brought some homemade bread and a ham. Y'all are probably going to have a lot of visitors today."

"Yes ma'am, I suppose so."

By this time, Tammy was on her way to Beulah's aid, rescuing her from her father-in-law, the Defender of the True Faith. I heard them talking and was glad for the focus to shift away from me and Drew for a moment. I leaned in close and whispered, "I don't blame you for hiding away; I might be doing the same thing. You don't owe me anything, but you know Tammy needs you." His head sunk further down until his chin was almost touching his chest; it wasn't much, but at least it was some sort of reaction. I repeated what I'd said, stressing her name: "*Tammy* needs you."

He lifted his head a little, and a few seconds later he nodded. He took a deep breath, blew his cheeks out as he exhaled, and stood up. Without another look at me, he went to Tammy, who'd invited Beulah into the house. The two women were hugging each other when Beulah saw Drew coming and pulled herself free. Drew just stood there until Tammy burst into tears and opened her arms for him to step into. They were both sobbing by the time Beulah came over to me, still sitting at the kitchen table.

She kissed the top of my head and murmured, "You okay?"

"Yeah," I claimed, reminding myself this is not about me.

She paused until I looked up at her, then searched my eyes and said, "Liar."

I've never been any good at lying; maybe I just haven't had enough practice. No, that's a lie: I've probably lied about as much as anybody, but I've never been much good at it, never been comfortable with it. Anyway, for better and for worse, Beulah has always been able to see through me. And of course she was right: I was not okay.

I whispered, "I'm just a little out of whack," and she whispered back, "Yeah, and you can't just go to the store and get more whack." I answered, "Let's talk about it later," and immediately regretted saying it—she wouldn't stop until she made me confess my crisis of faith, and I didn't want to do that. I didn't know if I would ever want to talk about that, but certainly not any time soon.

She said, "Later, then."

I said, "I'm so glad you're here. I tried to call—how did you find out that Callie . . ."

"I got a call at the office from the sheriff's office. They didn't know I knew Callie; they were just filing the report of a child who was killed with the social work office. I took Gracie over to Charlie's and came on over. Charlie said she'd pick Jude up from school."

"Good. Did they tell you what happened?"

"Yeah. Tammy had gone to pick her up from dance practice, was waiting in the car on Walnut Street, and was watching Callie crossing the street when she was hit by a hit-and-run driver."

"That's terrible."

"She was dead before the ambulance got there. They had to pull Tammy's arms apart to make her let go."

"Oh, dear God. Have they found the driver?"

"No."

Drew went back into the kitchen, and I looked at Tammy. She nodded to me and mouthed the words, "Thank you."

Beulah was holding my hand and squeezed it, glad to think I'd done something helpful. I was feeling a little better about myself when Father Mullen decided he should acknowledge my presence.

He struggled to extricate himself from the couch—and from Drew's mother—and made his way across the room to where I was standing with Beulah. I held out my hand, which he took with lukewarm enthusiasm. I said, "Father Mullen, I'm not sure if you've ever met my wife, Beulah."

He inclined his head slightly in an oddly formal bow, but said nothing. She said, "It's nice to meet you, Father."

He bowed again, then turned his bleary gaze to me. "Hmm, well. Doris tells me Drew and Tammy have been coming to St. Thomas lately."

"Yes sir."

"I've known Drew since I baptized him as an infant, hmm, known his whole family."

"Yes sir."

"I guess you'll be wanting to do the funeral there, hmm?"

"I don't know. We haven't talked about any of that; that'll be something Drew and Tammy will need to decide."

"Well, we'd be glad to have the service at Sacred Heart. I know his family would be more . . . hmm, comfortable there."

I felt the heat come into my face. I wanted to yell at him that this shouldn't be about Catholics and Protestants, that this wasn't about some asinine argument bishops had started five hundred years ago.

Beulah put her hand on my right arm, just above the elbow, and squeezed it hard. She must have felt me tense up and wanted me to know she was there for me. She also wanted to help me not do or say anything that I would regret later. I covered her hand with my left hand and said, "Yes sir. I'll be glad to do as much or as little as Drew and Tammy want."

He wondered, "Have you ever preached at the funeral for a child?"

I had not, and I told him so. He said, "Well, I have. Hmm. There's nothing you can say that'll make it any better for anybody. I've been a priest for almost forty years, and I've preached maybe ten or twelve children's burial services. Nobody's ever liked anything I ever said at a child's funeral, hmm. I didn't like much I said myself."

I didn't know what to say, and I didn't say anything. Father Mullen took a deep breath and said, "When the little Spirelli boy died—what was that boy's name, just four or five years old—ah, well, it doesn't matter now, hmm. I told them God had needed another flower to bloom in the Gardens of Heaven, something I read somewhere, probably. I was embarrassed I'd said something so . . . shabby. But you know—hmm—you've got to say something, I guess."

It was oddly reassuring to me that this old priest had also struggled with his faith in the face of a child's death. I felt more sympathetic towards him, a sense of professional comradery. I said, "Well, if we have the funeral at Sacred Heart, I'll look forward to hearing what you have to say."

It looked like he was going to say something more, but he changed his mind and settled for one more "Hmm" before making another stiff little bow to Beulah and walking away.

She tugged on my arm and I leaned down so she could whisper in my ear: "What the hell was that all about?"

"An old turf war." Before I could say more, she saw that Tammy was looking for her, and she kissed me on the cheek, saying, "Gotta go—kitchen duty."

A minute or two later, as the room continued to fill with family and friends, Drew caught my eye and tilted his head toward the back door in a signal for me to come with him. As we picked our way through the kitchen, Tammy told him they were going to need more coffee and mayonnaise. Beulah, seeing that Drew was trying to get me out, told her she'd be glad to go to the store and pick some up. Then Beulah raised an eyebrow and nodded to me, sending us through the little screened-in porch, out into shelter of the backyard.

Their swing set was there, conspicuously without a little girl to swing or slide on it, her pink bicycle lying abandoned in the grass beside it. He walked over to the bike and picked it up, muttering, "I told her to . . . ," then caught himself and hugged the bike close to his chest, close to his heart. When he sobbed, the bike shook, the little red and white handlebar streamers shuddering with him.

I put my arm around his shoulder and pulled him into my embrace, and we cried together.

20

A PASTORAL BUD

After a while, Drew put the bicycle down, leaning it against the swing set lovingly. When he turned to face me, it seemed like his grief had been overcome by an anger he'd been holding in check. "Why, Buddy? Why?"

"I don't know, Drew. There's so much I don't know. I wish I did. But I'm not going to lie to you; I'm not going to tell you I've got it all figured out. I don't know."

He stood there looking at me, either waiting for me to say something more or digesting the fact that I didn't know. Then he said, "That's it? You don't know?"

I started to say something, but he cut me off: "Damn it, Buddy! This is the kind of stuff you're *supposed* to know, right? If you don't know, who the hell does?"

I thought for a moment, wishing that Beulah's hand was on my arm, wishing that I had the answers, for him and me both. Softly I said, "I don't think anybody knows. You can probably find somebody who'll tell you they can explain all of this, why terrible things happen, but . . . well, I wonder if they really understand. I just don't think God can be explained."

We stood there for a moment or two, both of us lost. I said, "Look, Drew—I'm not going to tell you that you have to have faith, or that you're going to hell if you have doubts. I think there are times when even the most faithful people have doubts."

"Yeah?"

"Yeah. Of course. And if we're going to have a real and honest relationship with God, there're gonna be times when we're mad at God. We get mad at everybody at some point or another. I'm wrestling with my own doubts. But . . ."

He waited, maybe hoping that I would have something profound and meaningful to say. All I wanted was not to disappoint him. I said, "We don't know, Drew. We want to know—there have been shelves and shelves of books written about why terrible things happen, but we don't know. All we have is our faith."

We were quiet for a minute, just standing there, and Drew said, "Buddy, you told us something I've always remembered."

"Oh—well, that's kind of scary. What was it?"

"You told us a story about a camper who told you that you might be wrong. You said it was one of the most important things you could say as a faithful person."

"Yeah, I remember. He wanted to smooch with his girlfriend, and I'd told him it was against the rules. What he told me was that I could be wrong."

"And a lot of times since then, you've told us that you could be wrong."

"Yeah. I think it's dangerous for us to think we always need to be right. Being faithful can't be about being right."

"That's hard on the engineers, you know."

"That I could be wrong?"

"Yeah. It scares them, scares us. I mean, we're all out here trying to be as precise as we can be, and you're saying you could be wrong."

I thought about it for a moment and conceded the point. "Yeah, I can see how that could be scary. But still . . . it's true. God can't be something that can be proven or defined. I could be wrong, about any of this."

"But Buddy—you really don't know? You don't know whether . . . whether she's in heaven right now?"

It was the moment I had to decide. I was going to swim or I was going to sink, right there in his backyard. I took a deep breath and said, "I believe it, Drew. I don't understand it, I can't prove it, I don't know it, but I *believe* it. I *hope* it. Sometimes it's easy to believe and sometimes it's not. This is not an easy day for us to believe in God, but it's on days like this that we most need to believe."

That wasn't satisfying to him, even though it did me some good to hear myself say it out loud. I plodded on.

"I believe that God loves Callie, and that the part of her that you and I love is not her physical self but her soul. I believe that God made her soul, all of our souls, and that God loves her still. Yes, I believe that Callie is in heaven, in the presence of God."

"But you can't say that you know it?"

"I believe it."

"I need to *know* it."

We sat there for a minute or two, until I had an idea.

"Look, Drew—one of the funny things about being a priest is that we're always facing the other way." He looked at me wearily. "I mean, when the people come sit in the pews, you're all facing east, right? But the priest is facing west."

"If you say so—what the hell difference does—"

"Hang on, hang on. So y'all are looking at me, or Father Mullen, or whoever's up there. But it's not like television: we can see you, too."

"So?"

"So most of the time it's the same people sitting in their places. Most of the time we're just preaching to the choir. But sometimes, like at weddings or funerals, people come who aren't usually there."

"Fine with me."

"Yeah, me too. But here's the point: some of those folks go to some other church, and some of them don't ever go to church at all."

"Okay."

"I wonder how it must feel for folks like that to come to a funeral, when they don't really believe anything. I wonder how it would be to live without faith."

"What the hell are you talking about?"

"I'm saying, what if we didn't believe in God?"

That caught him by surprise, but he recovered with a bluster: "Well, what if we didn't?"

"What would we say about Callie if we didn't have any faith at all? She's just gone, that's it—the end?"

He looked at me, thinking hard, and I pressed my point: "If we didn't have faith—not because we know it but because we believe it, because we hope it—what hope could we have for Callie?"

He shook his head and muttered, "I don't know."

I said, "I don't want to live without hope."

He said, "No. I don't, either."

"So we will hope together."

"Okay."

"I really loved Callie, Drew. This has made me wonder what I believe. But I think the best we can do is to be is faithful, even when we don't understand."

"Yeah, well—I guess that makes sense."

"I hope so. That's the best I got. So here's what I think: I don't understand all of this, either. But I choose to trust God. Not because I understand, but because I don't."

He stood there, his hands locked behind his bowed head, his eyes shut tight. I said, "And because if I don't have faith in a good and loving God, then the whole world is a cruel and hopeless place. I don't think I could stand life with no hope in it."

He dropped his hands and opened his eyes, but kept his head down. "Yeah, well—I don't see much hope this morning."

"No, I know. I don't either." I took a deep breath. "But it's still there, whether we can see it or not."

We stood quietly, not needing to say anything else for the moment, until Beulah opened the screen door and called out, "Buddy, can you go and get us some ice?"

I called back, "Yes ma'am." Then I asked Drew, "You want to go with me, or go back in there?"

He replied, "Let's go."

He was about to open the door to the screen porch when I caught him by the elbow and suggested that we might walk around the house rather than going back through it. He took a moment to imagine all the people in his house, then nodded and said, "Good idea, thanks."

We got into my car and drove to the little convenience store that sold ice from a machine out front. The name of the store was on the sign: "The Bee Quick." There was a cartoonish honeybee, outlined in orange neon lights. I told Drew that Beulah had called it "The Be Quick or Be Stabbed" ever since the kid behind the counter had been held up at knifepoint two years before. It didn't quite get the laugh I was hoping for, but he did smile. We went in to pay for the ice, and on a whim I turned back to Drew and said, "How about a beer?"

"It's not even eleven in the morning yet."

"Well, yeah, but it's sort of a different kind of day, though, y'know?"

He smiled more broadly then. "I don't guess we'd have to tell our wives everything, you think?"

I returned the smile. It was like we were back in high school, doing something our parents had told us not to do. "Surely there are some things they'd rather not know."

So I paid for a bag of ice and two tall cans of Budweiser. We sat there in the parking lot, drinking our beers and soaking in the moment as the ice slowly melted. Just then it seemed a little less urgent to solve the mysteries of the universe, and a little more important to have a friend.

We took the ice back to the house and saw that the number of cars along the street had increased dramatically. Drew hesitated. I opened the car door and said, "C'mon, man. And try not to breathe on Tammy." He looked at me questioningly, and I said, "Beer breath."

I took the ice to the kitchen, hugged Beulah, who said, "You been drinking?" They don't have to know everything, but usually they do anyway.

I whispered, "Just one beer." She looked at me dubiously, and I continued, "For pastoral purposes."

By the time I made my way back into the room where Drew and Tammy were, now so jam-packed with family and friends that you could hardly lift your hands, I saw that the men from the funeral home were there, talking to Drew and Tammy, with Father Mullen and Drew's mother Doris and Cappy close by. A moment later, Doris tapped her coffee cup with a spoon to get everybody's attention, then announced that it had been decided that Callie's requiem mass would be at two o'clock that Saturday afternoon, at Sacred Heart Roman Catholic Church, and that "Reverend Hinton from the Episcopalian Church" would give the funeral sermon. I looked over at Father Mullen and thought I saw just a hint of a twinkle in the bastard's eye. He'd worked it out so that his parish would host the service, but he didn't have to preach a child's funeral.

I didn't sleep much that night, and it was no better the next: my brain wouldn't slow down. I was filled with my own doubts, filled with fear that I was going to make things worse by saying something stupid at the funeral. And I was filled with anger: anger at God for letting Callie die, anger at myself for not having better answers to impossible questions, and anger at Father Mullen for setting me up.

The sun was coming up when Beulah came into the kitchen; Jude and Gracie were still asleep. "How long have you been up?"

"I don't know, long time. I couldn't sleep."

"Are you worried about your funeral sermon?"

I thought about lying so she wouldn't worry about it, too, but I knew she'd see through it. "Yeah."

"You'll be fine, Buddy. You always say the right thing."

"That's not true."

"Well, almost always."

She offered to make pancakes, but I told her I didn't want anything to eat. This was a surprise, since I was almost always hungry in the morning and am especially fond of her pancakes. She sat down with me. "Is it just the sermon?"

"Yeah." I took a deep breath. "No. I just . . . I don't know. I don't know what's going on with me. I don't know if I . . ."

She waited, but I didn't have anything else to say. We hadn't really talked about all of this, but she knew. After a minute or two, she said, "This is about Callie. This is like that old priest said—it's the death of a child."

"Yeah. I just don't understand. If God's really God, how could . . ."

"How could God let Callie die?"

"Right."

"Where's the justice in that?"

"Right."

"You're trying to hold on to your faith, when it doesn't make sense."

"Well, yeah. Right. Well, it's just . . ."

"Welcome to the human race, pal."

"What?"

"That's how most of us feel most of the time. We want answers to questions that we can't get, and we don't understand."

"Well, yeah, but—"

"You think you're special because you're ordained? You think God owes you something because you're a priest? This is what you've been saying for as long as I've known you—that all we have is our faith. Sometimes God doesn't make any sense. That's what you've been saying for as long as I've known you."

"Well, yeah, but—"

"So, do you believe all this stuff or not?"

I looked at the kitchen clock: it was seven twenty-six. I had a little more than seven and a half hours to answer the essential question for all faithful people: Do I believe all this stuff or not?

21

Coloring Book Saints

I wasn't sure what sort of vestments I should take to Callie's funeral, so I brought my whole liturgical wardrobe: alb and white stole in case I was invited to participate as a Eucharistic minister, cassock and surplice with black tippet if I wasn't. I understood that Father Mullen was very traditional, and I didn't want to push him. The official line from Rome is that Episcopal clergy—any clergy but Roman Catholic clergy—are not validly ordained because the Apostolic Line of Succession has been broken. That's an awful oversimplification, but it's pretty close, I think. If he held to that convention, I would not be asked to take part in Communion.

I was there early to have a chance to talk with Father Mullen and make sure I knew what I was supposed to do and where I was supposed to sit. And I guess I was looking for some sort of inspiration, or at least a change of scenery. I still didn't know what I was going to say in the sermon, and I knew that Beulah was getting more and more worried about me.

The first two doors I tried at Sacred Heart were locked, and when I tried the third, I was surprised that it was opened for me by a priest I'd never met before. He looked like he was about fifteen.

I said, "Hi, I'm Buddy Hinton. I—"

He said, "Yes, I know. You're the rector of the Episcopal Church, St. Thomas, where Drew and Tammy are members. I'm Father Haggerty, the associate here. Call me Sean."

"Thanks," I said, liking him immediately. "My friends call me Buddy."

"Buddy it is, then," he said with an easy and seemingly genuine smile. "Come in, come in."

He led me down several passageways, up a flight of stairs, and down a long hall. I was completely lost and felt relieved when we finally arrived at a door with a sign on it that read, "Vesting Sacristy."

He said, "You can hang your vestments in here."

I said, "I didn't know what to bring, so I tried to cover all my bases."

I hung them all in a closet, and he started leading me down more corridors and hallways and another set of stairs. I couldn't have been more lost; all I could do was follow him. At some point, one of the children's Sunday school class bulletin boards looked familiar: the kids had colored either St. Peter or St. Paul—two biblically bearded old guys who looked the same in crayon.

I said, "I'm so lost."

Sean went into a long explanation that on the way to the Vesting Sacristy, we'd come from the East Wing through the Central Transept, but now we were on our way to the Office Complex—I'd lost my way and my interest long before he'd stopped explaining it. He saw that my attention had waned. "It took me a couple of years before I learned my way around."

"A couple of years?" I said incredulously, and immediately wished I hadn't.

He laughed and said, "Twenty-seven."

"What?"

"I'm twenty-seven. I've been a priest for a year and a half. Before that I was a deacon, and a seminarian before that. The bishop in his wisdom put me here right out of seminary, and I did an internship for a year here while I was still in school."

"In his wisdom?"

"Well, yes. I don't know you all that well. Sometimes I say that he put me here for my sins."

"Oh, wow. You must have had a lot of sins, huh?"

"So you've met Father Mullen."

We both laughed and kept walking. After a while we came across another bulletin board, with more coloring book art from Sunday school students. I pointed and said "Hey, wait a minute—have we been here before?"

He said, "Have we?"

He was lost, too. "Well," he said, "sometimes I still get a little turned around."

He looked around and then went to a window and said, "Ah." Then, motioning for him to follow him, he went back the way we'd just come.

Out of curiosity, I asked, "What did you see out there that helped you in here?"

He looked a little sheepish. "The steeple at the First Baptist Church." I understood: the Baptist steeple was the tallest structure in Greene, our most visible landmark. If you could find the steeple, you knew where you were. It was like finding the North Star in the night sky.

We came into the office area, and Sean knocked on the door labeled "Rector's Office."

The voice that answered sounded tired. "Enter."

Sean opened the door, and we entered. Father Mullen was sitting behind his desk. He looked like he'd been up all night: his sparse hair needed brushing and his shoes were off, the heels of both his socks wearing thin.

"Ah," he said. "Hmm. Good afternoon. You're early."

"Yes sir. Sean here was good enough to take me on a tour. I didn't know this place was so big."

"Hmm. Well, yes. Did you want to process in before the casket?"

I'd prepared for a moment like this, and I liked my answer: "This is your shop. I'll be glad to do whatever you want me to do. If you want me to process, I'll be glad to. If you want me to sit in the pews and just come up to give the sermon, I'll be glad to do that, too."

He glanced at Sean and then back to me. He said, "Well, hmm. Why don't you, hmm, vest and process in with Father Haggerty. You can sit in the chair by the prie-dieu next to the pulpit."

I nodded and said, "Thank you." I wasn't sure I knew what a prie-dieu was, but I felt sure Sean would help me out. Then I asked, "And what vestments would you like for me to wear?"

"Well, hmm. What vestments did you bring?"

"I brought an alb and stole, and a cassock and surplice."

Father Mullen looked a little surprised. I glanced at Sean and said, "Well, okay—we stole all that stuff from you guys." Sean kept his smile to himself and didn't say anything.

I stood there and waited for Father Mullen to come to a decision. I understood his dilemma: he didn't want to seem inhospitable to his Protestant guest, but he didn't want to minimize the divisions between the Catholics and the Anglicans, either. To invite me to wear an alb would sort of put me on the same ecclesiological footing with the two Roman Catholic priests.

It really didn't matter to me. I offered, "Why don't I just wear my cassock and surplice?"

Sean looked disappointed; Father Mullen looked relieved. He said, "Well, hmm. If that's what you would prefer."

I'd thought about this too and said, "Actually, it is not what I would prefer. I would prefer that our Lord's holy church wasn't all broken into pieces. You didn't do that, and I didn't do it, either. But that's where we are; that's what we've been given. I won't be serving at the altar, so I'll wear cassock and surplice. And a tippet."

A tippet is a preaching scarf, black and somewhat wider than a stole, which is worn by ministers of the Eucharist. I was telling him that I was stepping out of any expectations of being part of the Mass. He nodded and said, "Well, yes. Hmm. Thank you . . . Father." This time it was Father Haggerty's turn to be surprised.

The older priest said, "Do you drink coffee?"

"Yes sir—thank you. With cream, if you have any," I said, answering the question before it was asked.

He nodded to the younger priest, who left the office as Father Mullen showed me to an ancient chair that smelled like it had spent several decades in somebody's grandmother's attic. I thought it might have been happier there.

He sat in another antique, which wobbled precariously as he trusted his weight into it. There was an awkward pause, which he broke by saying, "Well, hmm."

I couldn't think of an appropriate response to that, but it was clear that it was my turn to say something. I asked, "How long have you been at Sacred Heart?"

He thought a moment, trying to recall. "Almost thirty-six years, I think—hmm—thirty-six years next month."

"Wow. That's a long time."

"Long time."

"Where were you before that?

"Notre Dame. South Bend, Indiana. I thought I wanted to go into academia, but I—hmm—I couldn't stand it. This is the only parish I've ever served."

"Wow," I repeated. "I'm on my third parish, and I've only been ordained eighteen years."

"Can't hold a job?"

I was stunned and trying to marshal my defenses when I saw a new twinkle in his eye: Father Sullen had made a joke!

He said, "Listen, Father Hinton . . ."

"You can just call me Buddy."

He thought about that for about two seconds before replying, "No, I can't." Then he continued, "Listen—I shouldn't have said anything to you about preaching at a child's funeral, and certainly you didn't need to hear any of the stupid things I've said in the past. You just say what you believe, all right?"

"Yes sir." I thought about confessing that I didn't really know what I believed just then, and I was arranging the sentence in my mind when Sean came in with four cups of coffee and a Southern Baptist preacher.

Brother Ewell preached at the First Baptist Church of Harmony, Alabama, where Tammy had grown up. He'd driven her parents up for the funeral and said he "just wanted to come and pay his respects to the senior pastor." Sean and I looked to Father Mullen, who said, "Well, hmm."

I took the ensuing awkward moment as my opportunity to introduce myself, telling Brother Ewell that I was the priest of St. Thomas Episcopal Church. He in turn took that as his invitation to start talking. He told us that he had grown up in Harmony and graduated from high school the year before Tammy: "She was just the cutest little thing back then."

He told us about his time in the Air National Guard and his call to be a preacher, and he was starting on what I'm sure was going to be a riveting account of his seminary experience when Sean rescued me and himself by asking if I needed to go back to the vesting room to get ready. I almost asked what time it was before realizing he was offering us both a way out of the "senior pastor's study."

I stood up and told Brother Ewell how nice it was to have met him, then nodded to Father Mullen and said, "Father," as I gave him a little wink. He knew I was deserting him; he nodded and said, "Father," conceding that he'd lost that round but that we would play again, another day.

Brother Ewell was oblivious to all of that and was talking about his first congregation when I left the office. The door to the office closed, and I said to Sean, "Thanks for delivering us from hearing Brother Ewell's entire life story."

He nodded and said, "Thank you for saying what you said, about the church being broken."

I said, "That might be the only thing we can all agree on."

He smiled his easy smile. "Even Brother Ewell."

We began navigating the meandering passageways back to the Vesting Sacristy. We passed several sets of coloring book saints, but each set looked sufficiently different that at least I didn't think we were walking in circles. Eventually we got back, and after I was appropriately vested, I told Sean that if he could just lead me to the back of the church, I would sit there quietly. I promised I wouldn't cause any trouble until the service started.

He asked me if I needed anything, and I said, "Just a sermon."

Incredulously, he asked me, "Don't you have it all written out already?"

"No," I said. "It messes me up to write them down. But usually I know what I'm going to say—not so much today."

The look of panic on his face was almost worth the stress I felt as I tried to conjure up a sermon. He recovered his composure and said, "Well then, I'll just leave you to your thoughts. I'm looking forward to hearing your sermon."

As he was leaving, I asked, "What time is it?"

He looked at his watch and answered, "One fifteen."

Forty-five minutes until I would stand in front of God's fractured church and tell them I was broken, too.

22

About Who You Trust

Forty minutes later, I still didn't know what I was going to say.

The organ was playing quietly, and the nave was filling up. I wondered how many flavors of Christianity were represented there. The Turrells who lived down the street from us were there, and they were forever telling me all the good things that were happening at their big Baptist church. If I hadn't known the people from St. Thomas, I wouldn't have been able to tell the difference between the Episcopalians and all the rest of them.

Beulah came in and saw me sitting in the back of the church, which was unusual—usually I'm scurrying around just before a service starts. She said, "Are you okay?"

I nodded, and she kissed me on the cheek. She whispered, "Go get 'em, Buddy."

Desperate now, I asked, "What should I say?"

She sat down beside me and said, "Do what you always do: make 'em laugh, let 'em cry, talk about hope."

I didn't know I'd always done that, but it sounded pretty good right then. I asked her to repeat it, and she did, then added, "Just tell us the truth." She looked at me and said, "New dress?"

I looked down and realized she'd never seen me in a cassock and surplice before. As I was thinking about how to explain it all, she said, "What have you got on?"

"Oh, it's a long, boring story." Over four hundred and fifty years long, and just as boring as ever, I didn't say. "It's a more Protestant set of vestments—morning prayer, that kind of thing."

She realized she didn't really care about any of that and moved on, saying, "You'll be fine."

"Beulah," I confessed, "I don't know what to say."

Once again, as it has so often happened, my sweet tough wife threw me a lifeline. She said, "Who are you talking to?"

"What?"

"Who's your target? Who are you here to comfort, or challenge, or whatever you're going to do?"

"Catholics?"

"You don't know who you're talking to?"

"Well, I . . ."

"You're talking to Tammy and Drew, who just lost their little girl."

"Yes, I know. Sure. I mean—of course."

"They trust you. They need you to speak from your heart to their hearts, to give them something to hope. Don't let all that theology get in your way, Buddy. Just tell them what you want to say."

"I don't know what I want to say!"

"You remember that day at camp when Edward jumped off the high dive?"

"Yeah, so?"

"You remember what you said about being up there in the dark, thinking you're all alone, and all you can do is jump in?"

"Yeah, but—"

"So that's you, silly man. That's where you are right now—you're up there all alone, and you can't see a thing. And do you remember what you said when you preached that sermon?"

"No."

"No?"

"Well, I probably wasn't listening."

"Well, I was. You said our faith has never been about making things make sense. It's about who you trust."

"Yeah," I said, remembering.

"You're never up there alone, you said—and the one who's up there with you, standing there in the dark and in the pain, has been there before. Remember?"

"Yeah. I remember. And I believe that. But . . ."

"But nothing." She stood and squeezed my hand, kissing me on the cheek again. "You've got this, Buddy."

A few minutes later the acolyte led the procession up the aisle, followed by the pallbearers carrying the pitifully small casket on their shoulders. Father Haggerty and I followed, with Father Mullen walking behind us as we sang "Dear Lord and Father of Mankind." The older priest conducted the service, which was generally similar to the funeral service in the Episcopal Church: we started with the opening prayers, and then the readings, and then it was time for the sermon.

I stood up in the pulpit, at the edge of panic. There was a glass of water on a shelf below the place where the preacher could put a manuscript; I took a sip, just to buy some time. I cleared my throat, and then, because I knew I ought to be saying something, I told them that I was honored to be there, honored to be invited to preach, and honored to have been Callie's friend. I'd already found Beulah in the congregation during one of the readings; I looked at her and she nodded her assurance. "You've got this," she'd said.

I told them that Callie's death had caused me to reconsider what I believe, that it had triggered a crisis of my own faith. I felt the people leaning in, listening closely. I looked at Tammy and Drew and felt them hoping that I'd say something they needed to hear.

I told them I wished I could tie all of this up into a tidy doctrinal bow, but I couldn't. I told them I wanted to be reassuring, but I didn't want to lie to them or resort to clichéd bumper-sticker theology. I told them I don't have all the answers but that I understood some of the questions they might be asking. Looking out over the congregation, I could tell they'd never heard a sermon like this before. I saw Beulah nod again, her face encouraging me to get on with it.

So I told them the story of Edward and the high dive. I told them a little about Special Session, a summer camp session for adults with mental and physical challenges, and about Edward, a first-time camper who'd been born blind. I told them about me worrying about assigning Zach, a sixteen-year-old who'd been sort of a knucklehead the summer before, to be Edward's counselor, and that I was glad the two of them had gotten along and had a good week. Then I told them that on the last full day of the session, someone came running to tell me that Edward was about to jump off the high dive.

When I told them I "sprinted up the hill" to the pool, some of them laughed, mostly Episcopalians: at more than six feet five and well over three hundred pounds, I am clearly not built to sprint anywhere.

I said, "Well, okay—I waddled with some sense of purpose up the hill," and almost everybody laughed. Drew's mother, the thoroughly Roman Catholic, didn't; she sat there not looking at me, looking straight ahead.

I told them that the people at the pool were chanting his name: "Edward! Edward!" so I couldn't really hear, but I imagined Zach talking to Edward the whole time they climbed up the ladder to the high dive, encouraging, offering help, being Edward's eyes as he climbed and reached the platform for the diving board. And when I said that Zach must have said to Edward something like, "Okay, now let go of the rail," I invited the congregation to imagine with me the immensity of the decision Edward had to make, the incredible decision we all have to make to trust the guy who's up there with us before we gather the courage to let go of the rail and jump into the darkness.

It was one of those moments when a dropped pin would have been loud. It was the moment for me to bring the sermon home, to make my point and steer the homiletical plane in for a landing. It was that magic moment for me to say something profound, and I found I couldn't talk—not because I didn't know what I wanted to say but because I had choked myself up. I was fighting against the tears in my eyes, and it felt like something large was trying to make its way up and out of my throat, and I could not speak.

We all waited for a moment, and then I said, "So here we are, up here in the dark. And all we can do is let go and jump in, or stand here for the rest of our lives. But we're not alone—we're never alone. The One who's up here with us has been through all of this before. That's what Good Friday and Easter are all about, right?" I looked right at Beulah when I repeated what she'd heard me say before: "Our faith has never been about making things make sense. It's about who you trust."

When I saw that she was crying, I had to look away quickly or I knew I'd be crying, too. I told them Edward jumped into the darkness and came up spluttering and splashing, to the cheers of the crowd around the pool. "And I was cheering, too—and crying, because for the first time in my life I realized that faith is not about understanding. Faith is about who you trust."

That choked me up anyway, and as I stood there trying to keep my tears at bay and hoping to restore my throat to a state that encouraged easy speech, I looked out over the people at the large rosary stained-glass window in the back of the church. Through the window, transposed behind the depiction of the Blessed Virgin Mary holding the broken body of her dead Son Jesus after his crucifixion, I could see the silhouette of the steeple of the First Baptist Church, a landmark, a navigational guide.

I said, "A while ago, Father Haggerty was taking me from one part of this old beautiful church to another, and we got lost." Sean looked at me like he was wondering what I was doing; some of the people in the pews, no doubt having also been disoriented by the labyrinth of halls and wings at some point, chuckled. "Well, we all get lost sometimes. But he looked outside and saw the First Baptist Church steeple, and then he knew where we were." Catholics and Episcopalians nodded together; most people in Greene, Alabama, navigated by the steeple at First Baptist Church. "I didn't have to know where we were—all I had to do was to trust my friend Sean."

I let that sit for a moment and said, "Even when we don't know, even when we're lost, we have each other. Even when we are filled with doubt and we are afraid, we're not alone: our Lord Jesus is up there with us in the darkness saying, 'Let go, step out, jump in. Even when you can't trust yourself, you can trust Me.'

"The landmark Christians steer by is not in us, not what we know, not what we understand. We have to look outside of ourselves to know where we are—to know who we are. You and I, as followers of Jesus Christ, whether we're Roman Catholics or Episcopalians or from some other part of God's one holy catholic and broken church, are called to set Jesus Christ as our landmark, our guiding star. In Greene, Alabama, once you know where the Baptist steeple is, you know which way is which—where you are and which way you need to go. And in our journey of faith, once we trust our Lord to be our landmark, we know where we are and which way we need to go."

I paused and then added, "Even when our faith is in crisis, even when a sweet little girl dies way too young, even when it doesn't make any sense at all, our Lord Jesus is still our companion and guide, up there in the darkness with us." Then I said, "When you're ready, let go, trust Jesus who is with us and who has been here before, and jump into the mysteries we cannot understand."

It felt like a good place to stop. The silence was broken by Father Mullen blowing his nose, which I thought was pretty rude until I realized he was crying. A few people laughed, and a lot of people stopped themselves from chuckling; I said, as I always say at the end of a sermon, "Thanks be to God," and, in a moment of ecumenical unity, the people said, "Amen."

I looked at Beulah, who held up one finger, then two, then three. It took me a second before I realized she was checking off the boxes—"make 'em laugh, let 'em cry, talk about hope." She nodded, and the world became a better place for me.

We all said the creed together, the same Apostles' Creed we say in the Episcopal Church. After the prayers, when the two priests went up to the altar, Father Mullen motioned that I should come up with them, which surprised me. I stood at the altar through the Eucharistic Prayer—so similar and at the same time so different from what I was familiar with.

When it came time to receive Communion, I crossed my arms over my chest to receive a blessing instead of the bread of the Eucharist. Father Mullen looked me in the eye and surprised me by whispering words from St. Paul's Letter to the Ephesians: "One Lord, one faith, one baptism." But still I resisted, whispering back, "Aren't you going to tick off some of your folks?" He gave me the bread and said, "What are they going to do, fire me?"

23

So Eager to Make
an Old Lady Happy

At some point in the fall of 1999, a conversation between our ten-year-old son Jude and our friend Sinclair apparently turned to the topic of drinking hard liquor. I'm not sure how they got there—they conspired one another into secrecy forever afterwards—but in that moment it was revealed to Sinclair Graham that Jude's father can't stand Scotch. It was further revealed in that same conversation that Jude's father went to see an ancient lady every month who made him drink Scotch anyway. For some reason, Jude thought this was just hilarious, and so did Sinclair.

As I was trying to get Sinclair to tell me why he was talking to our son about different types of booze, he said he would love to meet this powerful woman who made me drink Scotch. "She sounds like my kind of woman." Miss Edith was no longer able to come to church every Sunday, and Sinclair had never met her.

We had an uncomfortable conversation about a gay man going to visit a ninety-something-year-old woman in Alabama, and he assured me that if I would take him to meet her, he would keep himself in check as much as possible. He said, "I'll wear drab clothes, like you." I looked at my gray pants, black shoes, and black clergy shirt, and then I looked at his much more colorful, overstated attire, and all I could do was thank him.

A few days before my next visit with Miss Edith, I called her house and told her caregiver Pearlie that I would like to bring someone with me. She said that would be fine, that Miss Edith was always glad to meet new people. Three or four minutes later, Pearlie called me back to find out as much as she could about Sinclair, so Miss Edith could "talk to the bridge club girls" and find out what she could about her visitor. I have to admit I was worried about what her network of informants and gossips might uncover or speculate about. Sinclair would certainly be an interesting case for them to investigate.

The afternoon we were to visit, Sinclair came to my office dressed about as somberly as his lively wardrobe would allow. The white button-up shirt was a little too large, but it was the best he could find in the Little Theatre costume closet. I recognized the pants as his; he wore them every Sunday. They had been part of a suit he'd bought years ago to audition for a part in a "serious play." His tie was pure Sinclair, though: pink and bright green paisleys on a bright yellow background. Remembering Nathan Lane's pink socks in *The Bird Cage*, when Albert, his flamboyantly gay character, was trying to play it straight, I asked, "A hint of color?"

"Well, I didn't want to feel like I was going to a funeral."

"Is that the way I always look, like somebody's died?"

"Well, yeah—but you make it work."

We walked the half block down the street, and Pearlie met us at the door. She and I were well acquainted, as I'd gone to visit Miss Edith at least once a month since we'd moved there. I hugged her and said, "Pearlie, this is my friend Sinclair Graham." He held out his hand, and when she put hers in it, he took it and kissed it as if she were the Duchess of York. Pearlie giggled and led us to the parlor where I knew Miss Edith and her dreaded Scotch would be waiting.

I went over to the chair where she was sitting, the same chair I'd left her in the month before, and leaned over to kiss her on the forehead. When I introduced Sinclair, he kissed her hand, too. She did not giggle. Instead, she looked at me and sternly said, "Is this the little pansy boy who's started coming to St. Thomas?"

I was mortified. I couldn't believe she was saying that out loud, in front of my friend. "Miss Edith, you can't . . ."

But she smiled and said, "Oh hush, Buddy. I don't give a fig about any of that. You think we didn't have homosexuals back in my day? They weren't so honest about it, but they were there. I had a cousin who was a poof—went to New Orleans with some kind of Negro ragged-time band, and we never heard from him again." A pause as Sinclair and I both wondered what we could say, and then she mused, "He was my favorite cousin, too—so bold, so full of life and fun. He was a rascal, my cousin Milton."

I hadn't even sat down, and I was already off kilter. I stammered, "So why did you—"

She laughed—a large, strong laugh from a woman who looked so small and frail. "Oh, it's just something I've heard from one of the members of your Vestry."

"Richard Chambliss, I assume."

"Of course. He is no fan of yours."

"Yes ma'am, I know. He's a pain."

"You need to watch out for him. He doesn't like the idea of Negroes coming to church, and he really doesn't like your friend Sinclair, who I hear is charming and courteous." Then she turned to Sinclair and added, "Although I was expecting you to be more . . . colorfully dressed. I admit I am somewhat disappointed. I suppose he told you to tone it down for the old lady?"

"Yes ma'am."

"It is a nice tie, though."

"Thank you."

"Now you listen to me, Mr. Sinclair Graham, Program Director of the Greene Little Theatre. Don't let Father Buddy or anybody else tell you who you are, you hear?"

"Yes ma'am."

"You can't allow other people to tell you how to shine your light."

"Yes ma'am—thank you."

I was forcibly reminded of my friend Thed's grace toward me: "You are where you belong—just be who you are." It was a grace I had not so fully offered to Sinclair. It occurred to me that when it came to Sinclair, even back when I knew him as Michael, I'd violated one of my basic principles: I'd been treating him more as a problem than as a person.

Miss Edith turned her raptor gaze to me. "You know better."

Now it was my turn: "Yes ma'am."

Sinclair said to me in a whisper intended to be loud enough for Miss Edith to hear, "Ooh, I do like this woman."

"Now," she continued, a queen holding court, "would you boys care for a little splash of whiskey?"

I said, "Yes ma'am," trying to convey an enthusiasm I didn't feel. Then I was surprised and concerned to hear Sinclair ask, "Would you happen to have any good bourbon?"

She answered flatly, "No." We were both disappointed—for different reasons—and then she said, "There is no such thing as good bourbon. I do have a nice Tennessee sour mash, though—George somebody."

It took me a second or two, but I caught up with what was going on: Sinclair was toying with me, pointing out none too gently that I could have been drinking George Dickel Sour Mash Whiskey all this time if I'd only been honest with Miss Edith from the start.

Sinclair barely stifled a laugh. He knew that George Dickel was my favorite—and here I'd been gagging on Scotch once a month for years. He said, "Thank you, Miss Edith, but as I expect you know, I've given up the booze. I believe it's bad for my complexion."

She laughed at that and retorted, "Yes, I'd heard that. Congratulations on getting your two-year coin. Some iced tea, then?"

"Yes ma'am—some tea would be perfect."

"Sweet?"

"Of course."

Miss Edith nodded to Pearlie, who came back in less than two minutes with a Scotch, a George Dickel, and a sweet iced tea. Miss Edith held up her glass to us and said, "Cheers." Then she said to Sinclair, "As you can see, I've given up on my complexion."

We all laughed at that, and she said, "Father Buddy, so eager to make an old lady happy, am I to assume that you prefer the Tennessee whiskey?"

It was time to tell the truth. "Yes ma'am. I'm afraid I don't much care for Scotch."

"Yes, I saw that the first time you came to see me."

I was stunned. I thought I'd been careful to keep my dislike of Scotch to myself. She scolded, "Why didn't you just tell me?"

"Well, I—"

"You didn't want to disappoint me."

"Well—"

"You didn't want to refuse my hospitality."

"Well, I . . . yes, ma'am." There was a pause before I continued, "The first time I came, I was scared of you. But now . . ." I thought about what I wanted to say. "Now I trust you, and I enjoy our visits. Except for the Scotch."

The two of them laughed a little, so I ventured out a bit further. "I think I was thinking of you as a problem and not as a person. I think I just put you in the Grouchy Old Lady slot and didn't stop to see that you are . . ."

"That I'm not as bad as you'd heard I am?"

"That you're a real person. And, I think, a friend. And yes, also not as bad as I'd heard."

"And what do you think now?"

"I think you're a tough, intelligent woman, and much sweeter than I thought you would be."

She smiled her most inscrutable Mona Lisa smile and whispered, "Well, don't let it get out—I've got a reputation in this town."

Then I turned to Sinclair and said, "It's a terrible thing to think of another person as a problem, or a label, or a slot to fill, instead of as another person. I think I've done that to you, too—I am so sorry."

His pale face quickly flushed red, and his eyes filled with tears. He nodded and mouthed the words, "Thank you."

Then Miss Edith said, "Buddy, you're a fine young man, and I expect that you'll be a good priest someday. It was very sweet of you to endure my Scotch, just to please me. But you've got to learn to stand up for yourself."

"Yes ma'am. I'll work on it."

"I'll be watching."

"Yes ma'am, I expect so."

We talked about things in the parish and around town. Her sources were unfailingly accurate; I wondered how she had time to play any bridge at all.

Sinclair asked her where she'd grown up, and she said, "Right here in this house, my whole life."

He said, "So, Old Lady—I'm thinking maybe you've seen a thing or two."

She answered, "Oh, you *are* a charmer. Yes, I have seen this town grow up around me. I'll be ninety-four at my next birthday: December twenty-third, nineteen-oh-two."

Sinclair and I both did the math automatically—if she'd been born in 1902, she would be ninety-seven in December. We glanced at each other quickly and silently agreed that neither of us were going to mention that she'd lost a few years along the way.

And then she told us the story of her life.

24

THIS RAPIDLY CHANGING WORLD

Miss Edith told us that one of her earliest memories was of her parents talking about two young men in North Carolina who claimed they'd invented a flying machine a few years before; her father was absolutely convinced it was a hoax. "Now," she said, "there must be a hundred huge jet airplanes that fly over us every day on their way to Birmingham or Atlanta, full of people in a hurry to be somewhere else. Every day I wonder what Father would say if he could see them all up there."

She told us she remembered some of the men at church in her childhood who were missing arms or legs or eyes, and the terrible stories they told about fighting for the Confederacy. She said she was afraid of those men, not just because they were missing parts of their bodies but because she thought they were missing parts of their souls.

She remembered workmen taking the gas lines out and putting electrical wires in the house. She remembered the week another group of men had brought the plumbing inside, over her father's strenuous objections. "Father thought it was needless extravagance. He said, 'Why would anybody want to do that inside their house?'"

She remembered when a friend of hers got one of the first telephones in town, and the first time she saw a television in a store window downtown.

She remembered World Wars One and Two, the Korean War, and the conflict in Vietnam. "Such a waste," she said.

She remembered with some emotion that her father wouldn't allow her to ride in one of those newfangled automobiles, saying that they were noisy, dangerous, and unreliable contraptions, and that they were nothing but an expensive passing fad. "He couldn't understand why you'd want to buy gasoline to fuel a foul-smelling machine, when your livestock could take you wherever you needed to go and plow your fields and just eat the grass in your field. He used to tell me he couldn't understand why anybody would ever really need to go thirty miles in an hour!" She said he might be forgiven for that, as he had made his living selling and trading horses and mules, as his father and grandfather had before him.

Before Mr. Ford began selling his Model Ts in bulk, Miss Edith said her father had been doing very well, well enough to build this big house on Main Street. But then the world changed, and he did not. He continued to sell horses and mules, watching as automobiles replaced buggies, tractors took the place of mules, and gas stations and garages were built on corners where stables and smithies had been. When the Ford dealership offered him a job selling cars, he self-righteously refused it. She sighed and said, "So he died proud and penniless, because he was too stubborn and too short-sighted to keep up with this rapidly changing world."

Sinclair said, "And now it's our turn."

Miss Edith and I looked at him, and he continued, "As much as the world has changed since Miss Edith was a little girl, it's changing even more quickly now." He turned to me and asked, "What stories will we tell when we're ninety, about how much the world has changed?"

Miss Edith nodded wisely and wondered, "And who will listen to you?"

While I was still wondering about that, she said something that has stuck with me, a prophetic utterance that's haunted me ever since.

"The world has changed an awful lot in my time, and I think it can only just keep on changing. I suppose that's the way it's always been, the way it'll always be, but I'm thinking it'll spin even faster in your time. Buddy, I believe you'll be working for the church for a very long time, long after I'm gone. Part of your work in the church will be to strike the balance of keeping us supported and grounded in our traditions and at the same time helping us see that the world is changing, and . . . encouraging us to keep up."

I told her I knew change was inevitable, and I also knew how difficult it was for Episcopalians to accept any change, large or small. Maybe it was hard for people in other denominations, too, but I knew firsthand how challenging it could be for us.

Miss Edith nodded patiently, and then she told us about her father and the 1928 Book of Common Prayer.

"He had grown up in the days of the 1789 book, and when the one after that came along . . ."

"1892," I said, glad to put my seminary education to use.

". . . He hadn't let it worry him. I think he probably hadn't ever really thought about it until our minister back in 1928, Mr. McSherry, told us one Sunday morning that the Episcopal Church had voted to change the Book of Common Prayer.

"Father said he didn't want a new book. He said there wasn't anything wrong with the one they had. It seemed like the more he hated the new book, the more he loved the old one.

"He utterly loathed the '28 book and tried to get others to join him, to refuse to use it. He stomped around and pouted and argued with the minister. Mr. McSherry told him he didn't like it either, but said we didn't have any choice about it. Father even took us to the Methodist church for two Sundays in a row, but he couldn't stand that either, so we came back to St. Thomas.

"After a while, he got to where he could stand the '28 book, and then he admitted that he liked it, and then for years he loved it, just like I did. He died before we started talking about this new prayer book; I don't know if he could have taken another change like that. But he told me, one time, that he knew we'd be changing the book eventually."

"What did he say?" I asked, caught up in this rare glimpse of church history.

"He said, 'Your day's coming.'" She paused, allowing herself a moment to live in the memory of it, and then she said, "And he was right, of course—just as I am right when I tell you two the same thing: your day is coming."

"What day?" Sinclair whispered.

"The day when a change doesn't seem like progress anymore but seems like a threat to the way you've lived your whole life."

Sinclair turned to me and asked, "You think the Episcopal Church will change the prayer book again?"

"Well, sure we will," I answered. "I don't know when, but of course we'll change it. Language changes, theology shifts, and we ought to keep the words we say in church so we can stay"—I was trying not to say *relevant*—"lined up with the people around us."

Sinclair asked her, "Do you like the new prayer book?"

She shrugged. "Oh, it's all right. I loved the old one, but the new one's fine. Father Buddy knows I stopped going to church a couple of years ago—it's just such a distraction to everybody else, with people trying to get me up to the altar rail and back without falling on those steps, and kneeling at the altar." She sighed wistfully, and continued, "Father Buddy is good to bring Communion to me now. He always does Rite One, which is close enough to the old prayer book for me."

I teased, "I'll be glad to use Rite Two next time, if you want to see whether you'd like it better."

She answered, "No, thanks. Rite One is just fine with me. I'm too old for any more changes. But let me tell you this. All my life I've gone to church, pretty much every Sunday, until the last few years. Every year or so when the bishop would come to visit, we all dreaded it. You knew it was going to be a long service. The bishop's sermon was always longer, then you have to have all those confirmations, the announcements were longer, and we always had to have Communion, because the bishop was there. Even the blessing was longer when the bishop came. And whichever bishop it was, he would say the same blessing at the end of the service."

Sinclair asked, "The one Father Buddy says?"

"No, I don't think so," she answered. "I think it was a blessing that only bishops were supposed to use. I don't remember all of it, but I always thought it was funny that somewhere in there it seemed like the bishop would always say, 'Hold fast to that which is good.' I just thought it was funny that the bishop would tell us—each one of us just absolutely determined to keep everything the way we think it's always been—to hold on to what is good."

Sinclair looked at me, trying to remember. "That's in the Bible somewhere, right—about holding fast to what's good?"

I knew it was, and was trying to figure where it might be, when Miss Edith said, "Romans chapter twelve."

I nodded, just to make clear that I couldn't disagree with that, and Miss Edith continued, "But there's another verse that I think ought to go with that one. Buddy, if you're ever a bishop, I want you to put it in your blessing."

"Oh, Miss Edith—I'm never going to be a bishop."

"Why wouldn't you be?"

"Because bishops are so . . . serious, so dignified all the time. I'd hate it. Surely the church has more sense than to elect me. I wouldn't vote for me."

Miss Edith said, "You don't know what's going to happen, Buddy—you might be a bishop someday."

I squirmed a little, not wanting to disagree with her but not wanting to get too close to the idea of becoming a bishop, either. I started to say so, but she said, "Oh hush, Buddy. You don't know what the Lord has in mind for you."

I was aware of Sinclair looking at me closely, as if he was trying to see if I had any purple in me, when out of the blue Miss Edith asked, "Is your mother's father bald?"

I was startled by the question and couldn't find any words that seemed appropriate. Sinclair asked, "Why?"

She answered, "Surely you know that male pattern baldness is inherited from the mother's side of the family."

Still wondering what we were talking about, I managed to say, "No. He had hair until he died. It got thinner as he got older, but he didn't have male pattern baldness."

"Well, that's too bad," she said.

Sinclair helped us both out, asking, "Why?"

"Because the best bishops are bald. People expect a bishop to be bald."

I said, with more force than I intended, "I don't want to be a bishop!"

She said, "That's good. I don't think we should ever elect somebody who wants to be a bishop. Well, we'll have to see how that goes. But if you ever are elected, I want you to add a verse to the blessing that bishops say, right after 'Hold fast to that which is good.' Will you do that?"

"Yes ma'am. Which verse are you talking about?"

"It's from the Psalms. I think it's in there two or three times." We waited, and then she said it just the way she wanted me to say it if I was ever going to be a bishop, in a solemn, dignified tone: "Hold fast to that which is good; *sing to the Lord a new song.*"

25

THE *FAIS DO DO*

A few months passed, and I was starting to get concerned about Sinclair. Every week he seemed more guarded, more cautious, more cynical. I tried to get him to talk about it, but he didn't bite at any of the bait I put out in front of him, and I didn't feel like I ought to press it.

One Sunday morning in early December, he was excited to tell me about something he'd heard on National Public Radio. "On the winter solstice this year, there'll be a full perigee solstice moon." I knew the winter solstice was the longest night of the year, but I didn't know what perigee meant, so he told me. "The moon's orbit around the earth isn't perfectly round. Perigee is when the moon's orbit brings it closest to the earth. This year on the solstice it'll be a full moon, and it's at its perigee. This hasn't happened for a hundred and thirty-three years!"

I love looking up into the night sky, and while I was regretting that I don't take the time to do it often enough, Sinclair declared, "We could have a big Saturnalia party!"

The more he talked about it, the more excited he became and the larger his visions for the imagined party grew. Soon he was talking about having a huge bonfire and threatening druid rituals. As he was imagining the potential for all-out bacchanalian revelry, JoJo came up and asked what we were talking about.

Sinclair told him; JoJo was not overwhelmed, so Sinclair tried hard to impress him with the rarity of it. When Sinclair mentioned a bonfire, JoJo said, "No, man. If you're looking up into the sky, you want to see the stars and moon and such. You don't need no extra light. You ought to come out to Siloam. They ain't much light out there at all."

For Sinclair it was kismet—everything was lining up perfectly. He started talking to JoJo about having a big celebration at the spring, and JoJo said he'd be glad for people to come out. He said, "I can cook up a big pot of gumbo."

At that moment Beulah walked up, having put both of our kids in the parish nursery for the morning. She'd heard JoJo offering to make gumbo, and that's all she needed to know: "Count me in."

While Sinclair and JoJo were debating the possibility of having a fire and how large it might be, I told Beulah what I could about the phenomenon of the winter solstice full moon at perigee. She listened patiently and said, "Okay. I don't care about any of that. I'm just interested in a night out and having JoJo's gumbo, really." Then she turned to JoJo and said, "Maybe this would be a good time for us to invite Wanda Stovall to come visit, maybe stay for Christmas. She's welcome to stay with us. What do you think?"

This was the first Sinclair had heard of Wanda Stovall, the deputy sheriff in West Branch, Mississippi, whom JoJo had been dating before he'd moved to Greene, and it seemed to him that inviting Wanda to join us was the icing on our karmic cake: "It's predestined!" I was glad to see him excited about something, and I thought the idea of going out to Siloam for gumbo and a full moon sounded like fun.

After church that day, JoJo came to our house to call Wanda and left a message on her machine. After a while, she called back and Beulah invited her to come to a party we were having just before Christmas, and then to stay for a few days and spend Christmas with us. Wanda said she didn't think she'd be able to stay through Christmas, but she'd love to come to the party and stay that night with us. Then Beulah handed the phone to JoJo, and we tried not to listen to his end of the conversation, as awkward as it was endearing.

Sinclair wanted to call the party the Solstice Soiree, but after Beulah told JoJo what a soiree was, he said we ought to call it a *fais do do*, because that's what the Cajuns call a party, and we were having gumbo.

Sinclair said he thought a *fais do do* was when everybody was drunk and got into fights. JoJo shrugged and declared that since I would be coming to the *fais do do* with Beulah, and since Wanda was coming too, Sinclair would need to bring a date. Sinclair said he wasn't dating anybody at the time, but JoJo was sure he'd be able to find somebody—"a good lookin' guy like you, all sophisticated with the way you dress and all, you ain't gonna have no trouble findin' somebody."

But as the solstice grew closer, Sinclair told me he wasn't having any luck convincing anyone to spend a cold night just before Christmas out in the woods looking at the moon, whether there was a bonfire or not. Apparently, a full moon at perigee on the winter solstice wasn't as big a draw as he'd thought.

The Sunday before the solstice party, he told me that he'd persuaded his friend Troy to come up for the night. He'd met Troy back when they were in college and they'd "had a moment or two." Now Troy lived in Mobile with his sister, and he was excited about coming up for the soiree. Sinclair was eager to renew his friendship with Troy, and it seemed like everything would work out just the way it was supposed to.

Then, little by little, things started to fall apart. First, the weather prediction was that it was likely to be cloudy. Then Troy called to say that his sister had refused to loan him her car, so he couldn't come. Wanda called to tell us that her work schedule had changed because the sheriff was taking the week off to visit his grandchildren in Florida. Then, as the last vestige of kismet faded away, the weather report on Wednesday morning warned us about the possibility of impending snow and ice.

Now, in case you're not from Mississippi or Alabama, I need to tell you a little about forecasting the weather in the Deep South. "Hot and humid again today," day after day and month after month, just doesn't bring in the advertising dollars. So when the weather people have a chance to say something else, especially if there's a chance of calamity and disaster—tornadoes or ice and snow, something exciting—they lay it on pretty thick, often giving their viewers the worst-case scenario. And it seems to work every time: people rush to the stores and buy up all the milk and bread as if all the prophecies of St. John of Patmos will come true later that afternoon.

After a while you start to wonder how much is true and how much is exaggerated, so it becomes something like the Boy Who Cried Wolf in front of a green screen, with doppler radar providing a dazzling array of barometric information to support the likelihood of impending doom.

So we knew there was a possibility of snow, but we decided we should have the party anyway. We'd arranged for a babysitter, and we knew JoJo would already have the gumbo simmering away. I was determined that we should celebrate the winter solstice whether we could see the remarkable moon or not, mostly for Sinclair's sake. It had been wonderful to see him excited about something going his way, and I hated to cancel it.

Then Carey, our regular babysitter, called to say that she had pink eye. After Beulah said it was too late to find another babysitter, I told her I'd tell Sinclair and JoJo we weren't coming. She said she thought I ought to go anyway. "It'll be a boys' night out for you guys." I told her I'd rather stay home, that the best part of the whole thing was that she and I were going to enjoy an evening out of the house, but she insisted: "For Sinclair's sake."

She had baked a big loaf of garlic bread and wrapped it in aluminum foil; Sinclair had gathered all the ingredients of a salad that he would put together with the dressing he'd made when we were ready to eat. Sinclair came to the house at about 4:30, and we drove out to Siloam. Beulah told me to take her Ford minivan, since her heater worked better than mine.

We had to stop at the Bee Quick for a bag of ice and a tank of gas, and by the time I'd parked the minivan on the side of County Road 14 and walked Sinclair down the gravel driveway, the sun was going down, giving up on the shortest day of the year. It was cold and getting colder; we were both glad to see that JoJo had a fire going in his old cast iron wood-burning stove. He opened the door for us; as we stepped into the warmth of his cabin, we were embraced by the pervasive aroma of simmering gumbo and the big arms of its cook.

I put Beulah's bread on the warming surface of the wood-burning stove and looked around at the cabin. Sinclair had never been to Siloam, and it had been a few months since I'd come inside; we were both impressed. I told JoJo it looked nice, and he said, "Well, I was thinkin' that Wanda was gonna be comin', so I fixed things up a little."

There were blue and white gingham curtains on the windows—JoJo said, "They ain't nuthin' but a couple of Walmart sheets I cut up." A framed picture of JoJo with his brother Bobbo and an older woman I assumed was their mother stood on the mantel next to an old Bible and a kerosene lantern. An old-looking Regulator clock, its brass pendulum ticking and tocking in well-practiced rhythm, hung on the wall. Sinclair went over to look at the clock and told JoJo it might be worth a lot of money; JoJo told us his granny had given it to him, and it was something her grandmother had given to her. When Sinclair told him again that it might be valuable, he said, "I ain't sellin' it."

Either Tom or Bob Cat graced us with his or her presence for a moment, rubbing JoJo's ankles before going back into JoJo's room. He said, "They don't like all this cold, that's for sure."

'Twas three days before Christmas, and all through the house were dozens of Santas in overwhelming variety: old and new, black and white, hand-crafted and store-bought. There were Santas made of paper and painted on wood, and a foot-tall figurine of Black Santa in the middle of the table in the kitchen, which JoJo told us he'd painted and fired in the kiln, stood next to a beautiful crèche that JoJo had also made. Two red-and-green-striped stockings were hung by the stovepipe with care—one for JoJo and the other, I imagined, probably for Wanda.

Bits and pieces of pottery were everywhere: candleholders and vases and plates and bowls, and on a shelf over the doorway to the bedroom were about twenty little figurines, including a group of four figures set a bit apart from the others, one taller than the rest and wearing a black shirt and a white collar. It was me, of course, a little caricature of me in clay; he'd painted the shirt slightly untucked with a little gap for the belly to show, and one of my shoes had a tiny clay shoestring untied. Next to me was a remarkable facsimile of Beulah, wearing jeans and a white shirt, holding baby Grace in one arm and trying to constrain Jude with the other as he attempted to escape, presumably toward whatever trouble he could find or create.

There was a figurine of Sinclair, too: wearing a purple shirt and yellow pants, one red shoe and the other green, bright red hair in a fragile clay ponytail, holding a script in one hand and a megaphone in the other.

It was Sinclair who noticed them first and realized what they were. "This is brilliant!" he exclaimed, pointing. JoJo beamed. Then Sinclair said, "Would you sell these?"

"Naw—they just for fun."

"I bet you could sell these," I piped in. "Actually, I'd love to buy the Hinton family and put them on our mantel."

JoJo said the figures were made from little bits of clay that the pottery ladies had left lying around, and Miss Judy had taught him how to use the paints and fire them in the kiln. "It was just somethin' I been doin' to pass some time in the evenins'." It took me a while to talk him out of giving the figures to me, but finally we agreed I could buy them for fifty dollars, which he thought was ridiculously high. I told him I thought they'd make the perfect Christmas present for Beulah, and I was right.

As I was starting to write JoJo a check, I realized Sinclair wanted the little clay stage director, too, but he didn't have any money with him. So I negotiated with JoJo a little more, wrote a check for seventy dollars, and gave Sinclair his caricature in clay to deflect JoJo's objections. Sinclair was delighted; he thanked me and said, "Really, JoJo—you ought to make these and sell them."

I agreed, and as the idea was becoming a little more solid, Sinclair took it further: "We could have a store out here!"

JoJo was taken completely off guard. "A store?"

But Sinclair was seeing it now. "Yeah! And you could sell these little guys"—gesturing toward the figurines—"and your rocking chairs, and . . ."

Now I was starting to see it, too. "And vegetables from your garden," I added. JoJo was trying, but he couldn't see it yet, so I continued: "And Judy and Allie could sell things they make, too."

JoJo declared, "Y'all are crazy. Must be the full moon."

That seemed like the end of the conversation, but Sinclair murmured, "Just think about it, though," so quietly that JoJo didn't have to respond, but he'd have to think about it.

We talked for a few minutes about the Christmas Eve service coming up. I'd invited JoJo to sing "O Holy Night," and he'd agreed but was nervous about it. He'd sung it a couple of times when we were in West Branch, Mississippi, and I assured him that the congregation would love it. "But they gonna be a lot of people there, people I don't know," he worried. I told him he'd do just fine.

We went outside to look for the moon that had led us out there, but we couldn't tell much more than where we thought it probably was, hidden behind the clouds. The temperature had been dropping steadily since we'd arrived; now it was bitterly cold and starting to sprinkle. "Maybe we better go back to town," Sinclair suggested, "while we still can."

The regret in Sinclair's voice and the look of disappointment on JoJo's face decided me against what was obviously a reasonable plan. I looked at my phone to check the weather; Judy said her husband had worked on it, but the cell phone signal was weak in the best of times and nonexistent at the moment.

I said, "Well, let's just have some gumbo and see if the clouds move on later tonight, so maybe we can see this magical moon before we have to go."

We went in and stood around the old stove to warm ourselves up. As JoJo stepped out onto the porch to get more wood for the fire, Sinclair found a big pottery bowl in one of the cabinets to mix the salad, and I got three beautiful clay bowls and plates and put them on the table for the gumbo. I saw either Tom or Bob Cat, just checking out what was going on before going back into JoJo's room.

When we'd sat down, JoJo asked me to say the blessing, but I told him he was the host, so he said, "Jesus, thank you for this food, and for this night, and for these friends."

We all said "Amen," and JoJo said, "Well, I guess this ain't really much of a *fais do do*; this is just three guys out in the woods, lookin' for the moon we can't see 'cause of the clouds. I guess this might be a soiree after all. But I'm still glad y'all are here."

We passed our plates and bowls around; I broke the bread with my hands and gave both of my friends a large piece. Sinclair put some salad on each plate, and JoJo ladled some aromatic gumbo into each bowl. It reminded me so strongly of a night long ago when I'd eaten from bowls that Preacher Jake had made that tears came to my eyes for the memory of it, and with my mouth watering for the gumbo, I was having my own private flood.

It was, I was thinking, an almost perfect moment. If only Beulah and the kids were with us . . .

And then we heard a grim voice from outside the cabin: "Hold it right there."

26

A Game of Insults and Innuendo

When I followed JoJo and Sinclair onto the porch, the first thing I noticed was that it was snowing. This itself is pretty remarkable in North Alabama. The second was that two men were walking toward the porch, the second one holding a rifle on the first, who was holding his hands over his head. JoJo and I stood and stared; Sinclair, rarely at a loss for words, said, "What the hell is this?"

The first man was wearing a jacket with a hood that hid his eyes, and it wasn't until he was almost to the cabin that I realized two things: that it was Richard Chambliss and that he was drunk. When he looked up at me, he said, "Hello, Father." As always, his use of the title was drenched in sarcasm.

Behind me I heard JoJo's rich baritone voice saying, "Hey, Sutty. You're out huntin' late tonight."

I hadn't seen Jimmy Sutter since I'd taken him to the police station a year and a half earlier. Beulah had told me that he'd been released after a couple of months in a Veterans Administration rehabilitation program, and then I'd lost track of him.

Richard slurred, "Father Buddy, tell him to put the gun down."

Sinclair said, "What's going on? Who're these guys?"

JoJo and I waited for Sutty to answer, but it was Richard who spoke. "Damn it, Buddy—I don't like having a gun pointed at me. Tell him to lower the goddamn rifle!"

"You got no call to talk like that," growled JoJo.

Things were not far from getting out of hand, and I knew they could easily get worse. I said, "Okay, everybody calm down. Sutty, stop pointing that at him. Let's all go inside, all right? JoJo, is that okay with you?"

"Yeah, but I ain't havin' no cussin' in here."

"I'm sure Richard will be more careful what he says. Won't you, Richard?"

Richard didn't answer but turned to see if the rifle was still trained on him. When he saw it wasn't, it looked like he was going to take a swing at Sutty. In that moment I wondered if that would be the last thing Richard ever did, but apparently he had the same thought; he backed down.

Sinclair opened the door to the cabin, and JoJo tried to get us all to go in quickly, to keep the cold out and the cats in. Sutty and Richard were reluctant to step inside, both for their own reasons, so some of the warmth of the cabin spilled out anyway. I didn't see Tom or Bob.

When we were all in, JoJo brought two more chairs from the bedroom, and we all sat around the table: me at one end, JoJo to my left, Sinclair to his left, then Richard, and finally Sutty to my right.

Nobody knew where to start; I think most of them were waiting for me to say something. So I said, "JoJo, I believe our friend Richard needs a cup of coffee—can you make some for us?" JoJo didn't seem happy about doing anything for Richard, but he got up and went into the kitchen.

Richard groaned, "I think I need to lie down."

From the kitchen, JoJo grumbled, "If he's gonna be sick, take him outside. I mean it, now—I just mopped in here."

Richard put his head on the table, and Sinclair, Sutty, and I exchanged glances. I said, "Mr. Sutter, it's good to see you. You doing okay?"

He looked down at his hands folded on the table. "Yeah."

"Are you back here now, out here in the woods?"

"Yeah."

I was reminded that Mr. Sutter was a man of few words.

I persisted, "Even though Sarah Jo and the kids are in town now?"

Sutty shrugged and mumbled, "Yeah."

Apparently, he was also a man of few syllables.

I heard the coffee maker spitting out the last of its percolation cycle. JoJo was getting homemade mugs for everybody from the cupboard.

I said, "Okay, Richard—naptime's over. Sit up; let's talk."

He ignored me, which was a surprise to no one. Sutty grabbed him under one arm and Sinclair under the other; they hauled him into a sitting position. He tried to put his head back down, but Sutty held him upright. I nodded my thanks to Sutty and asked Richard, "Why are you here?"

He responded with a torrent of words you don't hear on network television, what Beulah calls "cable TV language." It was rude and aggressive; I'll leave it to your imagination.

JoJo growled threateningly, "I tol' you before—I ain't gonna have no cussin' in my home."

Sinclair leaned over to Richard and said, "All right, Bucko—I think one more nasty word out of you and you're back out in the snow, capeesh?"

It seemed like Richard capeeshed a little and that he still had enough sense to be afraid of JoJo. JoJo thumped down a mug of coffee in front of Richard so that a bit spilled out. Then he asked who else wanted coffee, and Sutty and I said we did. I wondered when Sutty had last had a cup of coffee. I tried again with Richard. "Why are you here?"

"What—it's against the law to take a walk now? You need to be talking to that guy." He pointed at Sutty. "He's the one with a gun!"

I repeated, trying to impose a sense of calm on all of us, "Richard, why are you *here?*"

He snarled, "Why are *you* here?"

"I was invited to dinner."

"With these two . . . losers? With this . . . mountain man? What's really going on out here?"

Sutty didn't move a muscle, but both JoJo and Sinclair clearly had something to say. I really didn't want this to escalate so that we got trapped into playing Richard's game of insults and innuendo as conversational intimidation. I held up my hands, patting the air down in front of me and saying matter-of-factly, "We're really having dinner. JoJo and Sutty live out here. Why are you here?"

Now Sutty spoke up, his voice flat. "Lookin' in the window." We sat for a moment, trying to make sense of it, and Sutty continued. "Takin' pictures."

Richard tried to look as innocent as he could, and then he spoiled his effort by saying, "That's bullsh-"—he glanced at JoJo—"that's baloney. I don't have a camera."

Sutty intoned, "He dropped this." He laid an expensive-looking camera on the table.

Richard shrugged. "There's no law against having a camera."

"So you been snoopin' around out here," JoJo said. "What're you lookin' for?"

Sinclair had steel in his eyes as he glared at Richard and spoke what I knew was true as soon as I heard it: "He's just out here trying to catch you doing something wrong, Buddy—something he could get a picture of that would be embarrassing to you, something with a black man and a sissy boy. Is that about right, Richie Rich?"

JoJo—sweet, guileless JoJo—protested: "But we just havin' supper out here. We ain't doin' nothin' wrong, I swear." He looked around for me or Sinclair to confirm his innocence. "It's the winter solsters or somethin', see, and the full moon s'posed to be great big tonight 'cause sometimes the moon's closer and this is one of them nights like that. Sinclair said it's real rare what's happenin' tonight, so that's why we're out here."

I realized that JoJo had lived under accusations and suspicions all his life; so had Sinclair and Sutty, for that matter. I said, "JoJo, you're okay. We haven't done anything wrong, none of us."

As I looked over to see Richard smirking at the ease with which he'd put JoJo on the defensive, I felt my calm evaporating; when he met my eyes, I realized that he wanted nothing more than for me to lose my temper. I wanted nothing more than to slap that smirk off his face.

"Haven't done anything wrong?" Richard scoffed. "You call pulling a gun on a man nothing wrong? And no telling what you and your . . . friends are doing out here—Father Buddy and the three wise men."

Sinclair said, "Okay—you caught us. It's the winter solstice and there's a full moon, so of course all of us homos are going to be out here dancing naked around a bonfire and sacrificing goats to the druid gods of fertility and thunder."

As I was telling Sinclair that was not helpful, I heard JoJo whisper to Sutty, "I ain't really a homo at all."

I turned to Richard. "But how did you even know I . . . you followed us out here! You saw me and Sinclair coming out here, and you followed us!"

Richard said, "Oh, well done, Sherlock."

"But why?"

Sinclair said, "Because he's out to get you, Buddy! Don't you get it? He wants to make your life miserable; he wants to run you out of town!"

"But why? Why would anybody want to make me miserable?"

"Because he's miserable, and misery loves company so much that miserable people try real hard to make the rest of us miserable. He hates you because his life is falling apart. He has to blame somebody, and he couldn't stand to take the blame himself, so he's blaming you. He's started drinking and stopped thinking, as we say in the program, and the more he drinks, the more his career as a shyster is disintegrating. And he's mad because people like me and JoJo—people who are black or gay—aren't being kept in our place anymore, and he blames it on liberals like you." He turned to Richard, itching for a fight. "Ain't that right, Richie Rich?"

"No, that ain't right, princess."

Sinclair was finding his stride now. "So you're okay with homosexuals and African Americans?"

"I didn't say that."

Sinclair doggedly held on. "So: you're *not* okay with gay people and black people?"

Richard smirked. "I didn't say that, either."

Suddenly, oddly, I felt an unwelcome sense of compassion for Richard. He and I had grown up in the same South and seen the world changing around us. I tried to ignore the unwanted empathy, but it was too late; I was seeing him in a new light: he was like Miss Edith's father, who couldn't let go of the way things had always been to open his mind to the way things were now. I wanted to hate him, but I just felt sorry for him.

Mostly I wanted him to go away.

I said, "Okay. Well, Richard—nothing suspicious or immoral going on here, sorry to disappoint you. Just some friends eating gumbo. You can join us if you'd like, or you can leave, but I do believe it's time for us to eat."

JoJo was surprised when I invited Richard to join us; Sinclair was fuming that I'd taken the wind out of his sails; Richard was taken off guard, distrusting what I had said. Sutty didn't say anything. While I was waiting for Richard to respond, I saw JoJo mouthing an invitation for Sutty to stay for supper; Sutty just nodded.

Richard sputtered, "You . . . you want me to . . . you're inviting me to eat with you?"

I nodded. "JoJo makes the best gumbo I've ever eaten." I looked at Richard and said, "You're welcome to join us—I think we have plenty." There were only three bowls on the table, the ones I'd put out. I turned to JoJo and asked, "Have you got a couple more bowls?"

JoJo wasn't sure about Richard eating with us, but he mumbled, "I got lots of bowls." He picked up the three bowls on the table, now filled with lukewarm gumbo, and was in the process of dumping them back into his Granny's cast iron gumbo pot when Richard stood up. He looked like he was losing an argument with himself; he was trembling.

"I'm not—there's no way I—you can't really think I'd . . ."

I said as soothingly as I could, "Richard, there's no trick. We have plenty of gumbo, and you are welcome to join us."

He stood motionless for at least ten seconds, deciding what to do. It was a turning point that none of us saw in that perilous moment; I really wish he'd chosen to stay. Instead, he picked up his camera and went to the door. He opened it wide and pronounced, "You and your wise men can all go to hell!" before going out into the snow.

27

Two Perfect Fools

We sat there, stunned and relieved: four men in search of something to say. JoJo put down the bowl of gumbo in his hands and closed the door, but not before Sutty went out quickly. I had time to be afraid that Sutty had gone out there to do Richard some sort of harm, but in a few seconds he came back in holding an armful of wood for the stove. He put in a few small logs, and when he saw us watching him he said, "Gettin' cold."

JoJo put a bowl of steaming gumbo in front of each of us, and I gave Sutty a big piece of Beulah's bread. He shook his head when Sinclair asked if he wanted any salad. The gumbo was delicious, the bread was perfect, the salad was fine, and the conversation was strained.

JoJo said, "Anybody need Tabasco?"

I answered, "No, thanks."

Sutty said, "No."

Sinclair didn't answer, still sorting through it all.

I was wondering what I should have done differently, Sutty was somewhat uncomfortable around so many people, Sinclair was spoiling for a fight that had walked out the door, and JoJo was uncomfortable because the rest of us were.

I said, "Well, I feel sorry for him."

Sinclair responded, "Sorry for him? Because he's such a snooty, bigoted jerk?"

JoJo added, "Because he's so full of hate?"

We all looked at Sutty to give him a chance to play along, but he asked, "Why?"

I said, "Because he's missing out on an incredible bowl of gumbo!"

Sinclair said, "Well, he's still a snooty, bigoted jerk."

I tried a little laugh, but I didn't sell it very well, and nobody else bought it. "Yeah, he's a jerk, and he's full of hate, and he's scared of how he sees the world changing. There are a lot of people like that out there."

They agreed, even Sutty, and I went on. "But we can't let any of that ruin this good supper for us." I took another spoonful of gumbo and another bite of bread, and then I said, "I hope he makes it home."

Sinclair said, "He's not going home."

"Where's he gonna go?" JoJo wanted to know.

Sinclair looked at each of us in turn before telling us, "Candy kicked him out of the house."

I was surprised at the news and startled that Sinclair knew it before I did. "Where'd you hear that?"

"Miss Edith." I looked at him blankly, and he continued, "Hey, you're not the only one who can visit an old lady from time to time. And she and the bridge club network know everything that's going on in Greene."

"What did she tell you?" I asked.

"Well," Sinclair said, relishing this moment, "Miss Edith said Candy was scared for her children to grow up with him in the house, drunk and yelling at them all the time. She said she packed up all his stuff on Thanksgiving Day, while he'd gone with some of his fraternity buddies to the Egg Game in Starkville." I'd watched the Egg Bowl that night, the annual football game between Ole Miss and Mississippi State; State had scored seventeen points in the fourth quarter to win a thriller 23-20. Sinclair continued, "While he was at the game, Candy kicked his ass out!"

He glanced at JoJo and said, "Sorry. Anyway, Miss Edith said Candy called Officer Meigs at the police station—you know Danny

Meigs, right?—and he was waiting for Richard when he got back around midnight, standing there with all of Richard's clothes and stuff out on the front yard. Ole Miss lost; Miss Edith said Richard was already drunk as a monkey when he got there, so Meigs took him to spend the night in jail. The next day Richard moved in with his sister."

The only sound in the cabin for a few moments was Sutty trying to get the last drops of gumbo, his spoon scraping the bottom of his bowl. Then JoJo asked, "Why did he call us wise men?"

I answered, "He was just trying to make fun of us, like we were the wise men visiting Jesus in Jerusalem."

JoJo wasn't comfortable with the idea. "I ain't no wise man."

"You're smarter than you think you are," answered Sinclair.

"Being wise is different from having a lot of schooling," I said. JoJo was not convinced, and I added, "The tradition is that one of the wise men in the Bible was black. And I'm pretty sure none of them were as pale white as I am!"

Sinclair said, "Their names were Balthazar, Kaspar and Melchoir."

That surprised me, and I looked at him, wondering how he would know that. He shrugged and said, "Amahl and the Night Visitors."

I said, "Oh."

JoJo asked, "Which one was black?"

"Balthazar, I think."

JoJo repeated the name, enjoying the feel of it in his mouth: "Balthazar."

Sutty asked, "You got more?"

I wondered for a moment if he was asking for more gossip about Richard or maybe more information about the wise men from the East, but JoJo stood up beaming. "Yes sir—we got a whole pot full."

JoJo ladled some more gumbo into Sutty's bowl and was about to give me some more when Sinclair said, "Buddy, we might better drive on back into town. I'm getting worried about this weather."

I stood up and went outside, opening and closing the door as quickly as I could. It was snowing pretty hard, and there was some sleet mixed in as well. Soon the roads would get too treacherous to drive. I went back in and said to JoJo with genuine regret, "Sinclair's right—we'd better go."

JoJo was disappointed but insisted that I take some gumbo home for Beulah and the kids, and he scooped some out into a plastic container. Sinclair and I put on our coats, hugged JoJo, and said goodbye to Sutty, promising that we'd come back for the next winter solstice. Holding the plastic container of hot gumbo and the figurines that JoJo had made, we carefully made our way down the steps from the cabin porch. The snow was not melting; I felt my foot slip a little on the porch steps before I caught myself.

We walked the gravel driveway back out to the highway, marveling at the snow like we were children. When we got there, I saw that another car had smashed into Beulah's minivan from behind. The headlights and the interior lights of the other car were still on; the driver's side door was open. Then I saw a dark shape on the snow-covered road. It was Richard, passed out facedown on County Road 14, lying awkwardly on top of what turned out to be a bottle of tequila that he was still holding with his left hand. It was nearly empty—there was no way to know how much he'd drunk and how much of it had been spilled. The car was pinging politely to let the world know that the keys were in the ignition with the door open.

I handed Sinclair the gumbo I was carrying and felt Richard's neck for a pulse like you see people do on TV. When I found it, I said, "He's alive."

Sinclair said, "Is that good news or bad news?" Before I could answer, he looked at the bumpers of both vehicles and said, "It's not too bad." Then he put the gumbo and figurines on the back seat of the minivan and fumbled around a bit before turning off Richard's car and lights. He told me that he was going to leave the keys in the ignition.

I was trying to get Richard to sit up, but he wasn't responding. It felt like I was trying to get a grip on a cold, wet bag of mashed potatoes, and the ice-covered road was slippery. I said, "Sinclair, go back and get JoJo and Sutty, would you? We've got to get him back into the cabin."

"Are you serious? Let's call the police and let them deal with him."

"There's no cell phone signal, and I'm not sure they could get out here before he freezes to death, if they can get out here at all. He's cold and wet and soaked in booze. And . . . I think he probably peed on himself or something."

Sinclair said, "Damn!" as he jogged away into the icy woods, back the way we'd just come.

I was trying to roll Richard over onto his back when he opened his bleary eyes, and in a heartbeat or two he got them focused on my face. "Leave me the hell alone!" He tried to shrug out of my grip, and I held on.

I'd parked the minivan on the shoulder of the road as it curved away from JoJo's cabin. It was banked somewhat there, and an incline sloped away from our vehicles. A ditch ran along the other side of the road; it was usually filled with muddy, stinky water, and that night I knew it would be filled with ice-cold, muddy, stinky water. As Richard struggled to get away from me, he slid away from the car a couple of feet, toward the ditch. I caught him by the shoulder of his heavy coat, and we slid out into the middle of the road together. I was hit by an incoherent barrage of verbal abuse and physical resistance, and a fresh wave of stink took my breath away.

Trying to break through his drunkenness to find whatever vestige of rational thought might still be lurking inside his tequila-drenched and foul-smelling exterior, I said, "If I leave you alone, you will die out here."

"Then let me die!" It was partly an angry cry, but I thought it was full of despair as well.

"I can't do that."

"Leave me the hell . . . you goddamn . . . you son of a . . ."

He passed out before he could tell me what I was a son of. I figured he'd come back to his car and drunk several gulps of tequila out of the bottle before starting the car and crashing it into Beulah's minivan. Then he'd gotten out to see the damage, probably taken another swig or two, then slipped on the ice and fallen.

I tried to get him to sit up so that when Sinclair came back with JoJo and Sutty, we could pick him up, but all I really accomplished was getting the two of us to slide a few more feet away from our vehicles. If Sinclair didn't come back with help soon, I was afraid that Richard and I would slide off into the ditch.

Richard tried to struggle out of the grip I had on the shoulder of his wet, slippery coat; I pulled him back and we both slid a little farther down the slope. I listened for Sinclair or JoJo but didn't hear any help coming.

Now I will admit that I am more likely to remember to pray when I recognize that I'm desperate; maybe that's how we all are. As I lay there on that slippery ice, clutching a hostile, stinking, drunk antagonist, I whispered, "O Lord God, look down in love and mercy on all of your children . . . especially this dumbass." I thought about it a few seconds and added, "I mean him—he's the dumbass," just to be clear. Then, because I think we ought to be honest when we pray to the One who knows the truth, I admitted to the Almighty and to myself, "Well, I guess it could be either one of us, really."

In the absurdity of it, I started to laugh. It began as a little giggle but grew into a set of full-scale chortling guffaws I couldn't control. It was all so utterly silly. I imagined if the Lord God was answering my prayer, and looking down on us, we must look like two perfect fools, lying on a rural highway with a winter storm happening all around us, sliding inch after inch toward an unwelcome icy bath. I couldn't stop laughing, even though I knew every chuckle threatened to bring us closer to the frozen ditch.

Richard muttered, "What the hell are you *laughing* about?" and that made me laugh all the more because there was no way I could explain it to him. This made him furious, and he yelled, "Get off me, you goddamn faggot!" I didn't let go and he tried to push me away. I held on, not wanting to abandon him to the ditch, and we began to slip and slide again; this time we didn't stop until we made the inevitable icy plunge.

Richard hit the water first, and I sort of slopped in on top of him. It was mostly my left side that went underwater, but he was fully immersed. In that moment, it stopped being anything like funny, and Richard came sputtering up a lot more sober than when he went in. He was completely furious. I stood up and reached down to help him stand as well; he slapped my hand away and stood glowering at me, as if this was all my fault somehow.

He tried to take a step out of the ditch, but when he put his foot on the icy pavement, it slipped away and he fell back, plunking down into the freezing water again. This time I didn't offer to help him at all. I was thinking that we'd have to get out of the ditch, moving away from the cars, and then walk along on the other side of the road until we could find a place to cross, when the cavalry arrived. JoJo had come prepared: he yelled "Buddy, catch!" as he threw a rope to me.

It took a second for me to understand what he had in mind: they were going to pull us across the ice. I caught the rope and handed it to Richard. He took it as if it were an insult to his dignity, but when Sinclair called out, "Now sit down on the road, and hold on to the rope," he did. They pulled him so that he slid across the road, and then they stood him up, against his several and various objections. Sinclair put a blanket over his shoulders, which he accepted grudgingly. JoJo tossed the rope back, I sat on the road, and they pulled me across. I was glad to get a blanket; my teeth had started to chatter.

We trudged our way back through the woods to JoJo's cabin, with Richard grousing and complaining every step of the way. The part of me that had gotten wet was freezing cold; I could only imagine how uncomfortable Richard must have been. When we got to the cabin, as Sutty and Sinclair were helping Richard up the icy steps and across the porch, JoJo leaned in to whisper to me, "*Now* it's a *fais do do!*"

28

Who Loves You?

Richard was led into the bathroom and instructed to take off his wet clothing; JoJo gave him a pair of jeans and a sweatshirt, both ridiculously large on Richard. I went into JoJo's bedroom, where I put on a pair of well-worn overalls and a flannel shirt, also large on me but not quite so comical. When we came out into the larger room, we were both given a pair of heavy socks JoJo had warmed on the wood-burning stove and told to stand next to the heat. I felt like the marrow in my bones had ice in it, and I thanked JoJo for his care.

Richard and I rotated slowly in front of the stove, doing a sort spinning self-rotisserie; when one side got warm, we'd turn to heat the other. JoJo gave us both a cup of hot coffee. After a while, when we turned so that we were face to face, Richard said, "Were you laughing out there?"

I kept turning so he couldn't see me as I dodged his question. "Why would I be laughing? We could have died out there!"

I rotated until I was toasty warm, and then I sat down at JoJo's table, joining Sutty and Sinclair; JoJo poured some more coffee in my cup and sat down with us. None of us said a word. After a while, Richard asked us, "What now?"

I asked the group, "What time is it?" before recognizing that Richard was the only one wearing a watch. He didn't move, so JoJo looked at his Regulator clock and said, "Nine forty."

Richard said, "I'm getting out of here."

JoJo laughed and asked, "How?"

Richard didn't answer, as if JoJo wasn't there. I asked again, "How are you getting out of here?"

"I'm going to get in my car and drive home."

I replied, "The car that you crashed into my wife's minivan?"

He seemed genuinely puzzled, as if this was news to him. "I hit your wife's . . ."

"That's right," I answered. "Our insurance people will be in touch with your insurance people."

Richard persisted, "But I can still drive it, right?"

Sinclair declared, "No, you can't. You might be able to get back to your car, but there's no way you're gonna be able to drive it home with all this ice and snow on the road. Looks like you're stuck with us for the night, Richie-boy."

JoJo grumbled, "And I ain't gettin' back out in all this just to save you from bein' stupid again."

Richard looked at me, as if he hoped I could tell him he had a way out. I said, "Maybe somebody could come get us, with chains on their tires or something, but we're probably here for the night. So," I added, "come sit down."

He considered, weighing his options. "No thanks—I'll just walk. How far is it back to town?"

I guessed, "About ten miles, I think."

JoJo said, "More like twelve."

Sinclair added, "On icy roads every step of the way."

Richard said, "Goddamn it!"

JoJo growled, "Next time you take the Lord's name in vain, you see if I don't slap you upside your head, you hear me?"

Richard was standing there by the stove alone, with the rest of us looking at him, waiting to see what he was going to do. It was not his nature to be chastised or contrite; it was not in him to back down. The only direction he knew was full speed ahead, damn the torpedoes. He managed to muster up a swagger in the few steps between the stove and the table and sat down like he owned the place, daring any of us to say anything.

Sinclair said, conversationally—and so nonchalantly that Richard had to have known that he already knew the answer before he asked the question—"So, how're Candy and the kids?"

Richard looked at him with steel in his eyes and answered, "Fine, thanks. How's your love life?"

"Oh, I do just fine, thank you."

Richard feigned surprise. "Oh. I didn't think there were that many of you"—he looked at me—"in this part of Alabama."

"More than you'd think, actually. Most of them are just hiding from bigots and scared little men." Sinclair left the "like you" unspoken, but I think we all heard it anyway.

I watched as Richard tried to come up with a snappy retort; he couldn't bear the idea of losing a battle of wits with the town's most conspicuous homosexual. But what he decided to say next was just plain strange: "Who loves you, baby?"

It caught Sinclair off guard. I knew he'd been struggling with isolation and loneliness, and he'd been disappointed that Troy hadn't been able to come up for the solstice. I thought for a heartbeat that Richard's comment had rubbed salt into Sinclair's biggest wound, but he was quick to recover. "Everybody, Kojak—everybody loves me." Richard smiled at him spitefully, until Sinclair continued, "Your wife loves me." Then, just to twist the knife a little more, "Your children love me, too."

JoJo, misreading the rhetoric and thinking Sinclair was the one under attack, said "I love you, Sinclair." Then he turned to Sutty and said, "We're just friends, though."

Richard had been leaning on his bravado and swagger, his defenses firmly in place, but I could see that Sinclair's words had cut him deeply. It was like watching a knife fight, each of them trading cut for cut; I looked at JoJo and saw that he was wishing they would both just stop. I suppose that was what I was hoping for as well.

JoJo stood up saying, "'Scuse me" as he left the table and the room. He knew he couldn't stop the fight or the pain, but he didn't have to witness it.

For most of my life, one of my primary motivations has been to include people who've been left out, to bring the outsiders in, to bring the fortunate out to where the less fortunate are. I think that's why working with teenagers at a summer camp for adults with mental and physical challenges has been such a major thing for me; why it's been such a big deal to take upper middle-class Americans on medical missions to help some of the desperately poor people in Honduras. Part of being compassionate is the willingness to see the world through somebody else's eyes.

So I can't say I was surprised in that moment to feel my instinct for inclusion and compassion coming into play. I also can't say I was happy about it. Again, and very much against my will, I felt myself feeling sorry for Richard Chambliss. In that moment, I was aware that I was looking for something likeable about him or at least to give him a chance to show us something that we didn't all have to hate.

I remembered a moment of the first Special Session at the summer camp in Alabama, when Richard had helped a camper named Tommy take some things up to dining hall window after lunch. It wasn't for his benefit or gain; as far as I knew, nobody had even seen it but me. There had to be something in Richard, some spark of decency or virtue. I wasn't so naïve that I thought Richard was ever going to be my friend—neither of us wanted that—but I wanted to believe that deep down under the selfish conceited persona he presented was something more: that little spark of goodness in all of us.

I've always believed that even the best of us are selfish from time to time and that the worst of us have some good in us, even though we may try to hide it. But Richard was challenging that belief—either he was hiding that original virtue too well, or it wasn't there. But still, he had helped Tommy that day at camp.

I said, "Richard, we're not trying to hurt you. We don't have to be your enemies."

"What, you think I'd be friends with . . . these people?"

"These people who just saved your life?"

"I don't seem to remember asking for any help, from any of you."

"They saved you anyway."

"You want me to give them a medal?"

"I want you to stop treating them like you think they're something you need to scrape off your shoes!" He stared at me, and I continued, "It's like you think you're better than us."

"Well, I am. I mean, look at these clowns."

"You don't even know these guys."

"I know everything I need to know."

"What do you think you know?"

Richard thought about what he wanted to say and decided to say it anyway: "I know I'm stuck out here in an ice storm with a black guy, a faggot, a mental case, and a liberal."

Everybody bristled except Richard, who smiled his satisfaction at our outraged reaction—it was just what he'd been hoping for. He had tossed his rhetorical hand grenade and was enjoying the explosion. I said to the table, "Look, y'all—we're all going to be here all night, okay? It's going to be a long, miserable night if we're doing this all night."

Richard said, "Oh, I don't know—I'm sort of enjoying it myself."

I asked, "What do you want, Richard?"

He looked at me like I was insane and replied, "Oh, I don't know, Father. A million dollars, maybe—can you help me with that?"

"No, I can't," I said with all the kindness I could scrounge up. "Do you think that would make you happy?"

He was taken aback, not by my words, I think, but by the simple, gentle honesty behind them. He had prepared himself for a contentious conversation—attack, defend, strike, deflect. He wasn't prepared to deal with someone who wasn't trying to win the fight.

For a moment, it looked like he was going to change his strategy. He said, "Well, no, I . . ." But then he caught himself and reverted to the character he'd been playing for so long. "Well, you could buy a lot of tequila with a million bucks."

Sinclair was quick to jump in, galvanized by his own painful history with alcohol. "And you think a million dollars of tequila will make you happy?"

Richard caught the hostility and responded in kind. "I think a million dollars of tequila will make me drunk."

"A million dollars of tequila will make you dead."

"Then I'll be dead—that way, everybody gets what they want."

JoJo had come back into the room, and as he was sitting down at the table, he said, "You got two children. What about them?"

Again it was as if Richard couldn't hear JoJo, and again I repeated what he'd said. "What about your children?"

Richard looked down at his hands for a long while before responding, "They don't need me."

"Bull." To everyone's surprise, including his own, it was Sutty who had spoken. We all stared at him, and he felt led to expound on his one-word eloquence: "Kids need their daddy."

Again, Richard looked at his hands, quiet for such a long time that I was looking for something to say just to break the silence. Then he said, "Well, they don't want me."

Sinclair looked at me before saying whatever he was going to say, but he didn't say it after I shook my head slowly. He sat back in his chair and I gave him a slight nod—just letting the moment sit there. It sat, and we waited—maybe a minute. Then Richard said, "She sure doesn't want me around."

Sinclair looked at me again, and it seemed like he was sending the message that if I didn't say something, he would. As gently as I could, with all the compassion I could scrape together, I said, "Candy doesn't want to be around somebody who's drunk and abusive. She doesn't want her children to be yelled at all the time. I don't blame her. You understand that, don't you?"

Again it seemed to me that I was watching a man in conflict with himself. He loved Candy and their children and wanted the best for them. He knew his drinking was hurting them and that he was hurting himself, but he couldn't stop. Jake Jefferson, my old friend and mentor, had been an alcoholic in recovery for many years. He'd been so concerned that I would become an alcoholic when I was in college and seminary, he wrote me that "alcohol will take over your life if you let it."

Richard had let it take control of him, and now he didn't know how to get his life back. Or maybe he understood the how but had lost sight of the why.

I repeated my earlier question: "What do you want?"

The internal struggle was clear to see, tearing him apart. Then it was like he remembered who he was and where he was—he could not back down. "I want you to leave me the hell alone."

All of a sudden it seemed to me that there was nothing more to say or do. I wanted to leave Richard alone, too.

Sutty stood up and went outside without saying a word. I looked at Sinclair and shrugged. JoJo got up and brought the coffee decanter, pouring a little more in each cup without asking if anybody wanted any. Sutty came back in with more wood, and after he put a couple of pieces in the stove, he sat down. When we all looked at him, he said, "Pretty moon."

Sinclair said, "It's a full perigee solstice moon!" He stood quickly to go out and see it, with JoJo right behind him. I stood and looked at Richard, saying, "This is why we came out tonight. It's the winter solstice, and the moon is full. It's also closer to the Earth than usual, at perigee. You want to see it?"

"No."

"You just gonna sit there?"

"Yeah."

I left him sitting there with Sutty, stewing in his self-pity, and went out down the steps into JoJo's yard. All the ice and snow had frozen solid, and I broke through the crust with every step, but the clouds were dispersing. The moon was riding through the patches of clear night sky so brightly that the stars were lost in its glow.

We stood there, Sinclair, JoJo, and me, each lost in his own thoughts. It was a nice, peaceful moment, especially as it contrasted with the chaos of the evening to that point. I wished Beulah was there; I hoped she took the kids outside to see the moon. I wished I could call her to let her know I was okay. All three of us sighed at the same time, grateful for the beauty of the moon, regretting that it was too cold to stand out there for long, and waiting for somebody else to say what JoJo said: "Let's go back in."

When we came back into the cabin, I saw that Sutty was holding his rifle pointed at Richard, who was holding JoJo's cherished antique clock in his hands.

29

All Kind of Choices
I Don't Want to Make

JoJo went over and took the clock out of Richard's hands, gentle and firm at the same time. He looked at Sutty and demanded, "What's going on?"

Sutty, still holding his rifle on Richard, said, "He's messin' with your stuff."

We all looked at Richard, who said, "I was just admiring it, looking to see when it was made. I know a lot about antiques; this could be worth some serious money."

JoJo said what he'd said earlier, but this time with considerably more force. "I ain't sellin' it."

Richard turned to me and said, "Could you tell G.I. Joe to lower his gun, please?"

I stared back. "I'm not his boss. Maybe it would help if you could show a little respect." JoJo put the clock back on the mantel, and Sutty lowered his rifle but didn't put it away.

Then Richard looked at me and asked, "Have you got anything to drink?"

I answered, "Water."

"Have you got anything . . . stronger?"

"Nope." It had never occurred to me that JoJo might have any wine or beer out there, although of course he could if he'd wanted.

Richard said, "Well, I've got something in the car."

JoJo responded, "You ain't drinkin' no kind of booze in my home." Richard ignored him and kept moving toward the door.

Sinclair asked, "Are you thinking you'll drink the rest of that tequila?"

Richard looked at him from the edge of panic, and Sinclair continued, "It's gone, Richie-boy. Whatever you didn't drink, you must've spilled."

"It's . . . gone?" There was desperation in his voice.

Sinclair abandoned his customary slouch and stood up straight. "Hello, my name is Sinclair, and I am an alcoholic."

"Oh, God," Richard groaned.

"Two years sober."

"Good for you, princess." Richard smirked. "You're making all kind of choices I don't want to make."

Sinclair took a deep breath and plunged on. "Take it from a drunk: you will either choose to stop drinking, or you will choose to let it kill you."

"Well," Richard said to his hands on the table, "I guess that's my choice to make."

I said, "Richard, you can still make everything right."

He didn't respond, so I continued. "It's not too late. You can get help with your drinking. You can get Candy and your kids back. She still loves you. It's not too late."

He looked at me suspiciously before saying, "It's none of your business, Father."

"No," I said. "I suppose it's not."

JoJo jumped in. "He's just tryin' to help!"

"Why?" Richard snapped. "What's it to him?"

"He just . . . he just helps people, everybody."

"Oh, because he's a righteous man, a man of God, right?"

JoJo said, "That's right."

Sinclair was going to say something, but Richard held up his hand to stop him. "So what has this God done for you, JoJo?"

JoJo found himself in an argument he was not prepared for. "Well, God made ever'thing, like all of us and my mama, and the trees and flowers . . ."

"For you, you fool!" Richard hissed. "What the hell has your precious God ever done for *you?*"

I wanted to jump in, to rescue JoJo, but I held myself back. He was a grown man, and I didn't want him to think I viewed him as a child. He looked at me, and I nodded my encouragement.

"Well, he made me somebody who could love people, and made me somebody somebody else could love. Like my mama, and my brother, and Buddy and Beulah. I guess there ain't nothin' better'n that, to love and to be loved."

This time Sinclair would not be denied. "So who loves you, Richie-boy? Who do you love?"

It seemed to me that Richard had been punched in the face, and now he was punching back. "Love" he said with practiced disdain, "is overrated."

"You can't believe that," said Sinclair, horrified at the idea of it. "You can't really believe that."

Richard looked at Sinclair with venom in his eyes. "You hear about love, read about it, watch movies about it. But that's all just Hollywood bullshit—that's not really the way life is." Nobody said anything, and he continued. "At some point, we all have to grow up, princess. Real life is not a fairy tale. So you, and all your fairy tale friends, can go . . . to . . . hell."

I said, "Hell is life without God.

"God can go to hell, too!"

Quietly, I said, "You don't believe in God, Richard?"

"Oh, sure—of course I do. And I believe in the Easter Bunny, too—and the Tooth Fairy and the Goodness of Man!"

JoJo said, "Richard, you don't . . ."

But Richard didn't want to hear it. "Shut the hell up, fool!"

JoJo turned to me in disbelief and said, "He don't think God is real. He thinks God is just a story for children?"

I said, "That's what he's saying. He doesn't think God is real—he doesn't think love is real. I suppose he wants to think he's never been loved. That's gotta be a scary place to be." I turned to Richard and asked, "Have I got that right?"

Richard made no response, and JoJo said, "You think your mama didn't love you?"

No one moved a muscle. It seemed like Richard was holding his breath until he exhaled and said, "Oh, I think all dear Mother really loved was a good dry gin martini. And before you ask, I'll tell you that as far as I could tell, my daddy never loved anything or anyone."

I said with real compassion, "And Candy? And Noelle? Belk?" He didn't answer. "You don't think they love you, Richard? You don't think you love them?"

Sinclair said, "What a lonely, scary idea—no love, no faith, no hope. It's like you're on your own personal desert island, Richie."

Richard had been looking down at the table blankly, but now he looked up. "Oh, that's priceless, coming from you, Tinkerbell. I see you in church when I have to go; you hate it almost as much as I do. No, I'm not alone on that desert island."

Sinclair looked at me guiltily. I said, "No, he doesn't hate church, or he wouldn't come. I'm sure he's bored sometimes; I'm bored sometimes." I let that settle in for a moment—"Priest Confesses to Being Bored in Church"—and then I said, "So, Richard—in the real world there is no love, no God?"

He didn't answer, so I went on. "So what is there, in your real world? What makes anything worthwhile?"

Then it seemed like he was trying to reach out to me, to convert me to his bleak understanding of the real world. I guess I was the only other white, straight, non-crazy person there, and he was feeling a need for an ally. "Aw, c'mon, Buddy—it's all about money. You know that. It's all about what you can get."

I don't think it was a surprise to me that Richard thought this way, but I was truly surprised to hear him say it out loud, and it made me sad for him all over again. I shook my head, and Richard continued.

"Buddy, you know this. You know how the world works—c'mon, man."

"That might be how you think the world works. But for me, and for millions throughout history, the world has also been about faith, and love, and hope."

"You can't really believe that!"

"I do. I actually do believe in the Goodness of Man."

"You payin' your bills with faith and hope, Father?"

"No."

"You think Beulah is staying with you because of faith and hope?"

I laughed a little at that. "Well, she's sure not staying with me because I'm making so much money!"

Richard was about to say something else, but I cut him off. "We've been married for twelve years. Beulah is with me because she loves me. My children love me. And I love them. Sometimes it's hard. Sometimes they have to put up with me, and sometimes I have to put up with them—but it's worth it. It's always worth it. I'm sure I could be doing something else for a living; I do this because of faith and hope."

Sutty got up and went out again, taking his rifle with him, and came right back in with some firewood. JoJo thanked him, and they put more wood in the stove. Sutty sat back down and said to Richard, "You don't believe in God?"

Richard managed an air of sophistication. "No, the illusion of religion is not part of my reality."

Sutty looked at him like you might look at a snake in your shower. "You ain't never been to war."

Richard looked around the table. "You all believe in this God and Jesus crap?"

JoJo and Sinclair were stunned. Sutty was inscrutable. I said, "I do."

Richard was ready for me. "Well, of course you do, Father—you have to; it's your job."

"It's not my job to believe in God."

"Then what is your job, exactly?"

Actually, that turns out to be a difficult question to answer. I'd been ordained for eighteen years by then, and I'd done all sorts of things, from trying to repair a leaking faucet in the parish kitchen (unsuccessfully) to talking a young man out of suicide (successfully) to preaching hundreds of sermons (some better than others) to taking part in committee meetings and budget processes beyond count. There were liturgical seasons and rhythms, but every day held its own blessings and challenges. Several people had asked me to describe a typical week; my answer was that I would if I ever had one. How could I define my job in a sentence or two?

Well, I couldn't, so I told them a story.

A few years before, St. Thomas had started a big lobster fundraiser at the parish to fund our annual medical mission to Honduras, and some people had been skeptical about the whole thing. I told them my friend Bob had been opposed. He suggested that we could all just make a contribution to raise the money. I told him everyone needed to be involved, to get our hands dirty, to have some investment in what the parish was doing, more than just giving money. He repeated that it wasn't the most efficient way to raise money, and I agreed he probably was right before telling him that efficiency wasn't the primary goal, which I think made no sense to him.

Happily, his wife was one of our most prolific ticket sellers, and that kept him involved. He wound up organizing the counting of money and tracking how much was made in the different areas of the event.

In the third or fourth year of the event, I'd gotten to the church early to help get everything set up. At some point that morning, I had to go into my office to make a phone call. After I hung up, I took a moment to take a deep breath before I went back to my main job that day, wrapping the lobsters in newsprint. In that moment, there was a knock on my office door. It was Bob.

I thought, "Oh, man—here we go again. He's going to tell me one more time how much more efficient it would be to just ask people to give money."

But instead he said, "Buddy, I just want to thank you."

I asked, "For what?"

"For all of this, for the Lobsterfest."

I said, "Well, Bob, there're lots of people doing lots of work here: Charlie and his crew have been barbecuing all night, and Horton and Peter are out there cooking the lobsters. People are working in the kitchen and the concession stand and the children's games, all that stuff. And people sold tickets for months to get ready for today. Somebody told me your wife's sold almost two hundred tickets. And Rick's organized the live music, and—"

"Yeah," he interrupted, "I know. But you created the environment. Thank you."

I told the guys around JoJo's table, "Of all the definitions I've ever seen about being a parish priest, I think that's probably the truest one I've ever heard. My job as a priest is to create an environment for people to come together as a community of love, to share our faith and invite other people to live in the hope we find in our faith."

JoJo was the only one with any reaction; he turned to Sutty and whispered, "He's good at it, too."

I continued, "It's not my job to tell people they have to believe what I believe. It's not my job to tell anybody that they or anybody else are so sinful that they're going to hell if they don't shape up. It's not my job to change people, or fix people, or get people to do what I want them to do. It's not my job to tell people they're better than somebody else, or to give people permission to hate anybody at all ever. It's not my job to pretend I have all the answers.

"My job—the church's job—is to offer, to invite people into a deeper awareness of the love of God, so we can share it and shine the Light of Christ. The church exists to offer hope to the world."

Sutty was looking at me when he said, "Well, damn," but he turned to Richard when he said, "That's got you shut up, ain't it?"

30

MOON-GAZING AND THEOLOGIZING

But it didn't. Richard broke the mood harshly. "Yeah, well—it's all bullshit. If Jesus loves the little children, all the children of the world like that tedious song says, why is the world so messed up? Why do children suffer and starve? Why are babies born with birth defects? Why are there tornadoes and earthquakes and epidemics? Why—O wise men of faith—is there so much wrong with the world if God loves us so much?"

Whereupon JoJo McCain, eminent philosopher, answered, "It's the Theology of Gumbo."

Richard ignored JoJo but Sutty asked, "What's that?"

JoJo answered, "It's like a pot of gumbo. They's some things in there you like, and some you don't, and some you ain't sure about, like Buddy don't like okra and oysters. But we can't just pick out the parts we don't like, 'cause then it ain't gumbo anymore. Them things we don't like, things we might want to pick out, they just make the whole thing . . . whole."

Then JoJo remembered another thing we'd said over a bowl of gumbo, before he'd moved to Greene: "They's always gonna be things happenin' and people around we don't much care for, ain't they?"

I said, "Yes sir. They're part of the gumbo, too. And God loves all of us, all the time, no matter what."

Richard said, "Do we all sing Kumbaya now?"

I answered, "Feel free. I'm gonna check out that beautiful moon again." I did want to see the moon, but mostly I was thoroughly sick of talking to Richard and needed some fresh air.

I got up and walked out on the porch. The moon was shining brightly, illuminating the ice encasing every branch and limb of the trees, shining on the white ice and snow of the yard. The air was cold and crisp and smelled somehow cleaner than usual. There was a slight breeze, enough to make the icy branches click against each other. It was breathtakingly beautiful. I hoped that Beulah wasn't worried about me.

JoJo came out and put a blanket around my shoulders, hugging me warmly in the process. He looked up at the moon and said, "Wow."

I whispered, "Yeah."

We stood for a long moment, and JoJo said, "How can somebody see somethin' like that and say they don't believe in God?"

I whispered again, "Yeah." Then I said, "You remember me talking about my friend Jake Jefferson?"

"The preacher?"

"Yeah. He wrote me a bunch of letters when he was in prison, and I was in school. He said his father had taught him to look up into the sky at night. I think he was talking about how we all need to look outside of ourselves sometimes, you know?"

"Why?"

"Well, I'm not sure about this, but I think maybe part of it's because we're more likely to find God in the night sky than in ourselves. Jake said his father had told him, 'The mysteries is ever before us.'"

JoJo said, "I guess maybe God's all around us all the time, but most of the time we just ain't lookin'." I mm-hmm'd my approval of this spiritual insight, and he continued, "But He's there anyway, whether we lookin' or not."

I looked at him and smiled. "Amen, preacher!"

He smiled back, the teeth of his wide grin lit up by the light of the bright moon; the smile and the loving soul behind it reminded me so strongly of Preacher Jake that I teared up again.

I wished we could have stayed out there, but it was just too cold, and I was standing there with only JoJo's thick socks on my feet—my shoes and socks had gotten soaked in the ditch with everything else, including my cellphone.

We went back inside. It looked like no one around the table had moved a muscle; I got the impression that they hadn't said a word while JoJo and I were out on the porch moon-gazing and theologizing.

Richard said, "How's the moon?"

JoJo said, "Still beautiful."

I asked JoJo if I could have another bowl of his wonderful gumbo, which pleased him greatly. He asked if anybody else wanted more, and both Sutty and Sinclair were glad to accept the offer. We all looked at Richard, of course, and he said, "None for me."

By that time, we were all content to let Richard exclude himself from any sort of conversation or invitation. Soon JoJo had four bowls of steaming gumbo on the table, hot sauce and bread within reach. We all enjoyed the late-night repast; I suppose Richard enjoyed refusing JoJo's hospitality.

Sinclair finished his gumbo and proclaimed, "I have eaten at some of the finest restaurants in this country, from New Orleans to New York City, and this has to be the best gumbo I have ever eaten!"

Richard snorted his derision.

Sutty agreed, "Real good, thanks," with all the heartfelt sincerity you can cram into three syllables.

I joined in, "Nobody makes better gumbo than JoJo McCain."

"Oh, all right," said Richard, making his exasperation with us loud and clear, "I'll have some." He made it sound like he was doing us a favor.

But JoJo brought him a bowl, and he took a hesitant taste. Then he took another spoonful, and another. He looked up at me and said, "This really is very good."

I answered him, "I didn't make it. JoJo's the cook."

Sinclair, still spoiling for a fight, said, "What do you think about that, Richie?"

"What, eating food cooked by a black cook? We had a black cook when I was a kid."

I knew that a lot of white families had black cooks and maids, and that very often they loved the children of the people they worked for. I asked Richard, "What was her name?"

"What?"

"What was your cook's name?"

"I don't remember."

"Sure you do. What was her name?"

"Why do you want to know?"

"Just making conversation. What was her name?"

"Rosie."

"Rosie what?"

"Just Rosie . . . Rosie—I don't remember."

JoJo said softly, "Did you ever know her last name, Richard?"

Richard made no response, and Sinclair said, "We had a maid when I was growing up. Her name was Ruthie, Ruthie Lee Jones. She helped raise us, me and my sister. Ruthie said she wiped our butts when we were in diapers, wiped our noses when we were in elementary school, and wiped our tears when our hearts were broken. We loved that woman, and God knows she loved us. Sweet as honey, tough as nails. She's the first person I ever talked to about being gay."

Richard seemed glad to be talking about someone else's pain; he said, "You came out to your maid?"

Sinclair closed his eyes, remembering. "No, she was the one who told me. She just told me she knew. I was eleven. It scared me to death to talk about it out loud, for somebody else to know. But she just hugged me, so tight I could barely breathe. She said one of her sons was . . . like that, and that she still loved him anyway. She said it wasn't my fault."

After a moment, Sinclair said, "That was the best hug I ever got."

I said, "She loved you." Another moment, and then I went on, "Didn't she, Richard?"

"What're you asking me for? I don't know who his maid loved."

"He just told you. In one of the worst moments of his life, Ruthie was there to love him. It was the best hug he ever got. Did you hear him say that?"

"Yeah, but I don't know who he's been hugging since then."

Sinclair slapped the top of the table with his hand. "You son of a bitch!"

"Hey, don't get your tutu all in a wad, Tinkerbell. Your friend the padre asked me a question and I answered it."

Sinclair was furious. "Okay, look, Richie: I'm sorry your mama and daddy didn't love you and all, but you don't have to be such a damn . . ."

Things were close to getting out of hand, so I interrupted to speculate, "No, no—that's not true." They all looked at me like I was crazy, and I said, "His mother and father loved him, just not the way he thought they ought to."

Richard was dumbfounded. "You can't—you don't know anything about my parents."

"No," I answered, "I don't. But I do know something about people. Less than half of one percent of mothers don't love their own children." Well, all right—I just made that up, but none of them could disprove it, and I said it like I knew what I was talking about; that's probably part of the job of being a priest, too. I went on like I knew what I was talking about, and they believed me. "It's one of the strongest instincts we have. Mothers who don't love their children are almost always schizophrenic, sociopathic, or on drugs." You probably can't prove that's not true, either.

I said, "The odds are overwhelming that your mother loved you, Richard. You have told the sad story of your unloving parents for so long that you've started to believe it yourself, but it's just not true."

Richard stared at me. Clearly nobody had ever talked to him like this. I continued in my foray into amateur psychology. "They may not have always been good parents. You and I both know it can be really, *really* difficult to be a parent. But you can't truthfully say they didn't love you."

Richard glared at me, as if he hated me with impotent passion.

JoJo agreed, supporting my bogus psychology with a simple truth: "Ever'body's mama loved 'em, now—that's just as simple as up and down."

Richard addressed me as if I were the only person in the room, with acid in his voice. "What do *you* want, Father?"

I thought for a few seconds and answered him honestly. "I want to be a good father and a good husband. I want to be a good priest. I want to do what I can to help people to live in love and hope. It's a terrible thing to live without hope."

Richard repeated that last word with as much derision as he could put into it: "Hope." He said it with disdain, like it was a stupid, silly, childish idea.

But I believe hope is at the heart of life and faith and love and everything I think is noble and virtuous, everything that makes life worth the effort. And hope . . . hope is something worth fighting for.

"Yes, Richard. Hope. That's all I have when I have to go and tell a little boy that his mother's just died, when I sit with parents whose little girl was hit by a drunk driver, when I answer the phone and the young man on the other end of the line has a pistol in his hand and is about to pull the trigger because his girlfriend just dumped him. That's what I have when I preach at a funeral when most of the congregation is uncomfortable in church and distrusting everything I have to say because they think God has mistreated them by the death of somebody they loved enough to come to a funeral: hope. Not hope in me, not hope in the church, not hope in religion, but hope in what we can't see, what we can't count or control.

"I know that Christianity doesn't have all the answers. Neither does any other religion, and having no religion doesn't answer all those questions, either. You can toss the religion out if you want, but it doesn't change anything. Not believing in God just takes you away from any chance at making sense of any of this. Life is not simple. It's more than just the things we can understand or approve. I don't know why there are earthquakes, other than shifting tectonic plates. I don't know why there are tornadoes, other than weather patterns and barometric pressures. I don't understand all that stuff, and I probably never will. But it's not enough for me to just step back from it and make fun of people who are trying to do the best they can to live good and honorable lives even though they don't understand.

"So I choose to live in hope, in faith, in love. You are welcome to scoff at that if it makes you happy, but it doesn't seem like it does. I choose to live with the assumption that something more powerful and beyond my feeble understanding created all that is, seen and unseen."

Sinclair said, "A Higher Power."

I nodded to him before preaching on. "So maybe we've gotten some of the facts messed up. The church has taught things for centuries that a lot of us don't believe anymore: about women, about different races, about homosexuals. For centuries, the church taught that the world was flat and that the sun and the rest of creation revolved around the earth. The church taught that people born with mental or physical disabilities were not wholly people, that they were born with palsy or epilepsy because of their parents' sins or because they were children of the devil.

"Maybe—probably—we've still got some of it wrong. But we're *trying*. We're trying, not to understand, not to be in control, but to offer ourselves into the love and service of that Higher Power even though we don't know it all, even though the reality of existence and its Creator is beyond our limited capacity to comprehend.

"And because I believe there is hope for us all, I believe it's still not too late for you to stop drinking, for you to address whatever's going on with you and Candy, for you to reclaim your life. There is still hope. But nobody else is going to do it for you; nobody else can."

Richard had decided he was not going to be moved, not by anything I had to say. He chose this moment to play what he thought was his trump card: "You can't prove any of this. It's just what you want to believe."

I think I surprised him when I agreed with him. "You're right. I can't prove any of it. I especially can't prove it to somebody who doesn't want to believe it. If you don't want to believe it, I can't prove that water is wet. I can't make you believe that this table we're sitting at is made of wood. If you don't want to believe in God, you're not going to. And you don't have to. If you don't want to believe you have been loved, you don't have to. Your not believing it doesn't mean that water's not wet or that the table is not made of wood; it just means you don't want to believe it. Your not believing in God doesn't mean that God isn't there. Your not believing that you are loved doesn't mean you aren't. It just makes it harder for the people that are trying to love you."

JoJo reached over and squeezed my hand; I gripped his back. Then with his left hand he took Sinclair's; Sinclair seemed lost in his thoughts and kept his head down. I felt Sutty looking at me and wondered if he wanted me to reach out to him, so I did. He took my hand solemnly. I had the impression that it was an important moment for him, and then I realized it was an important moment for me. For almost all of us.

Even Richard felt the magic of the moment, although he couldn't stand it for long and tried to spoil it. He said, "Oh, so this is when we sing Kumbaya, right?"

Sutty was eloquent in his response: he extended his right hand, palm up, and laid it on the table. Without looking at him, Sinclair offered his left hand, a clear invitation to Richard to take it and complete the circle. It was a beautiful thing.

JoJo looked at me and asked, "What's Kumbaya?" Sutty turned to me, curious as well.

Sinclair said, "It's a sappy children's song, the kind of song they sing at Sunday school."

I said, "Well, they might sing it in Sunday school, but I learned it at summer camp. It's an African song, I think—'kumbaya' is a word from an African language that means 'come by here.' It's a prayer for God to come help us when we cry, when we pray. People make fun of it now, because I guess they think it's naïve, but I've always liked it."

JoJo said, "What's naïve?"

31

HONEST ANSWERS

Richard looked at Sutty and Sinclair's hands like they were spiders. He got up and went through the door onto the porch, slamming the door on his way out. Then Sinclair reached across the table to take Sutty's offered hand, completing the circle of friends. We all tightened our grips briefly around the table before letting go. It was sappy, simplistic, naïve, and very meaningful.

"Naïve means you want to see things as simple and sweet," I answered, "even when they're not. Naïve is when you choose to trust people who shouldn't be trusted."

JoJo said, "I guess I'm naïve, huh?"

"Sometimes," I said. "Sometimes I am, too. I think it's better than being cynical and suspicious all the time."

JoJo said, "Cynical is . . . when you don't never trust nobody?"

Sinclair said, "Yeah. Cynical, like me."

This confused JoJo, who said, "But you trust us, right?"

"Yeah, but it's . . . hard for me, hard to trust people."

I said, "JoJo, the truth is that we can't trust everybody. There are people who shouldn't be trusted. But we should give them a chance."

Sinclair said, "How many chances do we have to give them?"

Sutty said, "As many as seven times?"

I was surprised that Sutty was quoting a Bible verse, and I looked at him with a question in my eyebrows. He shrugged and said, "Sunday school."

I remembered how Jesus had answered a similar question about forgiving from one of his disciples, and I said it: "Not seven times, but seventy-seven times."

We sat there in companionable silence for a few minutes, pondering the enormity of our obligation to forgive, to keep giving people more and more chances, until Sinclair said, "You think Richie's okay?"

I hadn't been thinking about Richard, and realized that he'd been out in the cold a long time now. I said, "You think he's going to try to walk back into town?"

"Nope," JoJo said, and when I asked how he knew, he said, "He ain't got no shoes." Richard's shoes were still drying beside the stove, next to mine.

Sutty got up and went out and came back in with more firewood, saying, "He ain't out there."

Sinclair spat, "That idiot! Now we're going to have to . . ."

Sutty shook his head, stopping Sinclair's diatribe. "Car's runnin'."

Now I was alarmed. "You think he's going to . . ."

Again Sutty shook his head. "Just sittin' there."

Richard was sitting in his car, running his heater. I said, "Fine with me."

We talked for a while after that, about JoJo's life and work at Siloam, the Greene Little Theatre, and the Episcopal Church. We tried to drag Sutty into the conversation, but though he seemed to enjoy hearing us talk, he didn't seem interested in joining in. Eventually he stood and said, "G'night." I tried to convince him that it was much too cold for him to sleep out there, but he just shrugged. He went out into the cold, into the frozen night.

I stood and caught up with him on the porch. I said, "Sutty—listen—are you okay out here, man?"

"Yeah."

"Did it all work out with the VA, all that counseling and everything?"

"Yeah."

"You don't really like being around other people, do you?"

"Nope."

I guess I couldn't blame him; he'd been through circles of hell I couldn't imagine, and now he was living the life he'd chosen, out here in these woods. It wasn't really any of my business, but still I said, "Listen, if you ever—um—need anything, will you let me know?"

Sutty didn't usually look me directly in the eye, but in that moment he looked right at me, as if he had something he wanted to say. But all he said was "Yeah." I said, "Really?" and he said, "Cross my heart," making the motions over his chest.

"Okay," I said, "My wife is a social worker, you know, and there are people at the church who could help you, if you need something."

He said, "All right."

On an impulse, I put my hand on his shoulder and said, "We'd be glad for you to come to church with us, if you wanted."

He looked at me again, and it seemed like he was trying to read me, wondering if he could trust me. I felt myself shrinking from his scrutiny and had to force myself to maintain eye contact. He might have smiled a little—or I might have imagined it—and he said, "Thanks." And then he walked away, into the woods, and he was gone.

I went back inside, and Sinclair wondered, "Does Sutty have a house out here or something?"

"I don't know where he stay," said JoJo. "I don't really see him much. Every once in a while, he'll bring me some deer meat. Once he killed a big ol' wild hog, and I tried to cook us up some pork chops, but they weren't much good."

Sinclair and I helped JoJo clear away the leftovers and wash the dishes. The gumbo we put in plastic containers and took out on the porch to freeze, the bread he tore into little pieces to set out for the birds, and the salad we threw out for the raccoons and possums.

When we sat back down, JoJo could barely keep his eyes open. He'd probably been up since early that morning, getting ready for the big *fais do do*, and I knew he was tired. I told him it would be okay for him to go to bed. He argued with me, just for the form of it, before telling us good night.

I said, "It was a wonderful meal, JoJo—thank you."

He smiled and nodded, and went back to his room. In a few minutes we could hear him starting to snore; a minute or two after that we could feel it.

Sinclair chuckled and said, "Let's go check out the moon."

This time I put my shoes on, warm and dry from sitting beside the stove. I thought about taking Richard his shoes, too, but decided against it. I'd had enough of him for one night, and he'd probably had enough of me as well. He could get his own damn shoes.

Sinclair and I put our coats on and I took the blanket JoJo had wrapped me in earlier. We stepped out on the porch, and I was again overwhelmed by the beauty of the moonlit winter wonderland: the moon glimmering through the bare, ice-coated limbs, the stark bright white of the ice and snow covering everything, the crisp freshness of the piercingly cold wind that with each breath challenged me to take another. In the distance, we could hear a car running—Richard keeping warm, and keeping his own company.

Sinclair said, "Buddy, if I ask you something, will you answer me honestly?"

"Maybe."

"I'm being serious."

"Okay, I'll try."

"Don't you ever get mad?"

"Sure, I do."

"I don't think I've ever seen you angry."

"Well, honestly, I guess I try not to get mad, and when I am mad, I try not to let it show."

"What's that all about?"

"I just don't think it does much good."

"So you just . . . hide it?"

"Well, yeah, I guess so."

"Oh my God—how can you do that? Why *would* you do that?"

"I don't know. It just seems to me that we're more likely to say or do stupid things when we say or do them because we're angry." Sinclair was dubious, so I continued, "I guess I get just as mad as anybody, but I try not to say or do something I'll regret later, after the anger passes."

"Weren't you mad at Richard tonight?"

"Yeah, a couple of times. But mostly I just feel sorry for him."

"Sorry for him? I just wanted to slap the hell out of him every time he said anything. How can you feel sorry for him?"

"Oh, I don't know—I just . . . I just think he's such an angry, lonely, frightened little boy."

"He's an arrogant, manipulative snot who thinks he's entitled to wealth and power because he's a straight white man."

What he said and his angry passion made me smile. I reminded him, "You know I'm a straight white man, right?"

"Well, yeah, but you're . . . different."

"Yeah. Well, we're all different, you know?"

"But I meant—"

"I know what you meant. Listen, Sinclair: every person you meet—whether you talk to that person or not—everybody's got struggles, everybody's got their own issues and problems."

"All right. So?"

I was struggling to make my point; actually, I was having a little trouble figuring out what my point was, but it felt like it was important. I decided to try a new tack.

"Okay, let's try this: did you ever read comic books?" I'd read comics since I was in high school and happened to have kept them. Now, because some of them were valuable, it was considered a collection.

"What, you mean like Superman and Batman?"

"Yeah—perfect! Superman is invulnerable, strong, virtuous, good-looking. He can fly, he has X-ray vision—Superman's perfect, right?"

"Well, except for that green stuff that's poison to him . . ."

"Kryptonite, exactly. The writers of Superman realized that if the good guy is too perfect, the story they're telling is boring. The readers can't really relate to Superman, because he's too perfect. He's not like us. But Batman, now: Batman is dark and brooding. He doesn't have any superpowers—he's not exceptionally strong, a bullet could kill him. Sometimes he breaks the law to get the bad guy."

"So he's more interesting."

"Yeah, he's more interesting because he's more like us. We're all flawed, we're all broken somehow or another. We've all got struggles, everybody's dealing with their own issues. You are, I am, and . . ."

"Richard is."

"Yeah. The thing is, none of us are all good, and none of us are all bad." Sinclair was thinking about all that, and I drove in the last nail: "Richard is not all bad. I am not all good. You are not all good or bad, either. We're all mixed bags."

Sinclair was not convinced and unwilling to let go of being mad at Richard, not that I blamed him. I said, "Do you really think Richard came out here to get photos of me doing something embarrassing?"

He looked at me like I was a foolish child. "Of course. Why else would he be outside JoJo's window with a camera?"

"But really—why would he do that?"

Uncharacteristically, Sinclair thought for a moment before answering. "Because his whole life is falling apart: his marriage, his family, his work. It's all going sour on him, and he blames you."

"Me? Why would he blame me?"

Sinclair already had the answer for that one. "Because he can't blame the one who's really at fault: himself."

I couldn't believe that, but he continued, "He thinks you're stealing Candy away from him."

"What?"

"Well, she's a beautiful woman, and she likes you—she trusts you—and more and more, she's disgusted with him. He feels her slipping away from him and he thinks she's moving toward you."

"That's absurd!"

"I didn't say it makes any sense, but I do think that's what's going on."

"Why would you think that?"

He paused before confessing, "'Cause that's what Miss Edith said."

I had to admit that lent a little credibility to the whole scary idea, if that was the buzz among Miss Edith and her network; they were usually pretty accurate. I asked, "So what should I do?"

"Well, there's probably not much you can do about Richard. He's just going to hate you and do what he can to make your life miserable. I'd be careful around his wife, though."

I was wondering what I could do differently with Candy when he added, "And you need to tell Beulah what's going on."

Well, damn. I already had some explaining to do with being stuck out all night in an ice storm, and now I would have to tell her about Richard's crazy grudge against me, too.

Then, because he was on a roll, and because it was just the two of us, Sinclair asked, "You really do believe all this stuff, don't you?"

"What stuff?"

"All that stuff about God and Jesus, love and hope."

"Well, yeah. Yeah, I believe in God. I believe Jesus is the best way for me to have a relationship with God. I believe in love. I believe in hope. So, yeah."

"And God is more like Superman, and Jesus is more like Batman, right?"

I had to laugh at that. "Well, yeah—Jesus is more approachable than God, easier for us to relate to."

"More like us."

"Yeah—that's the whole point of the Incarnation."

"Like Christmas?"

"Right. We've sort of screwed up Christmas with all the shopping and decorating, but the point originally—and the point still—is that God became human so we can have a connection to God, somebody we can have a relationship with."

"And Jesus talked about love and hope. That's why you do, right?"

"Yeah, I suppose. And Jesus talked about mercy and forgiveness. He told us to love all of the children of God, even the lepers and the prostitutes. Even the Romans, though they all had good reason to hate the Romans."

"So God loves us all?"

"All of us, no matter what, all the time, forever."

"Even . . ."

"Even Richard."

Then he was bashful, embarrassed and frightened by his own thoughts. I waited, and he said, "No, I meant . . . even me?"

I guess I shouldn't have been, but I was surprised. I blurted out, "Of course God loves you!" I remembered another conversation with this same man, all those years ago when he was Michael, sitting on a porch listening to an orchestra of night bugs and frogs. I remembered him telling me that he'd been taught that God hates homosexuals—that it's in the Bible somewhere. Now we were on a different porch, listening to a different night symphony, this one of icy branches creaking and clacking together, and he was still struggling with God, the Bible, and his sexuality.

32

And Yet It Moves

The place and part of homosexual people in the church and in society is a difficult, complicated issue that has troubled the church on several different layers and levels for decades. I don't pretend I have all the answers, but it was something I'd thought about for a long time.

I told Sinclair, "When I was in seminary, I wrote a paper on the church's response to Copernicus's theory of heliocentrism."

He said flatly, "Okay."

I laughed and continued, "I'm not changing the subject. Bear with me, and hopefully this'll make sense in a minute or two. I didn't really care about the science of it so much as the church's reaction to a shift in how we see the world."

And then I told him the main points, or at least what I could remember from my seminary paper. The traditional view, known as geocentrism, was that the entire universe moved around the Earth—not just the sun, which was assumed to rotate around the Earth, but all the stars, everything. The assumption was that we are the center—literally—of the universe. They knew this was the truth because clearly you can just feel that the Earth itself is not moving, while the sun rises in the east and moves through the sky until it sets in the west every day, going round and round like clockwork.

Copernicus was a sixteenth century Polish mathematician who postulated that the Earth circled around the sun, spinning around on its axis every day. His idea was that the Earth is not the center of the universe but that it is moving all the time, with great speed, to circle the sun.

We take it for granted now, but the idea was quite controversial in its day. Copernicus's book containing his radical ideas wasn't published until just before his death, as he was hoping to avoid controversy and the church's denunciation. The legend is that he was presented with the finished manuscript on his death bed; he came out of his coma to see the book and died peacefully soon after. I don't know if that's true, but I like the story. His book did seem to cause some controversy, but not a lot; it was mostly contained to theologians and philosophers.

It wasn't until sixty years later, when Galileo Galilei came along using logic and the brand-new technology of telescopes to support Copernicus's theory, that the church reacted strongly. Galileo wrote an essay titled "Starry Messenger" in which he described what he'd seen through his telescope: that Venus has phases similar to the Earth's moon and that Jupiter has moons orbiting it like our moon orbits us. If that had been all he had to say, everything would have been fine, but then he went on to voice his agreement with Copernicus's theory of heliocentrism.

The arguments were ferocious. The church's scholars and theologians quoted several Scripture verses saying that the Earth had been fixed in its place, that it did not move. Sinclair seemed interested in that and asked me which Bible verses I was talking about. I told him there were several, but the one that I could remember is in Psalm 96. I could remember it because we were going to use that psalm for the Christmas Eve service in a few days.

I said, "Psalm 96 begins with 'Sing to the Lord a new song.' That's what Miss Edith told me I needed to add to the blessing if I ever have to be a bishop, remember?" Sinclair nodded, and I went on. "But later in that same psalm, the psalmist wrote that God has 'made the world so firm that it cannot be moved.'"

I told Sinclair that the people who disagreed with Copernicus and Galileo used this verse and a few other Bible verses to argue against

them. Martin Luther and John Calvin criticized the theory of heliocentrism and used Scriptures to support their arguments.

"Eventually Galileo was tried by the church's Office of the Inqui-
sition. They condemned him for 'vehement suspicion of heresy' and
sentenced him to prison, which turned into a sort of house arrest
for the rest of his life. They forced him to recant, to take it all back.
The legend is that after he recanted, Galileo whispered, 'And yet it
moves.'"

Sinclair said, "Wow." He was listening politely; he might even
have been interested. But he was still struggling to find my meaning,
as I suspect some folks reading this may be as well.

"The point is that the church was absolutely sure that the sun
moved around the Earth. The church had always taught that we—the
Earth—were created to be the center of the universe, the pinnacle
of God's creation. But it's like I told Richard earlier: sometimes the
church gets things wrong.

"For centuries the church has taught that homosexuality is wrong.
There are verses in the Bible that support that teaching. But I believe
the church has been wrong about this, like we were wrong about
the sun moving around the Earth—like slavery, like the equality of
women. We seem to want to make things complicated—looking for
loopholes, I guess—but Jesus told us what we're supposed to do: love
God with all we are and all we have, and love other people as much
as we love ourselves. Everybody, always, no matter what. It's scary for
church folks to consider that we might have been wrong, and it's hard
for us to change."

"So what do you do with all those verses about homosexuality
being an abomination and everything?"

"Well, I think we need to read all of Scripture seriously. I don't
think we ought to be able to just pick and choose the verses we like
and ignore the ones we don't. We have to read the Bible critically,
with the understanding that the generations of people that wrote
the words in our Bibles were mostly interested in their relationship
with God. They didn't know or care about history, or science, or
psychology. The cultures they lived in owned slaves and treated
women as property, and they didn't question those assumptions.

The unquestioned assumption was that Earth was fixed, that the sun moved around it, and the church wasn't interested in science proving their teachings wrong.

"But now we live in a different time. We've shifted from geocentrism to heliocentrism, over the church's objections. We no longer think it's right to own other people. We think that women should be treated like people, not property. The church has resisted all of those changes, but now we see that we were wrong."

Sinclair said, "But there are still some parts of the church that treat women as less than men."

"Yes. And some people in some parts of the church still regard black people as inferior. Some people still support the idea that creation was made in six days and use verses from the Bible to support that idea. But I think they're wrong. The church is not infallible; it never has been."

And then a thought occurred to me. "Part of the problem with recognizing that women and black people and homosexual people are not inferior to us straight white guys is that a lot of us just *enjoy* the idea that we are better than somebody else."

To my surprise, he quoted one of my favorite Preacher Jake sayings. I guess he'd heard me say it several times: "Ain't nobody no better'n you, and you ain't no better'n nobody else."

I laughed and answered, "Exactly. But most of us think we need to have somebody we think we're better than. It's like Kris Kristofferson sang: 'everybody's got to have somebody to look down on, who they can feel better than at any time they please.'"

He looked at me blankly. "Who?"

"Aw, c'mon man—Kris Kristofferson, 'Jesus Was a Capricorn.'"

"I have no idea what you're talking about."

I reached back into the dim memories of the music I'd listened to back when I was in college, and decided it would be a favor to both of us if I just said the words instead of trying to sing them:

Jesus was a Capricorn, he ate organic foods
He believed in love and peace, and never wore no shoes
Long hair, beard and sandals and a funky bunch of friends
Reckon we'd just nail him up if he came down again.

Again Sinclair seemed interested enough for me to continue, so I took a little chance and sang a chorus:

'Cause everybody's got to have somebody to look down on
Who they can feel better than at any time they please
Someone doin' somethin' dirty decent folks can frown on
If you can't find nobody else, then help yourself to me.

He made soft little clapping motions as if we were at the opera, and told me I should be on the stage. I told him I was flattered but that I already had more than enough of being in front of people.

Then I said, "It's hard for church people to change anyway, but the idea of giving up whole groups of people we can feel better than makes it even more difficult. But here's the thing: I believe we are all children of God, all of us children of our Father who art in heaven. I think Jesus said we should love every other person because God loves us all. But it is hard for the church to change its mind."

My friend seemed lost in thought, and I was afraid I'd lost him. But then he said, "And yet it moves."

"Yeah. Slowly, but it does move."

In that moment, he looked so frail, so lonely and afraid, that my heart went out to him. I leaned over and took him under my arm, hugging him gently. After a while I felt him sob, and then after another while he reached up and hugged me back, hard.

I whispered, "As much as I know anything, I know that God loves you just as much as He loves me."

Sinclair nodded, and after we broke the hug, he said, "And God loves that son of a bitch Richard too, right?"

I chuckled a little. "Yeah."

"That's hard to take."

I composed a different song, with a tune that was probably more familiar to Sinclair: "Jesus loves the sons of bitches, all the sons of bitches in the world . . ." and we laughed. Then he said, "And this particular son of a bitch is on your Board of Elders?"

"On the vestry, yeah. I think it's about the same."

"Well, can't you kick him off or something?"

"No. I don't think so. I've never heard of a priest kicking somebody off the vestry."

"Well, could the congregation vote him off?"

"No. That's congregationalism, and that's not the way the Episcopal Church works. Decisions like that come from the Diocese, or the bishop maybe. I don't really know."

"So how much longer does Richie-boy have on the vestry?"

"I think he's starting the third year of a three-year term. So the end is in sight. He's pretty much stopped coming anyway, actually."

"Why?"

"I guess he figured out that being on the vestry isn't getting him where he wants to go."

"How many people are on the vestry?"

"Twelve. I think most of them see through him."

"Well, that's good."

"Yeah."

"But still, he's going to cause trouble."

"Yeah, I know.

"That's what Miss Edith says."

"Yeah, I know. What does she think he could do?"

"Well, she doesn't really know. Maybe reduce your salary?"

"He knows he wouldn't have the votes."

"Well, maybe he could cut funding to something important, like the Special Session."

"Oh, I think he'd love to, but he knows he doesn't have the votes for that."

"So I guess maybe the only thing he can do is to make your life miserable. So he sneaks around hoping to catch you doing something that could make trouble for you."

We chatted a little more, about his work and his friend Troy who couldn't make it for the solstice party. "Just as well, really—Richard and Sutty would have freaked him out."

After a while the relentless cold drove us back in. The mantel clock said it was one-thirty. We put more wood in the stove and tried to find someplace comfortable enough to get a little nap. I was almost asleep, listening the frozen branches creaking in the wind, when Sinclair started laughing. I asked him what he was laughing about, and he snickered. "I was just thinking that Richard was right: you are sleeping with a gay guy after all."

33

Your Heart Is Bleeding

By the time the sheriff's deputies got out to the cabin the next morning, the ice and snow were melting. Sinclair was "not a morning person," so he was slow to get up, but JoJo and I were looking at the damage to Beulah's minivan when the deputies rolled up in a big black pickup with chains on the tires. As they got out, I heard one of them say into his radio, "We found 'em. Call Mrs. Hinton and tell her we found 'em."

I asked the deputy, "Was she real worried about me?"

"Yes sir."

I said, "She knew where I was."

"Well, she was afraid you might've run off the road with all this ice and stuff."

The deputies were looking at the dent on Beulah's bumper and JoJo was telling them what had happened. I heard one of the deputies ask, "Mr. Chambliss hit this vehicle?"

"Yes sir," JoJo confirmed. "The minivan was parked right here, and he slid up on the ice and hit it."

"Mr. Richard Chambliss the lawyer?"

"Yes sir."

"Where is his car now?"

"Well, I don't know nuthin' 'bout that, now."

"What was Mr. Chambliss doin' out here in the first place?"

I stepped in to say, "He was just here visiting with me and his good friend Mr. McCain here," gesturing to indicate JoJo. They were taken somewhat aback to think Mr. Chambliss the well-known attorney had been out in the woods visiting with a black man and a preacher. I decided it would be better if I didn't tell them about the gay guy still asleep in the cabin. I continued, "It was a bright full moon last night, and this is a good place to see the night sky."

JoJo had been just as surprised as the deputies to hear himself being referred to as Mr. Chambliss's good friend, but he caught on quickly and said, "But then them snow clouds rolled in before we could see the moon real good, so they just stayed a while, and then it snowed and they got stuck out here."

This seemed to satisfy the deputies; they offered to give me a ride back into town, but I told them if I just stayed a little longer, I'd be able to drive my wife's minivan and wouldn't have to come back for it later.

Before noon, the roads had cleared enough for Sinclair and me to drive carefully back into town. It was the Thursday before Christmas, the last shopping day before Christmas Eve, and the town was bustling. I dropped Sinclair off at his apartment and drove through the town, past the church to our house; there were several cars at the church, likely the altar guild and people decorating for the big services coming up.

Beulah was relieved to see me, upset about the minivan's bumper, furious with Richard, sorry she missed the gumbo, curious about all about the various conversations of the night, and happy to hear that Sutty was doing well. She agreed with Sinclair that I would need to careful around Richard and around Candy. Then she said, "You need to talk to Jude."

"What's going on with Jude?"

"I think some of the boys have been teasing him."

"About what?"

"About being a preacher's kid."

Jude was almost eleven by this point, in the fifth grade. He had friends, played soccer and basketball, and seemed well adjusted. I had asked him a few times if any of the guys gave him a hard time about being a preacher's kid, and he'd always said they didn't know or care. I was hoping that it wasn't going to be a big deal, but now it had apparently caught up with him.

He was out in the backyard with his sister Gracie, sitting on the slide of our swing set, trying to keep the little snowman they'd scraped together from melting in the sun.

I went out the back door and called to them: "Hey, kiddos!" Gracie came running to hug me, but Jude stayed where he was, gathering together some snow to build the snowman up some, fighting a battle he knew he could not win.

I hugged Gracie and told her to go in and ask her mother to wipe her runny nose, and then I walked out to my son, who was studiously ignoring me.

"What's up, kiddo?"

"Nothin'."

I said, "I got snowed in at Uncle Joe's."

He didn't say anything, so I said, "Mom told me some of your friends are giving you a hard time about being a priest's kid."

"Yeah."

"You want to talk about it?"

"No."

It was like talking to Sutty the night before, dragging out one syllable at a time. I said "Okay" and sat on one of the swings to wait for him. In a minute or two, he looked over at me, and realizing he wasn't going to win this battle, either, he said, "It's not just that you're a preacher, Dad."

"Oh. Well, what is it?"

"They're all saying your heart is bleeding."

"My heart is bleeding?"

"Yeah."

"What does that mean?"

"They're all saying it's because you don't really believe in the Bible."

"Well, did you tell them I do?"

"Yeah, but they're all saying you don't preach about sin."

"Well, I try to preach about God forgiving our sins. I think that's better."

"They say your heart is bleeding and that you hug trees."

"Are they saying I'm a bleeding-heart liberal?"

"Yeah. A bleeding heart."

"Okay. I guess our church talks about love and hope more, and some other churches talk more about sin and punishment."

Part of the back of the snowman's head fell off; Jude scooped it up and put it back. I stood up and gathered some snow from part of the top of the swing set that was still in the shade and made it into a little snowball head transplant. I handed it to him, and he said "Thanks" before putting it on top of the rest of it—the former head became the new shoulder.

He worked on that for a few seconds and then it came out. "Dad, are you gonna die?"

"What?"

"Is your heart bleeding or something? I don't want anything to happen to you or Mama."

"No, sweet little man. I'm fine, and Mama's fine. My heart is fine. 'Bleeding heart' is something people say when they think somebody's too nice, when they think somebody should be tougher about things. A 'bleeding heart' is somebody that looks after people who are poor or who don't have much power."

"But that's a good thing, though, right?"

"Yeah, that's what I think, too. Listen, Jude—you don't have to agree with all your friends about everything all the time. Your friends have probably heard that from their parents, and I don't always agree with them, either."

"Because you're a preacher?"

"Well, because I guess I have different ideas about God and the church. Our part of the church is different from some of the other parts, and some of those other parts are bigger than ours. So some of your friends go to different churches, right?"

"Yeah," he lamented, "all of 'em."

"Well, their parents go to those churches, and the preachers there tell them that if they don't act right, they'll go to hell."

Jude was horrified. "Is that true?"

I laughed and gave him some more snow I'd gathered. "Well, it's not what I believe." That didn't seem like enough of an answer, so I added, "I believe God loves all of us, all the time."

He worked on his little melting snowman for a minute more; I was content to watch. Then he pushed it over, stood up, and hugged me. "I'm glad you're my daddy. I don't care what they say."

I hugged him back. "I'm glad you're my son." He squirmed loose and I asked him, "Is it hard to be a preacher's kid?"

"Nah. Most of the time nobody cares."

"What do you think you'll be when you grow up? You think you'll be a preacher, too?"

"Was your daddy a preacher?"

"No, he was an engineer."

His relief was obvious; I think he was worried that it was something that was passed from generation to generation. I said, "You don't have to be a preacher. You can be whatever you want."

Two years before, we'd taken the kids to see Santa at the mall. This Santa was asking all the children what they wanted to be when they grew up. Jude told him he didn't know, but three-year-old Gracie said, "I want to be a damn astronaut!" It had been a little embarrassing at that moment, but it's been a family joke ever since.

So now Jude puffed out his chest and said, "I want to be a damn astronaut!" and we both laughed.

I said, "Really?"

He said, "Nah." Then he said, "I don't know what I want to do. Do I have to know now?"

"No."

"When did you know you wanted to be a priest?"

"When I was thirteen, we got a new priest at the church where I grew up. He had a son who was about my age, and we became good friends. Just after they moved there, we had a meeting of all the acolytes, to work out how the new priest wanted to do things. Well, my mother was going to come and get me and my brother, your Uncle Lee, after the meeting was over. The meeting didn't take as long as we thought it would, and Lee went home with somebody else, so I was left alone at the church with nobody else but just the priest, and I was scared. I mean, I thought priests were weird, you know?"

"Yeah."

"I remember looking out of the window, waiting for Mama to come. It was raining real hard, and the rain was hitting the window and running down in little rivers. Then the priest came up, and he just talked to me, not like I was a kid but like I was a person. He asked me about school and what classes I liked and which ones I didn't, and what sports I played and if I was an Ole Miss fan or a Mississippi State fan, and he just talked to me like I was somebody important.

"When Mama came to pick me up, I told her I wanted to be a priest in the Episcopal Church."

"What did she say?"

"She said, 'Oh, Buddy.' Actually, there are several stories that have your grandmother saying 'Oh, Buddy' in there somewhere."

"What did your father say?"

"He said"—I tried to talk in a deep voice like my father's—"well, you know, Buddy, you have to be good to be a priest." Then I said, "I've been proving him wrong for eighteen years now." Jude didn't get it; I had to tell him it was a joke, and he still didn't get it. We sat there a little awkwardly for a moment or two, and then he said, "I think I just want to be who I am."

"I think that's a great idea."

"I mean, I don't want everybody to think I'm just your son, or just Mama's little boy. I just want to be myself."

"Yeah, that's what I want, too. For both of us."

34

The Outrageous Bathroom Implements Duel

For Christmas Eve at St. Thomas, we had two services; the early service was for children and families, and the second service was fancier and more traditional. In Mississippi I'd started telling stories for children on Christmas Eve, and it was a tradition I was glad to continue in Greene. Every year the story at the children's service became more and more complicated, and the production involved more people.

This year the story for the early Christmas Eve service was an adaptation of the Christmas hymn "Good King Wenceslas." The king was a good man who'd been brought up by his gentle grandmother and his selfish aunt—the story is about him choosing the influence of his kindly grandmother and not the aunt who treated people like property.

Part of the script I wrote went like this: "Now Wenceslas's grandmother was kind to everyone, but his aunt was mean and selfish, the kind of person you hear about in stories like this. She enjoyed having servants, people she felt were 'beneath' her. She liked to have people do what she told them to do. Wenceslas was very much like his grandmother in many ways: kind, gentle, and loving. But sometimes, especially when he was tired, he could be like his aunt—proud and snobby, like he thought he was better than other people."

The service was beautiful, the church was filled with members and visitors, and the story went well. As the congregation was leaving, the reviews of the story of Good King Wenceslas were overwhelmingly positive. Beulah said she and Jude loved it, but it was a little too long for Gracie. Candy said her kids loved it too, and then she lowered her voice to say, "Richard's here, Buddy—drunk and angry. Be careful."

We had a light supper for the choirs between the services, the children's choir with the adult choir. We relived the telling of the story of Good King Wenceslas again, in no particular order, remarking on the actors' gestures and facial expressions and some of the congregation's reactions.

I kept an eye out for Richard, but I didn't see him, and I was relieved to think he'd probably gone home to sleep it off. Just before Beulah and our kids were ready to go home, Jude came to tell me that the toilet in the men's bathroom was running. It wasn't flooding, but he thought something was wrong.

I thanked him and told Beulah I'd see them later. It was easier if I stayed at the church between the Christmas Eve services. The late service had incense and chanting and all sorts of liturgical complications, and it was better if I was there to handle things like ushers not knowing what they were supposed to do and acolytes not knowing where they were supposed to sit and . . . toilets running. The guys who normally fixed such things weren't there yet, but I figured—how hard could it really be?

Well, I'm pretty sure it didn't have to be as difficult as I made it; I'd turned the water off and worked on the toilet for at least a half an hour, but nothing I was trying was working. Just as I'd decided I needed to step away and let the guys who were good at this sort of thing do it, I heard a familiar and contemptuous voice behind me: "Cute story, *Father*."

I was still on my knees, with my back to the bathroom door. There was a little water on the floor. It wasn't enough to cause any damage, but the knees of my pants were definitely getting wet. I grunted "Thanks," hoping that would be the end of the conversation, knowing it would not.

On a whim, thinking that we could do something positive together, or at least to change the subject away from Wenceslas, I said, "Richard, do you know anything about plumbing?"

I couldn't see his face, but the sneer in voice conveyed his scorn as he answered, "No. I guess I'm more like the king's evil aunt, who had people who did what she told them to. Actually, I pay people to do this sort of thing. Fortunate for me that I have money to pay them."

I hauled myself to my feet—not easily and certainly not gracefully—to face him. I didn't want him to ruin my Christmas spirit; I wanted to be more like the king's grandmother.

He was standing in front of the door to the bathroom, which was closed. I tried to walk past him, but he moved to block me. In an odd moment of fantastic speculation, I wondered what I would do if he tried to hit me—turn the other cheek? I could smell the liquor on him.

I said "Excuse me" and tried to get around him again. He didn't answer and didn't move, daring me to do something. I said, "Richard, this is ridiculous. Please get out of my way. I've got work I need to do."

"Other toilets to fix?"

I retorted, "Other drunks to pull out of icy ditches." I probably shouldn't have said that, but it felt scandalously wonderful to be spiteful, just for a moment.

That took the smirk off his face, but it was replaced by the rage of a wounded animal. He took a swing at me, and the answer to my earlier question came easily: it was a clumsy swing and I stepped back out of the way. He nearly fell down, but not quite. As it happened, his drunken stumble brought him almost to eye level with the brush to clean the toilet; he picked it up and brandished it like a sword.

I looked around and saw a plunger, my only defense.

Now, just by pure chance, way back when I was in college, I took a semester of fencing. I needed a semester in Physical Education, and fencing looked fun. Very uncharacteristically, I was pretty good at it, good enough at least to hold my own, largely because my arms were long and fairly strong, a benefit of having played tennis in high school. The instructor invited me to think about joining the fencing team, but it sounded like a lot of work, and I never did.

I picked up the plunger as if it were a ridiculous foil, set my feet in the classical fencing position, and said, "*En garde!*"

I guess I was trying to make him see how silly a bathroom sword-fight was, but it backfired. He tried to hit me with the brush, and I parried his blow with the plunger. He tried six or seven attacks—stabbing, slicing, lunging—and each time I blocked his stroke with ease. I had an advantage in size, the superior "weapon," and a semester of fencing to fall back on.

He stopped, panting. He didn't know what to do next—he wasn't going to win the outrageous bathroom implements duel, but he didn't want to quit, either. We stood and looked at each other for over a minute. I thought about dropping my plunger, because that's the sort of thing the good guy would do in a movie to show the bad guy that he meant him no harm, but I didn't trust Richard not to come after me with the toilet brush if I did.

I said, "Please get out of my way." He unleashed an energetic and colorful stream of late-night cable television invective, indicating that he had no intention of letting me out of the men's room. I was having a hard time imagining how this was going to work out. I decided that Richard would have to make the next move, and I had just settled myself to wait when I heard a man's voice calling out. "Boudreaux? You in here?"

Richard glared at me. "Not one word, or—"

"Or you'll attack me with a toilet brush? Wait, no—you already tried that . . ." I called out, "Polk! We're in the men's room!"

That confused Polk; he came and knocked gently on the door. "Everything all right in there?" I guess you never know what you might find going on in a bathroom.

I said, "Come in!" and he did, trying unsuccessfully to assess the situation. He looked at me questioningly and I said, "Richard's just helping me with a minor plumbing issue."

Richard glowered at me and growled so that only I could hear, "This is not over."

Before he could push his way past Polk to get out of the bathroom, I answered "I'll bring my plunger!" When the door closed, after I knew that Richard was gone, I sat down on the toilet and brushed my hair back with my fingers, exhaling noisily.

Polk said, "What in the world was that all about?"

I answered, "I'll tell you over a cup of coffee." We went into the kitchen and made a pot; I told Polk it was a long, sad, complicated story, and then I told him a lot of it. When I got to the events of this evening, when I started talking about the toilet brush and plunger fight, I was laughing so hard I could hardly talk.

Polk said, "Buddy, this is serious. You could file charges!"

"What charges—assault with a deadly toilet brush?"

"Well, all the same, you need to be careful about that guy."

"Yeah, I know. I will."

I asked him why he was there. He'd already been to church; I remembered him saying, "Good story there, Boudreaux," as he walked out with his wife Charlie. He said he'd gotten a call from Beulah.

"Beulah told you to come back to the church?"

"Yeah," he drawled. "Seems that Candy Chambliss had called her and told her she was concerned about Richard coming into the church. She couldn't do anything about it; she had her two children with her and all, so she called your wife. Beulah said she tried calling your cell phone, and then she called the church, but you didn't answer, and she was starting to get worried. She couldn't leave Jude and Gracie at home alone, so she called me and asked me to come check on you."

He chuckled a little and added, "I don't guess she could have imagined what I'd find when I opened that bathroom door, the two of you facing off like a couple of swordfighters, him holding a toilet honey dipper and you fending him off with a damn plunger! I don't think I'll ever forget that sight, I can tell you."

We talked a while, and eventually he asked if there really was an issue with the plumbing. I told him what I thought was going on; he went into the bathroom and in less than five minutes it was fixed. It's enough to make a preacher cuss.

By this time in my career as a preacher, the Christmas Eve sermons were the only ones I ever wrote out. Even so, I almost always wandered off script as my whims led me. And by this time in the development of God's holy church, we'd started recording the sermon at every service, which I was still not sure about. Volunteers transcribed them and we printed out copies in case somebody couldn't come and wanted to read it. My concern was that the device also recorded sermons when I said something I thought might be better forgotten.

As it turns out, I'm glad we recorded the sermon from the late Christmas Eve service that year, not just because I abandoned what I had written altogether but also because the sermon is part of this story I'm trying to tell, the story of a prodigal coming home.

The sermon I'd printed and carefully laid on the pulpit flew out the homiletical window when JoJo McCain sang the introit: "O Holy Night." He'd sung it beautifully several times at the Church of the Holy Incarnation in West Branch, but this was his first time to sing it here at St. Thomas.

People in the parish knew JoJo as the black guy in the choir, and they knew that he was quiet and polite. They knew he was a friend of ours and that Jude called him "Uncle Joe." They didn't know, and in all honesty I guess I didn't know either, what a commanding voice he had. The effect he had on the congregation that night during the Introit was powerful to the point of being magical.

Maybe I'd never really heard him sing it before; I'd probably been too busy with last-minute arrangements or something. Maybe it was because I was standing next to the thurifer, and the incense was making me a little light-headed. Maybe he sang it better that night than he ever had before. Or maybe, and most likely, I was just in a spot where I was ready to hear it.

Whatever it was, when the organ played a few notes to set up the song, the choir, the acolytes, the last-minute arrivals, and the people in the pews were all bumping around, getting their purses, coats, hymnals, and worship bulletins situated like they wanted them; but when JoJo sang, "O holy night, the stars are brightly shining," it felt everybody just stopped what we'd been doing to listen closely.

JoJo sang, "It is the night of the dear Savior's birth," and my eyes started to water.

He sang, "Long lay the world in sin and error pining, 'til He appeared and the soul felt its worth," and the tears were coming in earnest, partly because of my friend's intensely heartfelt rendition of the song and partly because of the remarkable idea of the soul feeling its worth.

JoJo sang, "A thrill of hope the weary world rejoices, for yonder breaks a new and glorious morn." I looked around to see that I wasn't the only one JoJo was touching; some of the members of the choir were crying along with me, and members of the congregation as well. I wiped my eyes to look up into the transept, wishing that Beulah was there. She was at home with our kids; I hoped she already had them "nestled all snug in their beds, while visions of sugar plums danced in their heads."

With his clear, rich, baritone voice, JoJo McCain commanded us to "Fall on your knees, O hear the angel voices! O night divine! O night when Christ was born. O night, O holy night, O night divine!" When he sang the line, "Here come the wise men from Orient land," I was sure he was looking at me; I looked for Sinclair but couldn't find him. And when he came to the end of the song, he didn't just hit the high note he'd been worried about; he knocked it over the fence.

The last note of the organ faded into silence, and it was one of those enchanted moments you get in church from time to time, when everybody seems to be connected, focused, in communion with each other. When the song was over, everyone was completely still and quiet. I thought about starting to applaud, to show JoJo our appreciation, but I didn't want to spoil the holy moment.

Our custom at St. Thomas was for me to nod to the organist when it was time to start the processional hymn, usually when the acolytes and choir were all lined up as best as possible in the chaos at the back of the church. On this holy night, this night divine, I let the moment linger, not so long that I thought people would be getting antsy but long enough for us to feel the magic. The organist looked at me and I shook my head and held up my hand, showing her my palm—not yet. We looked at each other for maybe fifteen seconds, and then I nodded. She nodded back and played the introduction to the hymn. The congregation stood, and we began the processional hymn with genuine gusto:

> O come, all ye faithful, joyful and triumphant!
> O come ye, O come ye to Bethlehem.
> Come and behold Him, born the King of Angels;
> O come, let us adore Him.
> O come, let us adore Him,
> O come, let us adore Him, Christ the Lord!

While the lesson from Isaiah was read, I took a moment to look into the congregation. The place was packed, with lots of visitors—not just the "Christmas and Easter" visitors but also visitors from other churches who didn't have a Christmas Eve midnight mass. I saw Richard sitting with a woman I didn't recognize. He was sitting up front so that I would be sure to see him, glaring at me; on an impulse I winked at him, just a subtle jab with a metaphorically invisible toilet plunger.

I looked further back and saw Sinclair sitting with Miss Edith. Sinclair was brightly colored, as befitted the occasion; Miss Edith was wearing a black dress and her familiar strand of pearls. Just beside her was Pearlie, her caregiver—she waved at me to be sure I saw her. I nodded slightly, and wondered why I had never invited her to come to church before.

Way off on the left side against one of the stained-glass windows, I thought I saw Sutty, but I couldn't be sure. When I blinked and looked again, I'd lost whoever it was, and I didn't see him again.

We sang "What Child Is This," which is sure to make me cry every time, and I read the Gospel, that passage we all love from the Gospel of Luke, the one Linus recites in *A Charlie Brown Christmas*.

Then I went to JoJo and asked if I could borrow his copy of "O Holy Night." I stepped up into the pulpit, took the manuscript I'd written and dropped it to the floor, and preached a sermon.

35

AFRAID TO IMAGINE MORE THAN WE KNOW

"In the Name of God the Father, the Son, and the Holy Spirit, Amen. Please be seated."

I started by repeating part of the passage from Luke: "An angel of the Lord stood before them, and the glory of the Lord shone around them, and they were terrified. But the angel said to them, 'Do not be afraid; for see—I am bringing you good news of great joy for all the people: to you is born this day in the city of David a Savior, who is the Messiah, the Lord.'"

I repeated, "'Good news of great joy for all the people,' and the shepherds were terrified. I don't think I've ever met a shepherd; we don't have many sheep around here, but I imagine that shepherds were not complicated people. You didn't have to engage in nuanced thought to be a shepherd. Just count the sheep, scare off the wolves, stay awake, move them to a new place when they'd eaten all the grass where you were—it wasn't complicated. There was no theology involved, no philosophy, no psychology—just count the sheep.

"So they weren't ready for angels, or prophesies, or Messiahs. But it was to them, regular people like you and me, that the angels came to proclaim the coming of the savior of the world, ready or not."

I held up the sheet music so the congregation would see that I was reading from it: "'Long lay the world in sin and error pining,' our friend JoJo McCain sang before the service. Thank you, JoJo." Here the congregation applauded, and I was glad to join them.

"The people of Israel had hoped and waited for generations for the coming of the Messiah, but I guess maybe they had started to think it was never really going to happen—maybe the shepherds had given up, thinking this was just the sort of thing religious people say, until all of a sudden one night, when they were minding their own business, the sky was full of angels!"

I read from the song: "'Til He appeared and the soul felt its worth.' The soul felt its worth, but the shepherds were terrified. What they had longed for was happening—and it scared them. It was absolute evidence of everything they'd ever hoped for, and it scared them. It was what they said they were hoping for, but it was outside their ability to imagine.

"I think the shepherds in this story are not much different from you and me. I think they were just afraid to imagine more than they already knew. Maybe that's how we are, too—afraid to imagine more than we know.

"When we were young, we were encouraged to imagine, remember? Santa Claus, the Tooth Fairy, the Easter Bunny. The boundaries that separated 'pretend' and 'real' were not so clear. One year my sister and I saw a rabbit in our backyard the day before Easter, and you could not have convinced me, or paid me, to believe that it wasn't the Easter Bunny. Now, sadly, I have to admit that I'd be sure it was just a rabbit.

"I think some of the pain of getting older—apart from the pain in our knees and backs—has to do with that sadness, that loss of imagination, the terrible clarity with which we divide pretend from real, fact from fiction, possible from impossible, spiritual from worldly.

"It takes some of us longer than others, but making these distinctions clear and sharply defined seems to be a part of how we define growing up. We get older and we think we're smarter and more sensible, when actually we have just limited our sense of wonder; mysteries become things we're supposed to solve, and we no longer recognize that there are some things we do not understand. And too often, if we can't prove something, it is labeled 'fantasy' or 'fiction,' and therefore 'not true.'

"There's a great movie out, I wonder if you've seen it: *Men in Black*. It's been out a couple of years, I think; Beulah and I just got it on DVD. The idea of the movie is that there are aliens living among us, and there's a government agency that keeps track of them. The Men in Black protect us from the aliens and protect us from knowing about the aliens.

"The older agent, who's played by Tommy Lee Jones, is trying to recruit a younger man, played by Will Smith, to join the Men in Black. Will Smith says that he knows there aren't really any aliens, and Tommy Lee Jones says something like this: 'Fifteen hundred years ago, everybody knew that the earth was the center of the universe. Five hundred years ago, everybody knew that the earth was flat. And fifteen minutes ago, you knew that humans were alone on this planet. Imagine what you'll *know* tomorrow.'

"I'm not suggesting that aliens live among us, as interesting as that idea might be. What I am suggesting is that we don't know everything and that some of the things we think we know, we might be wrong about. We have put ourselves in the insane position of not believing anything we don't know or think we can understand or prove—and just ignoring things we can't explain or control. We know we don't know everything, but it's easier for us to say we'll only believe what we know. But imagine what we'll know tomorrow.

"And that brings us to the problem of believing in God. The whole business of believing in something we don't understand has become contrary to how we see the world. It messes us up and makes us question our definitions. God is not verifiable, measurable, predictable, or controllable. For God to be God, He must be a mystery that cannot be solved or fully understood. For God to be God, He must be infinite, a concept that boggles our poor little finite minds.

"The whole point of Christmas is the Incarnation of God. The Word becoming flesh closes the gap between 'spiritual' and 'worldly' and smudges our imaginary line that keeps 'possible' safely distinct from 'impossible.' The infinite, eternal God becomes a person so we will be able to see and touch and understand, to invite us into a relationship with God, with Love."

I held up JoJo's music sheet to read again, "A thrill of hope the weary world rejoices, for yonder breaks a new and glorious morn!"

Then I said, "Here we are in the weary world, and we are afraid to look for the new and glorious morn—we are afraid to hope. I don't think I can imagine living without hope. I suppose that people who want to believe in God will believe, and those who don't won't. But I do wonder . . .

"I wonder how many of us 'religious people' really think God is 'real.'

"I wonder if we really believe what we say we believe.

"I wonder how Christians can say we follow Jesus and His teachings and still be so unwilling to forgive each other or to forgive ourselves.

"I wonder how we can treat other people the way we do—thinking that we are better than some people and others are better than us—if we really believe we are all children of our Father.

"I wonder if we're afraid of hope and faith because we really believe that God is 'fiction' or at least 'theoretical' or 'abstract.'

"I wonder what price we pay to keep all those 'religious, churchy, idealistic, Sunday morning' words and principles separate from our 'real world, pragmatic, business-oriented' lives."

I paused a moment before taking a deep breath and pressing on. "But what if God were really real? That's the question the shepherds had to be asking, and the question that you and I have to ask, too—what if all this stuff is real?

"What if God is real? What if we really believe that God is here and now? What if God is real right beside me as I say all this stuff; what if God is real right there with you as you listen? How would we live then; what would we do differently?

"The illusion of the real world needs to pretend that there is no God, that we make ourselves and that we can safely depend only on ourselves. There is no hope in anything but ourselves: what we can get, what we can make happen.

"If we live in that illusion, people are manipulated or frightened into coming to church, not to expand their understanding of God but to build up credit with an imaginary accounting firm in the sky. People are shamed or manipulated into coming to church so they won't burn if God turns out to be 'real' after all—it's all just fire insurance, just in case.

"I know some folks think I am naïve, idealistic, maybe even simplistic—maybe that's my job. But I want to tell you when I say I'm glad you're here, when I invite you to hear the good news of the love of God, when I invite you to come and receive the sacrament of the Body and Blood of Jesus Christ, it is because *I deeply believe that God is real.* I believe that with all my heart and soul; I am betting my life on it.

"I'm not asking you to play it safe; I'm not asking you to pay your fire insurance premium; I'm not asking you to mouth words you don't mean or do anything fake or false—I am asking you to consider the possibility that God is real. I'm asking you to take your place in this community of faith, to open yourself to the real presence of God Almighty on this holy night. 'Fall on your knees, O hear the angel voices! O night divine! O night when Christ was born.'"

I let the words sink in for a moment and took the time to think of what I wanted to say next. Then I realized we'd already said it. Or sung it, actually.

"So 'Come, all ye faithful, joyful and triumphant.' Let go of your need to limit yourself to what you think you understand, what you think is provable, measurable, and possible. Pay some attention to what the goosebumps on your arms are telling you, and come. 'O come ye, O come ye to Bethlehem.' Find your imagination again; it's still in there somewhere, hidden in all those layers of education and sophistication. 'Come and behold Him, born the King of angels; O come, let us adore Him.' There is more to life than what little we understand, so open yourselves to faith and come. 'O come, let us adore Him, O come, let us adore Him, Christ the Lord.'"

There was another pause, and I was thinking that would be a good place to stop, but then I thought there was something else I wanted to say.

"So—here's what I think, what I believe, and what I hope: God loves you. All of you. That's what I want you to know. God loves you as much as He loves any of His children. God loves all of us—whether we like it or not, whether we believe it or not, whether we believe in God or not. God loves you because love is what God is.

"There is nothing you have ever done, and nothing you could ever do, that will make God decide you are no longer His child. God loves all of us, all the time, no matter what, no matter what, for ever and ever. Amen."

Some of the people nodded, but it occurred to me that we needed to make more of a response than that. It seemed like the congregation had received the sermon pretty well, it felt like they were with me, so I decided I could push them a little bit. I said, "You know, if we were some other denomination, that would have been a good place for an amen." Some people chuckled, and a few said "Amen!" But I had a different idea.

"So maybe just this once," I continued, "on this Holy Night, we could put aside our stately Episcopal dignity and decorum, and say amen if you believe what I just said." More people laughed, and a few more people said "Amen!"

I playfully chided them and said, "No, not now—after I say it!" People sat up in their pews, waiting; most of us were enjoying the moment. I said, "Okay. 'God loves all of us, all the time, no matter what, no matter what, for ever and ever.'"

The people said, "Amen," and that was that.

36

Quite Possibly the Most Wonderful Christmas Gift

The Christmas Eve service lasted until almost one in the morning; by the time I got home it was after two. Santa had come while I was at church—all four stockings were full, and some of the kids' main presents were on display for that magical moment when they would come into the living room: a new gaming system for Jude with impressively complicated games to go with it; coloring books, a box of sixty-four colors, and an American Girl doll for Gracie, with sets of the doll's clothing and a book telling her story.

The children were angelic in their sleep, and so was Beulah; I could tell from her breathing she was sound asleep. I tried to crawl into bed without waking her—this almost never works and it didn't work at all this time. She said, "I'm awake."

"I'm sorry I woke you."

"No, I was awake."

I said, "Merry Christmas."

"Merry Christmas."

"It looks like Santa came."

"Yeah—Santa brought way too much this year."

"They're going to love it."

"And under the tree there's more—clothes and books and video games, and something special for you and Jude."

"Oh, Beulah—I hope you didn't spend a lot of money. I didn't get you anything real expensive. I hope you didn't . . ."

"It didn't cost all that much. And it's for you and Jude. And it's all I got you."

I kissed her and told her I loved her and put my head on the pillow and slept until what felt like a few minutes later, when both of the kids came bursting into the room. The clock said it was 5:27, but Gracie and Jude were filled with an urgent excitement that could not be ignored.

We got out of bed and marveled at what Santa had brought. I made some coffee and we all took out what Santa had stuffed into our stockings, announcing each item so the rest of the family could join in our good fortune. Then we started with all the gifts under the tree, including two cowbells and a pair of tickets to the 1999 Peach Bowl in Atlanta—the Mississippi State Bulldogs versus the Clemson Tigers. The earrings I got for Beulah were nice, and she said she loved them, but they paled in comparison to JoJo's figurines of our family and to the pair of bowl game tickets for me and Jude.

By the time the stockings were emptied and the tree was conspicuously bare underneath, it was almost eight. I connected the game system to the television and Jude and I raced Mario against Luigi while Gracie and Beulah learned all about her new doll, Samantha. Somewhere in there, Beulah had time to heat up some ham and the biscuits she'd made the day before, which I ate gratefully and the kids ate because their parents told them they had to eat something that wasn't chocolate.

The family tradition had become that we would eat a big breakfast—mostly to put some actual food in our bellies with all the Christmas candy—and a late lunch. This year Beulah had decided that we would invite Sarah Jo McCaskill and her children Mary Grace and Wil. Then I had suggested that maybe we could invite JoJo and Sinclair as well, and Beulah said that more would be merrier. So, a few days before Christmas, we spent time preparing for nine places at our table—four Hintons, three McCaskills, Sinclair, and JoJo. We owned only six chairs suitable for the event, so I had borrowed three folding chairs from the church.

On Christmas Eve, Sinclair asked Beulah if he could bring a guest, and she said we would be delighted to have whoever he brought. Then, while Beulah and I were trying to gather some of the wrapping paper in garbage bags without throwing any of our presents away, Charlie Guthrie called to say that she'd ruined their Christmas dinner—the turkey was burned to a crisp and the dressing was dry— and Beulah invited them to come, too. I went back to the church for four more chairs.

Beulah had made a huge pan of delicious cornbread dressing, giblet gravy, a ham, a sweet potato casserole, baked onions, and three desserts: a chocolate pie, my favorite; a pecan pie, her favorite; and a cheesecake, which the kids both loved. Sarah Jo brought Mary Grace and Wil, dinner rolls, and some sort of creamed corn dish that wound up tasting a lot better than it looked; JoJo had deep-fried a large turkey, which looked beautiful; Charlie and Polk brought their son Gideon, a pot of green beans, and another pecan pie because you can never have too many pecan pies; Sinclair's guest turned out to be Miss Edith Frank, who brought a bottle of what looked like champagne.

Miss Edith sat on our couch and summoned Wil McCaskill: "You there, boy. Come sit with me for a moment." He was afraid, I think—I know I would have been—afraid to sit with her and afraid to disobey the stern woman all dressed in black like she was the Wicked Witch's grandmother. But Mary Grace took his hand and went with him, and they both sat beside her. Miss Edith asked him what he'd gotten for Christmas—a new football, a pair of jeans, and a book about King Arthur and the Knights of the Round Table. His mother Sarah Jo was standing beside me, looking on; she murmured, "I wish it could have been more."

In a minute or two, Wil and Mary Grace relaxed a little and Miss Edith smiled at their chattering. Then she reached into her old black purse and pulled out an envelope with Wil's name written on it. When he opened it, he pulled out a crisp new one-hundred-dollar bill and showed it to his mother in disbelief, clutching it to his chest as if somebody was going to take it away from him. Sarah Jo stepped forward and said, "Oh, no ma'am—he can't possibly take that!"

Miss Edith looked at her levelly and said, "But of course he already has. I have more money than I know what to do with, and it would bring me great joy if you will allow me to give just this little bit to your brave son."

Then she pulled out another envelope with Mary Grace's name on it and gave it to her. It also held a hundred-dollar bill. Mary Grace thanked her and thanked her again, finally reaching over her brother Wil to hug her wholeheartedly, if somewhat awkwardly because of the squirming boy trapped between them.

I put my arm around Sarah Jo and whispered, "It's okay. Miss Edith doesn't have any family. She hasn't had anybody to give her anything on Christmas for years, and nobody to give anything to. It's okay. You'll be doing her a kindness if you let them take the money." Sarah Jo nodded, to me and to Miss Edith, her gratitude at Miss Edith's generosity outweighing her pride.

Then Miss Edith pointed at Gideon Guthrie and invited him to sit with her, in ominous tones. He perched on the edge of the couch, the fear of the old lady losing out to the prospect of receiving some money. And after he'd told her what he'd gotten for Christmas— clothes, books, a bicycle with ten gears, and a new game system, the same one Jude had gotten—it looked like he'd forgotten to be scared and was basking in her attention. After he'd told her at some length about his new video games—she couldn't possibly have understood or cared, but she listened patiently—she rummaged around in the old black purse and . . . looked up to motion me to come over to her.

She whispered, "I didn't know this kid was coming."

I murmured back, "His mother burned their turkey."

She nodded and whispered, "I've only got eighty-three dollars in cash. Can you spot me seventeen bucks?"

As it happened, one of the men in the parish had given me five crisp twenties after the Midnight Mass as a Christmas bonus. I whispered back, "I've got a twenty."

"That'll do—I owe you."

So as surreptitiously as I could, I took a twenty out of my wallet and slipped it to Miss Edith. We weren't fooling anyone, but at least we went through the motions.

She presented Gideon with five twenty-dollar bills, and he was delighted, until it occurred to him that he would have to hug the old lady. She said, "You don't have to," but he leaned over anyway and let Miss Edith hug him.

Then she called, "Gracie Hinton," and Jude took her across the room to sit with her. She asked them what they'd gotten for Christmas and they told her, and when she'd given both of them their envelopes with the hundred-dollar bills, Gracie blurted out, "Thanks, Grandma."

It stunned the room, until Miss Edith smiled at her kindly and said, "That . . . that is quite possibly the most wonderful Christmas gift I have ever been given. You may call me . . . Grandmother."

Gracie hugged her, and then Jude thanked her and hugged her, too. I was still standing close enough that during that hug I could hear Jude whisper, "Are you the old lady that drinks Scotch?" to which she replied, "Mm-hmm. But your daddy doesn't like it."

Gracie and Sarah Grace colored, and the boys took turns racing on Jude's new game system. Beulah and Sarah Jo pulled Charlie into the kitchen over her protests that she should never be allowed in a kitchen again after her turkey fiasco earlier that day, and we were well on our way toward a huge Christmas dinner.

Miss Edith and Polk were talking about large animal veterinary care—she was glad to know there were still horses and mules out in the pastures around town—and Sinclair was listening in. Miss Edith had an odd look on her face, an expression I hadn't seen there before: she was deeply content.

JoJo said we ought to help if we could, and he asked if we had another table. There was a wobbly old card table stowed away in the back of a closet; we pulled it up next to our old dining room table and put white bedsheets over both of them to make it look like we had a tablecloth over one huge, lumpy-looking table.

When we went to get the plates, knives, and forks, JoJo asked me how many places we needed to set. I counted it up in my head: four

Hintons, three McCaskills, three Guthries, JoJo, Sinclair, and Miss Edith—"Thirteen."

"Thirteen!" He looked legitimately horrified. "Aw, Buddy—you can't be havin' thirteen people sitting around a dinner table—that's terrible bad luck!"

I tried to tell him that it was just a superstition, but he was adamant. He said he would not set thirteen places, that he would go home before sitting at a table with twelve other people. It was like breaking a mirror or walking under a ladder, he said—"Some things you just don't *do*!"

He said, "If you set a table for thirteen, the first to leave the table will die before the year is up." I told him I thought the superstition had to do with Jesus and the Twelve Apostles, when Judas was the first to leave the Last Supper, but he was not going to be comforted. The more we talked about it, the more stubborn he became. I was telling him that we could get the children to sit at a separate table, or that I would eat in the living room, when the doorbell rang.

On my way to the door, I looked through the front window and saw an old motorcycle in the driveway. I wondered if I knew anybody who rode a motorcycle, and who would be visiting us on Christmas afternoon. I opened the door, and there stood James "Sutty" Sutter, carrying a cardboard box full of puppies.

37

The Prodigal

"Sutty! Merry Christmas! Come in, come in."

"No, I ain't gonna . . ."

Then I said something I never thought I was going to have to say. But it was Christmas, and we were overrun with Good Will Toward Men. I said, "Hush, Sutty, hush. Just come in. We're about to have Christmas dinner, and we need a fourteenth person at the table."

He had no idea what I was talking about, but he said, "No, I ain't . . .," so I said, with a note of command in my voice, "Come eat with us."

He looked at me and asked, "You want a dog?"

Well, that led to a tediously one-sided conversation, but eventually I dragged enough information out of him to piece together that he'd found these puppies by the side of County Road 14. Their mother had been hit by a car, and these four still were beside her dead body when he found them. Two other puppies had already died with their mother. He'd nursed these four to health and was hoping to find them homes, and hoping that he could give us one as a Christmas present. I knew just what to do.

I went back into the kitchen, told Beulah that Sutty was here, and wondered if we could invite him to dinner, too. "That'll make fourteen," I said, by way of justification. She laughed and said we had plenty of food. Then I told her he had four puppies he was trying to find homes for. She said, "No. We don't need a dog. I don't want a dog. No." Then, just to be clear, she added, "No, Buddy. After Jabbok died, I just . . . no. I couldn't stand loving another dog like that. No."

But then she, Sarah Jo, and Charlie went out to welcome Sutty, and by the time I'd introduced everybody all around, she already had the smallest of the litter in her arms. When I walked over to her, she said, "We'll call him Henry. Look at him—he was born to be a Hinton."

Sarah Jo's old dog Maggie had died a few months before, and after Mary Grace gave her solemn oath that she would take care of a puppy, they took one too. That left just two, a cream-colored female and the other a mostly black male with little white paws.

JoJo asked Sutty, "Can I have that black one?" Sutty said that he would be delighted for JoJo to take that beautiful puppy. Well, that's what he meant; what he actually said was "Yep."

Then JoJo announced, "I'm gonna call him Balthazar." Sinclair and I shared a glance and nodded; that was perfect.

That left just one puppy to be adopted, and it didn't look like anybody was going to take her. I tried to catch Beulah's eye, thinking maybe we could take both of them, but somehow she didn't seem to notice that I was trying to get her attention. Then Miss Edith said, "I'll be proud to have that last puppy." Then she said, "Buddy, if this dog outlives me, you will find her a new home."

It wasn't really a question, but I answered her anyway. "Yes ma'am."

Whereupon Miss Edith Frank asked little Gracie, "What should I name this beautiful puppy?" Gracie said without hesitation, "Sally," and the dog's name has been Sally from that moment to this.

Polk checked out each puppy and declared that they were all generally healthy. He thanked Sutty for saving them and told us that they all needed their shots, which he would donate and administer free of charge as his Christmas offering to the whole enterprise.

Our backyard was fenced in, and we sent all the children and puppies outside for a while with Mary Grace as overseer. JoJo was glad to set a fourteenth place, and in a few minutes, we were ready to call the kids and puppies in for lunch.

The puppies all cuddled together in their box, and the rest of us sat around the table in no particular order. I said the blessing, giving thanks for this family gathering and for the food that we were about to eat. After the blessing, Miss Edith nodded to Sinclair, who brought a tray of assorted cups and glasses and the bottle of chilled champagne, which he opened with a flair and a pop and a little fizzy wine dripping on the floor.

Sarah Jo said, "Oh, no—no wine for us!" but Sinclair said, "It's sparkling cider—there's no alcohol, I promise!"

Then he gave each of us a glass or cup or something—mine was a plastic Power Rangers cup, Beulah's had something to do with Barbie, all the children got wine glasses, and Miss Edith's plastic cup was something we'd gotten in a box of Cocoa Krispies. When everybody had something to toast with, Miss Edith held up her cup and said, "Here's to family, and friends, and long life."

Nobody planned it this way, but when Sutty repeated, "Family and friends," the rest of us said it again—"Family and friends."

We ate and ate, and talked and talked—it was chaotic and delicious and a very special moment for all of us: family and friends.

There was some negotiation about who would clear the dishes and who wanted what for dessert, and whether they wanted coffee with that or not, after which Miss Edith held up her Cocoa Krispies cup and said, "I do want to say, while we are all still sitting here, how grateful I am that you have invited me to be part of this remarkable family today."

Beulah said, "You're welcome any time . . . Grandmother."

Miss Edith went on to say, "It has been an extraordinary experience for me, starting with the service last night."

I said, "Oh, good. Thank you."

But she wasn't finished. She turned her raptor gaze to me and said, "I must say, young man, that was the finest sermon I have ever heard. And I have heard hundreds over the years."

Beulah raised her Barbie cup and said, "Hear, hear!"

Polk drawled, "Well, they're not all that good." Then, thinking he might have hurt my feelings, he added, "I mean, they're usually pretty good, but that one was extra good."

Then JoJo said with a sparkle in his eye, "But that ain't the best thing that happened last night."

We all looked at him, wondering what he was talking about, but Gracie knew: "Santa came!"

We all laughed, and JoJo said, "I'm talkin' about best thing that happened at church last night."

Gideon said, somewhat uncertainly, "Good King What's-his-name?"

JoJo shook his head.

Miss Edith suggested, "Oh, you must mean when Mr. McCain here sang 'O Holy Night'! That was simply magnificent."

JoJo blushed and murmured, "Thank you very much, ma'am, but that wasn't it, either."

Polk drawled, "So that leaves out the duel in the men's room, I guess."

Beulah turned to me and asked, "What duel is he talking about?"

I answered her, "Let's talk about that later." I felt Miss Edith looking at me—she had already heard the entire story, of course; the Bridge Club ladies never missed a thing, and they never took a day off.

JoJo was relishing the idea of knowing something that most of the rest of us didn't know. He turned to me and said, "It's like that story you told one time at camp, when Jesus talked 'bout that daddy who had two boys." When he saw it didn't register with me, he continued, "You know—he had them two boys and one of 'em wanted his money right now. When the daddy gave him half his money, he went off far away and spent it all on wine and women."

I said, "The story of the prodigal son." We'd acted out the story at several Special Sessions, with campers playing the parts of the two sons and the father, along with pigs and prostitutes.

"Yeah, that's right. Well, when that prodigal boy wound up feedin' pigs and all, he thought, 'Shoot, I ought to jus' go on home—it's gotta be better than feedin' pigs all the time.'"

He paused, we waited, and he finally said, "The prodigal is comin' home!"

At that, some of the people at the table looked at Sutty, who looked up from his plate and saw everybody looking at him. He said, "Me?"

JoJo said, "No, it ain't you."

I added, "But we were all glad to see you there last night, and we hope you'll come back. And we're all glad you came for dinner today."

Sutty looked relieved and said, "Me, too. Thanks."

Miss Edith said, "I think he might be talking about me—it has been a while since the last time I was in church, but I—"

"No ma'am," I interrupted. "You've never really left; even when you can't come, you're always there. I don't think he's talking about you." She nodded appreciatively.

I saw Sinclair looking around the table a bit self-consciously before he said, "No, he's talking about me."

Then JoJo let it spill out: "Sinclair asked me last night!"

Beulah asked, "He asked you what?"

"He wants me to stand up for him!"

Sinclair said, "I have decided that it's time for me to be baptized."

There was a general murmur of acceptance and approval, and after it died down, he continued. "Well, I saw how much it means to live with hope and faith. I want to live like that, too—I wanted to belong, too."

It was Sutty who asked the obvious question: "What stopped you?"

Sinclair took a moment to compose himself. "When I was in high school, my church family turned their backs on me in the name of God. Then my parents turned me out."

Jude was horrified. "Why?"

Beulah shushed him. "I'll tell you later."

"So . . . I think I've just been mad. Mad at the church, mad at God, mad at everybody who feels like they belong."

I'd never known that Sinclair hadn't been baptized, and was about to confess my assumption when Miss Edith said, "What made you change your mind?"

"Well, it was a change of heart, really. Last night when JoJo sang that song, I thought: this is why Jesus came—to show us the love of

God for all people, from the greatest to the least. And I heard myself say, 'That means me, too.'

"So, after the second service, after Pearlie had taken Miss Edith home, I sat in the pew and prayed for a while. I was crying when JoJo found me, and he asked me if I was okay, and if I wanted something."

JoJo broke in. "And he said, 'I want to be part of it.' I asked him part of what, and he asked me would I stand up for him when he gets baptized!"

Sinclair looked at me, tears streaming down his face. "I want to be baptized, Buddy. I want to belong. All these years I thought other people were keeping me out, but it was me all along. I was just keeping myself out."

Tears were in my eyes, too, and Beulah squeezed my hand. I said, "It will be my privilege to baptize you, Sinclair."

Even as I said it, I knew that there would be some—or at least one—who wouldn't be so happy about Sinclair being baptized at St. Thomas. The most relatable character in the story of the prodigal son is not the father or the son who came home but the older son, who objected. I took a breath and continued, "And I'm so glad you've asked JoJo to present you."

Sinclair said, "Can I ask somebody else, too?"

I said, "Sure—you can ask as many as you want."

"Well," he said, "I'd like to ask Beulah and Miss Edith."

Beulah said, "Oh, Sinclair, I'll be happy to do that."

Miss Edith was momentarily at a loss for words, but Sinclair helped her out: "So, Old Lady—will you be my fairy godmother?"

We all laughed, and Miss Edith nodded solemnly and said, "It will be my honor to be your godmother." Then she asked Sinclair to pour everyone "just a splash" for another toast. When everyone had something in their various cups and glasses, she said, "To the prodigal coming home."

We all drank, and Polk held his Spider-Man cup aloft and added, "Family and friends."

Then we all said it again, from the oldest to the youngest: "Family and friends!"

POSTLUDE

The Mississippi State Bulldogs beat the Clemson Tigers in the 1999 Peach Bowl, and Jude and I were in the Georgia Dome in Atlanta ringing our cowbells to cheer them on. We drove home the next day, and that night we went to the Guthries' for a Happy New Millennium Party, as we moved into the twenty-first century. JoJo was there with Wanda Stovall, who was visiting from West Branch; Sinclair had been invited but he'd made other plans—apparently, he and Troy were going to a big New Years' bash down in Mobile.

"Wow," Beulah said on our way home. Both kids had already fallen asleep on the back seat. "Welcome to the twenty-first century."

I said, "Yeah—happy new year!"

She mused, "I wonder what it's going to be like?"

"So far, it seems the same as the last millennium to me."

"I mean, I wonder what it's going to be like for our children, when they get to be our age."

"When they're our ages, in their forties?"

"Yeah, so . . . say thirty-five years from now. What do you think life will be like in 2035?"

I said, "I wonder if we'll still be driving cars."

"You think we'll still be using gasoline?"

"I hope not. Surely all the cars will be electric by then. Or maybe we will have figured out how to reverse gravity, and . . ."

Beulah wasn't interested in talking about science fiction. "You think they'll have friends? You think they'll get married and have children?"

"Well, sure—if people don't have children, the species will be extinct."

"But I mean, will our children want to have children? Will it be important to them to be married?"

I said I assumed so, and then I said, "I wonder if the church will still be around."

"St. Thomas?"

"Well, yeah—but I mean, the whole church. People don't come to church like they used to, you know."

"Everything changes, though, right?"

"Yeah. Everything changes." I thought about it and said, "We will have to hold fast to that which is good, and sing to the Lord a new song."

Then my wise, wonderful wife declared, "Everything changes but love. There's always love. That's always been there, and I guess it always will be."

"Yeah," I mused, partly to her and partly to myself, "there's always love . . . no matter what, no matter what."